"I'm going to be

Jen said.

"Drew is old enough to choose where he lives, and I really don't want him to choose to live with his dad instead of me." Tears sparkled in her eyes. She tugged out of his arms and stopped dancing.

"I'm really sorry," he said, following her off the dance floor. "I didn't mean to upset you."

"It isn't that," she said with a quick shake of her head as they got to the edge. She crossed her arms. "I'm more professional than this, I promise you. But I really need something comfortable by the time my son gets here. I need a *home* for him, by Christmas. You know?"

She didn't want to lose her son in this divorce, either. He could understand that, because it could happen when you weren't looking.

Dear Reader,

There is something enjoyable about writing a woman in her forties, because she's experienced a lot, learned a lot and has a whole lot more to lose in a failed romance. Sweeping her off her feet is a bigger challenge.

But she also has a lot to give once the right man earns her heart, and I wanted to show women getting that happily-ever-after with heroes who have just as much life experience and depth of emotion to offer.

I hope you enjoy the women of the Second Chance Dinner Club! They believe in second chances in life and in love, and there's always an extra spot at the table.

If you'd like to connect with me, you can find me on Facebook, Twitter or on my website at patriciajohnsromance.com. I'm always happy to hear from my readers. If you've enjoyed this book—take a look at my backlist! There are more stories waiting for you to discover.

Patricia Johns

HEARTWARMING

Mountain Mistletoe Christmas

—

Patricia Johns

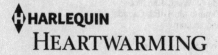

HARLEQUIN
HEARTWARMING

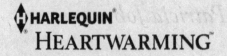

HARLEQUIN®
HEARTWARMING™

ISBN-13: 978-1-335-88990-4

Mountain Mistletoe Christmas

Copyright © 2020 by Patricia Johns

This edition published by arrangement with Harlequin Books S.A.

For questions and comments about the quality of this book, please contact us at CustomerService@Harlequin.com.

Harlequin Enterprises ULC
22 Adelaide St. West, 40th Floor
Toronto, Ontario M5H 4E3, Canada
www.Harlequin.com

Printed in U.S.A.

Patricia Johns writes from Alberta, Canada. She has her Hon. BA in English literature and currently writes for Harlequin's Heartwarming and Love Inspired lines. You can find her at patriciajohnsromance.com.

Books by Patricia Johns

Harlequin Heartwarming

The Second Chance Club

Their Mountain Reunion

Home to Eagle's Rest

Her Lawman Protector
Falling for the Cowboy Dad
The Lawman's Baby

A Baxter's Redemption
The Runaway Bride
A Boy's Christmas Wish

Love Inspired

Montana Twins

Her Cowboy's Twin Blessings
Her Twins' Cowboy Dad
A Rancher to Remember

Visit the Author Profile page
at Harlequin.com for more titles.

To my husband, my biggest supporter and
the love of my life.

CHAPTER ONE

WHEN UNCLE STU announced he was gay after thirty-five years of marriage, the entire family had been stunned. In Jen Taylor's family, Uncle Stu and Aunt Gayle had been pillars of marital success—both with great careers, financial security and the sweetest way of toasting each other from across the room to a successfully served Thanksgiving dinner.

"Gayle's the best!" Stu always said, raising his glass. "She's a real pal. Couldn't do it all without her."

So, looking back on it, there had been… signs. But what woman wanted to face that unless she absolutely had to? Jen could sympathize. Divorce was the most painful experience of Jen's life so far, too—almost like tearing off a limb. Trying it after thirty-five years of marriage was almost unfathomable.

But the tragedy for her aunt and uncle was

more than just Gayle's decades of marriage to a man who never truly desired her. It was Stu's decades of repressing who he really was. Painful as it was for everyone in the family, that divorce was for the best.

So when her favorite aunt called with a verbal invitation for her second wedding, to a local retired real-estate lawyer named Matthew Pickard, how could Jen not attend? Just because Jen was recovering from her own painful divorce, and her twelve-year-old son was spending Christmas with her ex-husband, didn't mean she couldn't be happy for other people. Right? Her therapist had said so, at least, and she'd been repeating that mantra to herself for weeks. Besides, Jen had just moved back to Mountain Springs, Colorado, and she'd recently purchased the old mansion on South Avenue. It wasn't like she couldn't make it to the wedding…

So here she was at Mount Springs Lodge—a lakeside lodge styled like a log cabin that had been redone to some real luxury in the past few years. Jen scanned the name cards. She had been marooned at a corner table with an arguably gorgeous view of the lake, with a bunch of women she didn't

know. Renata Spivovich, Angelina Cunningham, Belle Villeneuve and a couple—Melanie and Logan McTavish. Or siblings? She
had no idea. For being so eager to have Jen
come to the wedding, Aunt Gayle could have
at least put her at a table with family. Jen
picked up her name card and glanced across
the dining room to where her sister, Lisa,
was already chatting with some cousins.

"Hi."

Jen started and sheepishly put the card
back when a short, plump woman with a
sparkling smile came up beside her. She
wore a black sequined dress and her short
hair was done in a messy, spiky do that
suited her round face.

"I'm Renata," the woman said, holding out
her hand. "Gayle's told us all about you."

"Has she?" That was strange. "How do
you know my aunt?"

"We have a dinner club," Renata replied.
"She hasn't told you about us?"

"I think she mentioned a dinner club."
And her aunt had stuck her with *them*? Jen
was trying not to be insulted here, but...

"There's Belle," Renata said, looking past
Jen's shoulder, and Jen turned to see a lithe,

brunette beauty sailing toward them in a formfitting silk sheath. Jen felt positively prepubescent next to her.

"Hey, girl," Belle said, leaning down to give Renata a hug; then she turned to Jen. "Are you Jen Taylor?"

"Yeah—"

"Great to meet you," Belle said, and she enclosed her in a perfume-scented hug. "Sorry, I'm a hugger. I wasn't always, but I like it."

Jen stared at her in mute surprise.

"You okay?" Belle asked with a coaxing smile. "The hug was too much?"

"No, I'm fine," Jen chuckled. "Nice to meet you."

"Sit, sit," Renata said, pulling out her chair. "The food is going to be amazing. Angelina was supervising everything—she owns this place, you know."

"Oh—" *That* Angelina Cunningham. Jen should have placed the name. Angelina had bought the old hunting lodge and absolutely transformed it, turning it from an old man's hangout to a trendy tourist hub. Jen's sister, Lisa, had sent her some articles. This lodge had been covered in several travel magazines, and it had turned into a real hot spot.

Jen sat down. Any escape after being hugged and chatted up was going to be incredibly rude. Besides, a chance to pick Angelina Cunningham's brain about renovating an old building would be priceless. Perhaps Aunt Gayle had been looking out for her after all.

The string quartet was warming up across the room, and people were mingling, talking and laughing, finding their seats. Just then the McTavishes joined them. Definitely a couple. They were smiling and his arm was draped around her shoulder. His tie even matched her midnight blue dress.

"This is Melanie," Renata said, nudging Jen's arm. "And her husband, Logan. They're pretty newly married themselves. Mel, this is Jen."

"Jen?" Melanie raised her eyebrows. "Oh, *Jen*! Great to meet you."

Melanie put her hand out and they shook before the two took their seats.

Jen was getting the distinct impression that everyone had heard a whole lot about her. Was it her divorce that had garnered all this attention, or what?

"Good. You're all here." Gayle glided up to the table with a sparkling smile. "You've all met my niece, then?"

Gayle had chosen a floor-length lace gown with three-quarter-length sleeves and a bateau neckline. Her silver hair was swept into an updo, and she oozed old Hollywood glamour. She'd told Jen how she'd been nervous about this dress choice, convinced that a second wedding for a woman over sixty should stay "understated," but Jen had convinced her otherwise. Looking at her aunt now, she was glad she'd managed it.

"We have met," Renata replied with an equally brilliant smile of her own. "She's delightful."

"These are my particular friends," Gayle said, leaning down next to Jen. "They've been here for me through some tough times, and I really think you're going to like them."

"The dinner club, right?" Jen said uncertainly, and she leaned closer and lowered her voice. "What about Lisa and my cousins? I kind of expected to be seated with family—"

"Just meet these women first," Gayle

whispered. "Then go pull a chair up with the family. This wasn't meant to be an insult, I promise. It's just that they were all going to be here, and so were you, and I really wanted you to meet them properly—"

Someone called Gayle's name and she straightened and smiled as a flash went off. Gayle gave Jen's arm a squeeze and moved off to another table, leaving Jen with the women, who were looking at her with smiles and undisguised curiosity. Another woman slid into the remaining chair—an elegant, curvy woman with sleek blond hair and an ageless face. She wore crimson lipstick on plump lips and rivaled Belle for model status. Next to them, Jen was feeling just a little bit frumpy in her own knee-length red dress. She pasted on a smile. She'd make the best of this, and then escape to the family table.

"Is this Jen Taylor?" The blonde woman held out her hand. "I'm Angelina Cunningham."

"Pleasure." Jen shook her hand. "I'm happy to meet you. I understand you redid the lodge."

"Well, me and a small army," Angelina said, brushing off the compliment. "And you've purchased that old mansion that went up for sale. I had half a mind to buy it myself."

"Glad to have beaten you to it," Jen said with a chuckle.

"But getting to the point," Angelina said. "We understand that you've recently gone through a nasty divorce."

Jen swallowed and felt the blood drain from her face. "Right." *That* was the point? Her divorce? She was doing her best to press forward into her new life. Since when was a woman's marital status her defining quality?

"I'm just going to get us some drinks," Logan said, rising to his feet and slipping away. Melanie didn't even bat an eye. She leaned forward.

"I know how this sounds," Melanie said. "I'm sorry. It's a bit of an attack, isn't it?"

"A bit," Jen agreed.

"The thing is, we all know each other because we've all been through it. We've all had painful divorces and we get together for a dinner club with other women who understand. It's hard being the divorced one in your group of friends. There's always some level of judgment, so when we get together, we skip all that."

"Get together for dinner," Jen clarified.

"Right here," Angelina said, spreading her hands. "We deserve a nice dinner out with good wine and good conversation. It helps."

"Oh…" Jen smiled hesitantly, glancing around the table. "So you're all divorced, then?"

"I'm remarried," Melanie said. "But yes."

"And my aunt figured I could use this dinner group, did she?" Jen asked.

"Girl, we *all* need this dinner group," Belle replied. "For me, I was married to my agent. I was modeling at the time, and when I put on a little healthy weight, he replaced me with a younger woman."

Jen grimaced. "I'm sorry."

"It is what it is," Belle replied.

"My husband was cheating on me for some time when he finally confessed," Renata said. "He asked if he could move his mistress into the family home with our three children and we'd just…stay married."

Jen swallowed. "Ouch."

"So yeah…divorced," Renata said, some bitterness in her tone.

"I don't blame you," Jen said.

"My first husband had been a serial cheater for years," Melanie added. "I had no idea. When I figured it out, I left him, and everything I'd worked for, behind. It was the hardest thing I ever did. I'm still sorting out my relationship with my ex-stepkids."

"And I'm the one who was divorced with no cheating involved," Angelina added. "It was nearly a decade ago. We had a whirl-wind romance, got married and only after the vows did I find out the kind of money he came from. The family didn't approve, and we didn't last the year."

"I'm sorry…" Jen murmured.

"We did hear a little bit from your aunt," Angelina said. "She said you married your prof at college?"

Whatever. She might as well tell the story. The rest of them had told the worst, hadn't they?

"He was my political science professor," Jen said after a beat of silence. "We were married for fourteen years and we have a twelve-year-old son together."

"What went wrong?" Belle asked softly.

Jen felt tears mist her eyes and she blinked

them back. It must be the season and the fact that her son, Drew, was in Denver for the holidays. She was both childless and husbandless this Christmas.

"I don't know. We just started fighting more and more. He had all these academic friends, and I only have my master's degree in art history, so I was trailing behind all those PhDs. He wanted me to be something I couldn't be, and…there comes a point when being his cute, young student runs its course, you know? I'm neither cute nor young anymore, and I'm not about to pretend otherwise."

"You're beautiful," Renata replied. "Don't sell yourself short."

"I'm also thirty-eight," Jen replied.

The women all nodded at that. They got it, it seemed. Jen was a grown woman, and she wasn't going to be wide-eyed and in awe of her brilliant husband in the same way she used to be. Besides, Samuel wasn't exactly as brilliant as he liked people to think.

"Come to dinner," Angelina said quietly. "We dress up, we look fantastic and we enjoy each other's company."

It did sound nice. "Thanks. I think I'd like that."

Angelina smiled, then leaned forward, elbows on the table and a diamond bracelet glittering in the low light. "Now...what's the plan for that old mansion?"

Jen could feel herself relaxing now. "I want to turn it into an art gallery. I grew up here, you know, and I've loved that house ever since I was a little kid staring at it from the sidewalk. I'm putting everything I got from my divorce into this—but I really think it'll be amazing. With tourists year-round, and local people who might enjoy some art in their lives...it's what I wish we had when I was growing up."

"It sounds amazing," Mel said.

Jen smiled. "I hope so. The house is gorgeous. It has really good bones. The kitchen has servants' stairs going up from the back, so I can put a wall up blocking off the kitchen so that the rest of the ground floor can be used for the gallery. The first floor is just mammoth. I was thinking the second floor could be used for another showroom and some offices, and the third floor could be our living space. There's already two bedrooms up there, and a sitting room. And a bathroom, but I'm not sure it's functional right now. Anyway, my son and I don't need a lot of space to start. Presumably, once the gallery started supporting itself, I could buy another place to live in and expand the gallery. That might take a little while, though."

Jen stopped when she realized she'd been prattling on, the only one talking. Heat hit her cheeks. She tended to talk too much when she was uncomfortable, and she no longer had a surly husband to give her flat stares when she was doing it.

Logan reappeared just then with a platter of filled punch glasses, and he passed the glasses around with an easy smile.

"Sounds like you need a contractor," Angelina said once she'd taken her glass, smiling her thanks at Logan.

"I do," she agreed. "Do you have anyone you could recommend for a job this big?"

"Absolutely. He's at the wedding tonight, actually." Angelina straightened and looked out into the crowded room. "Hold on. I'll be back."

The quartet started up just as Angelina

left the table, a strings edition of a popular love song.

"Is Angelina talking about Nick Bryant?" Logan asked his wife.

"I think so," Melanie replied. "He's the one who worked on the lodge, so..."

"He's a nice guy," Logan said with a nod. "And he's good."

So this contractor came recommended by Angelina Cunningham and approved by a relative stranger's husband. Well, Jen didn't have a lot of time to be picky right now. She had to get this house into a livable condition so that when Drew came back after being spoiled by his father for the holidays, she could provide him with a proper home. It was the least she could do.

THE QUARTET WAS playing something classical but Nick couldn't quite place it. When he'd been married, his wife had tried to give him an appreciation for classical music, but it never stuck. He glanced down at his watch. He knew Matthew Pickard, the groom, from years ago when Matthew had been Nick's ex-wife's boss. They'd worked on a couple of charity projects together after the divorce, so they'd kept up a semiprofessional friendship since. That was how Nick had nabbed an invite to the wedding of the season. It was a gorgeous affair—Nick couldn't deny that. But he was ready to go home to his dog.

Nick's daughter, Amelia, was due to arrive in town tomorrow evening from college. While they had a tense relationship, he was looking forward to Christmas with his daughter. Amelia was brash, smart, opinionated and going places. She was in her third year of pre-law at Harvard, and her step-dad was footing the bill. That alone was a source of irritation for Nick—Chris, Nick's ex-wife's second husband, having the money to give Nick's daughter everything she ever wanted...not that he begrudged Amelia her dream college.

This year Nick had convinced Amelia to come see him for Christmas, since Shari and Chris were going to Europe. It had been a few years since he'd spent more than a few hours with his daughter, and he was nervous.

Nick glanced at his watch again, then rubbed a hand through his gray-flecked beard. He didn't feel like making nice and chatting with people, and he wasn't up to dancing, either. He wanted to head home and be alone with his thoughts. He turned toward the exit.

"Leaving so soon?"

Angelina Cunningham came up beside him. She was also an old friend, and he shot her a tired smile.

"Yeah, I—" Any excuse was going to sound flimsy. "I'm tired."

"Well, before you head out, there's someone I wanted to introduce you to," Angelina said. "It's Gayle's niece, actually, and she needs a contractor. She just bought the mansion across the street from you."

The petite woman with the sandy-blond hair. He'd only seen a glimpse of her when she was moving in—slim, beautiful, well-dressed. But that was it—just a glimpse. He'd had no idea she was Gayle's niece. But there were always unknown connections in a place the size of Mountain Springs. When you took out the tourists, the town was pretty tiny.

Nick raised his eyebrows. "And she's renovating?"

"She is."

His first client of the New Year had canceled on him, so it wasn't like he couldn't take on another project. Besides, that old mansion was gorgeous, and he'd love the chance to work on it. He did feel a twinge of guilt at considering this, since Amelia was coming for the holidays, but when he'd made plans with her, he thought he'd be working on another project anyway... What did it say about him that he'd rather work than face his own daughter?

"Just come say hello," Angelina said. "Then I'll even help you escape, if that's what you want."

Nick exchanged an amused look with Angelina. "Fine. A quick hello."

He followed Angelina between the tables toward the far side of the room. The sun had already set, leaving a glow of crimson along the mountains' jagged silhouette—visible through the bank of tall windows that flanked the room. He'd helped install every single one of those windows when he'd renovated this lodge, and he was proud of the work. The lodge was better than an advertisement—it showed anyone who'd seen it just what kind of work he and his team were capable of.

The table she led him toward was in the back corner, and when he approached he saw her, elbows on the table, her hands folded elegantly in front of her, and the low light sparkling in her blue eyes. She was wearing a sleeveless black dress, some lace around the collarbone that looked effortlessly sophisticated. She was stunning—not that it should even matter right now. He swallowed and arranged a professional smile on his face.

"Jen Taylor, this is Nick Bryant, the one who helped me renovate this lodge," Angelina said, and Nick leaned forward to shake her hand.

Jen's handshake was firm and strong, and after he gave a quick nod and smile to the others at the table, Jen rose and stepped to the side with him.

"It's nice to meet you," she said.

"Likewise," he replied. "Angelina said you need a contractor."

"Yeah…" She sucked in a slow breath. "I made an emotional purchase, I'm afraid. I have some good ideas for it, but it's probably going to be more work than I'd anticipated."

"The old mansion," he said.

"You know it?" she asked.

"I live across the street," he replied.

Her eyes widened at that, and he laughed softly. "You might not want to hire someone that close. I can understand if you don't want to see your contractor walking his dog in the morning."

"No, no..." But there was something in her voice that suggested otherwise.

"What do you need done?" he asked.

"Immediately, I need to get the kitchen renovated and the bathroom upstairs made functional again. Once those are done, it can be livable."

"When do you need that done by?" he asked.

"Christmas?"

He let out a low whistle.

She shrugged. "I know that's a lot to ask."

By Christmas...it would really depend on how much work would be required.

"I know that's probably wishful thinking," she went on. "The thing is, I'm newly divorced, and my son is spending Christmas with his dad, and then he's coming back to live with me right after. I wanted to have something decent for him, and when I bought this place, it was based on this huge idealized plan to open an art gallery in Mountain Springs, and I sank a lot of my divorce settlement into it."

A painful divorce and a kid in the mix. He knew that feeling all too well, and in spite of his better instincts, he found himself softening toward her situation.

"If we can have your attention, everyone," a woman's voice rang from the front of the room. "We're going to kick off the evening with the first dance! May I introduce to you Mr. and Mrs. Matthew and Gayle Pickard!"

Nick turned toward the dance floor, where Matthew and Gayle stood in the center of the room for the very first time as husband and wife. They both looked completely smitten, smiling into each other's eyes as they danced to a romantic ballad. Now was not the time to talk business.

"They're lucky," Jen said at his side, and he looked down at her. "I'm not sure a second marriage is that ideal for other people."

"How fresh is your divorce?" he asked with a rueful smile.

"Six months," she replied.

He nodded. That was a painful time. He remembered that first year post-divorce well.

It wasn't easy. His best friend, Bert, who worked with him now, had dragged him out for a few beers weekend after weekend. Bert had even brought him along to a book club for one very long month that spring before Nick had been able to politely extricate himself from the situation.

"For me, it's been eight years," he replied. "Since we signed the papers, at least. Ten since we split up."

"And you're more optimistic about second marriages now?" she asked.

"A bit. I've had time to figure out what I did wrong the first time," he replied.

She eyed him for a moment, but she didn't ask him to elaborate, which was just as well. The music changed and the woman at the mic invited everyone else to join the couple, and there was a rustling of dresses as people stood up to dance.

"Are you two dancing?" Logan asked as he and Melanie walked by, and Nick looked down at Jen with a half smile. He'd been meaning to escape before the dancing started, but now faced with Jen's clear blue gaze, it seemed rude not to ask… They were at a wedding, after all.

"Did you…want to dance?" he asked.

"Sure."

It had been a long time since he'd danced with a woman, and he was mildly worried he'd step on her toes. But the song was a slow one, and as they got to the dance floor and he tugged her into his arms, the music seemed to do most of the work. She was petite, and he could see a touch of gray mingling with her sandy-blond waves now that he was close enough to smell the sweet fragrance of her perfume.

She fit against him perfectly, and her fingers felt cool in his palm. She was beautiful, but not in the model-perfect kind of way. There was something about her, almost girl-next-door. Or girl-across-the-street, in their case.

"So what did you do before deciding to open an art gallery?" Nick asked, mostly to make conversation and distract himself from thinking too much about the type of pretty she was. She was a potential client, and Nick never did mix business with pleasure.

"I was a buyer for an elderly man's art collection. It wasn't full-time, but I did love what I did."

"Wow…" That was definitely out of his realm of experience.

"I miss it, actually," she said with a smile that lit up her face. "It was a good job and I got to use my master's in art history. Part of me wishes I'd just stayed in Denver and continued, but it wasn't full-time and I wanted to make sure that my part of the divorce settlement set me up for a life I could sustain."

"That makes sense," he agreed.

He kept his hand respectfully in the middle of her back, but even so, he liked the way she moved—without any thought seeming to go into it, their rhythm was in sync.

"I did do some research into people's interest in an art gallery around here," she said.

He turned on the balls of his feet, leading her into an open space and away from the other couples crowding in. She laughed softly as he swept her past Logan and Melanie, and he gave her a grin.

"You can dance," she said, giving him an impressed look.

"Yeah. I'm a surprising guy."

Her cheeks pinked. He hadn't exactly meant to start flirting, but he knew that he had. He'd have to rein that in.

"How old is your son?" he asked in an attempt to get things back on track.

"Drew's twelve," she said.

That was the same age his daughter had been when he'd gotten divorced, too.

"Is he...into art?" he asked hesitantly. It was possible.

"No." She laughed. "He's into science fiction, mostly. And video games."

"How's he handling it all?"

"He's really sad," she replied, sobering. "He loves his dad a lot, and he just wanted us to patch it up. For him."

"That's tough," he said. His daughter had wanted that, once upon a time, and he'd figured it wouldn't change. It had, though. Now Amelia didn't seem to have much use for him at all.

"But life goes on, right?" she said.

"It does," he replied. And while the divorce part got easier, parenting didn't.

Nick glanced up to see Logan McTavish and his wife dancing a few yards off. Logan held Melanie close, his hand moving slowly up and down her back, and it was like the air almost sizzled around them. Nick pulled his gaze away.

"I'm going to be honest with you," Jen said. "Drew is old enough to choose where he lives, and I really don't want him to choose to live with his dad instead of me." She stepped away from him, tears sparkling in her eyes. Cool air flooded between them, and he felt awkward standing there on the dance floor with empty arms.

"I'm really sorry," he said, following her off the dance floor. "I didn't mean to upset you."

"It isn't that," she said with a quick shake of her head as they got to the edge. She crossed her arms. "I'm more professional than this, I promise you. But I really need something comfortable by the time my son gets here. I need a *home* for him. You know?"

She didn't want to lose her son in this divorce. He could understand that, because it could happen when you weren't looking.

"I can't promise that I can finish it that quickly," he said.

"Just enough to make if comfortable?" she asked hopefully.

"I can take a look and give you an estimate."

A relieved smile spread over her face. "Thank you. I'd appreciate that. And if you can't do it, maybe you could recommend someone."

He wasn't in a hurry to just hand this off to someone else, but he wasn't going to say that. "I could come by in the morning, if you want. Say around nine?"

That was a nice professional hour, and he could see her when he was wearing a tool belt and he could get his balance again. He wasn't used to talking business with a woman while slow dancing. They needed to reboot this professional relationship.

"Nine would be perfect," she said. "Thank you. I do appreciate it."

His mind went to his daughter again, and he felt that pang of guilt. But Amelia had already told him that she was looking forward to catching up with some old friends, and she knew he'd be busy. Maybe he was running away from the inevitable with his daughter—that mutual acknowledgment that whatever fatherly relationship he'd been hoping for was too far in the past to resuscitate.

"I'm going to let you enjoy your aunt's wedding," Nick said.

"Of course. Thanks again."

He needed to get out of here, away from his beautiful potential client, away from the romance of a December wedding. Because he knew exactly what he'd done wrong with his first marriage—he'd followed his wayward heart and married a woman much higher on the social ladder than he was. And this Jen Taylor was beautiful, educated and had a passion for art. She was on a whole different level than he'd ever be, and that should be enough for Nick to shut down any kind of attraction he might be feeling.

Nick knew what he needed, and that was to stay solidly on his own level. He'd made that mistake once already, and he was no glutton for punishment.

CHAPTER TWO

JEN STOOD IN the middle of the old kitchen with a cup of coffee in one hand and her cell phone in the other. The kitchen had the same 1920s style as the rest of the house, with long counters, tall cupboards and a hardwood floor that was scuffed into paths that led to the servants' entrance, and to the main entrance into the dining room. How many people had served meals from this kitchen? How many had served only themselves?

She was dressed in a pair of jeans and a blue cashmere sweater that she knew brought out her eyes. And that wasn't because she had that contractor coming by in a few minutes, either. A woman could take pride in her appearance post-divorce. There was no rule against that. She moved the phone to give a panoramic view of the old kitchen.

"Okay, now the kitchen is going to be fixed up by the time you get here," she said to her son on the other end of the video call. "But look at these gorgeous old wood cabinets!"

"Uh-huh." Drew wasn't interested in the kitchen details, it would seem. "Where's my room?"

"Upstairs on the third floor, next to mine. It's full of boxes right now," Jen replied. "I'm going to clear it out before I show you. But this is an old mansion, son. It's a hundred years old, and the original owners were the wealthiest people in Mountain Springs once upon a time. This kitchen was used for servants, and the family dined in the other room."

"Do we get a maid?" Drew asked with a laugh.

"Not a chance," she said, and she flicked the camera around so she could see Drew again. "But it's going to be great. You'll see! This place is just amazing."

"Is it haunted?" he asked.

"Are you hoping?" She chuckled. "No, it's not haunted, but it's filled with history. This is going to be your home. It's cool. Trust me."

She could hear some voices in the background, and Drew's attention was drawn away.

"Is that your dad?" she asked, trying to sound casual.

"Yeah, he and Tiffany are back from their walk," Drew replied. "Tiffany says Dad has to get exercise, so he stays healthy."

Jen had been hearing about Tiffany a lot lately. Tiffany insisted upon green smoothies and she swore by hot yoga. Tiffany thought that Christmas was too commercial, and she insisted on making a wreath for the front door out of fresh evergreen sprigs and twigs of holly that she bought at the farmers' market. There was nothing Samuel liked more than humoring the young, beautiful women he taught and dated. Jen should know—that was how she'd met him—and having an enthusiastic young woman bounce into Samuel's heart and his life stung.

"Are you getting a Christmas tree?" Drew asked.

"Um—" Jen hesitated. "Without you here for Christmas, I wasn't planning on it."

"What? Mom! You've got to get a tree!" Drew said. "Have you seen Dad's? Let me show you."

The picture flipped around to display a massive Christmas tree decorated with what looked like popcorn strings and a mishmash of ornaments. These weren't the decorations they'd used as a family. She'd taken most of those with her—the ones that held particular memories, at least. This tree, for all its homey, natural look, was also color coordinated with red and white. Drew's face came back into the picture.

"It's nice, huh?"

"Really nice," she said, forcing a smile. Sam was moving on, apparently. Another woman was decorating his tree.

"Come on, Mom," Drew coaxed. "It's Christmas. And if you don't get a tree I'm going to feel awful. It's your Christmas, too, you know."

Jen pulled a hand through her blond waves. "I'll get a tree, okay?" she said. "And I'll leave it up so you can enjoy it when you arrive."

"You'd better!" Drew said. "And I got you something for Christmas yesterday when Tiffany took me shopping. You're going to love it."

Tiffany had taken him shopping. Jen hated

this. Her son, her life, were all getting covered in the fingerprints of this faceless Tiffany. And then as if on cue, a bouncing brunette popped onto the screen, her face pressed up next to Drew's.

"Is that your mom, Drew?" Tiffany flashed a glittering smile. She was beautiful—did she have to be so cute? "Hi, Jennifer! I've been taking good care of him. Everything organic!"

"Great," Jen replied, hoping her deep loathing didn't bleed through.

Tiffany ruffled Drew's hair and disappeared from view again, but Jen could still hear her voice. "Come on, Drew. Time for breakfast. No screens at the table. I'm sure your mom understands."

Drew winced. "Sorry, Mom, I've gotta go."

He never jumped that quickly when she told him to get off his screens, but then Tiffany was a novelty, and maybe Drew was a little smitten with his dad's girlfriend. Who knew?

"I love you, sweetie," Jen said.

"Yeah, me, too. Bye."

Drew hung up before Jen did, and she

stood there for a moment, her heart pounding in her chest. This Tiffany was everything that irritated Jen—pert, young, convinced of her own virtue because she was making nice with her professor's son. Jen idly wondered if Sam was still Tiffany's professor, or if he'd waited until she'd finished his class. Not that it mattered.

Jen put her phone on the chipped and faded countertop. Well, if Tiffany stuck, she'd be on the Samuel train, because that was how Sam liked things. He wanted a woman who was young enough to mold, and who wanted to be a part of his ambitions. Dr. Samuel Taylor was nothing if not focused. He taught political science at the University of Denver, and he'd written five books on various political topics, all of which were required reading for graduate-level political science courses across the country. Sam had been the top mind in his area of study for about twenty years, but he'd started to slip. There were younger, brighter, more innovative thinkers out there now, and while he'd contributed an intellectual gold mine to the subject, he now had competition.

Tiffany was a reboot for Sam. Jen could

see that. She was young enough to idolize him and was probably perfectly willing to support his career trajectory. Once upon a time, it had been Jen typing his chicken scratch notes and staying up with him late into the night so he could bounce ideas off her. All that was required was to say, "Sam, I think you've got something…" and he'd take it from there.

And yet, the one thing Jen couldn't get off her mind was the image of that tree in Sam's house. It was nothing the way she'd decorated it, a tree filled with unique ornaments, all with memories attached. Every year she had one treasured ornament that she carefully placed high enough that little fingers couldn't reach it—a silver ball of mistletoe. It had been a gift from her grandmother when she was a child, and like the mansion that she'd stared at wistfully from the road when she was a little girl, that ornament had represented something to her—all of her hopes and dreams for love of her own. Those unique ornaments were with her now, and that little ball of silver mistletoe was waiting for a new tree.

Jen looked around the old kitchen. One

bank of cupboards had been painted white, but not professionally. The old 1920s wood-burning stove remained in one corner but a newer stove had been installed next to it, a wide range hood hovering over them, suggesting that both had been used once upon a time. Would she ever try her hand at cooking over a woodstove? Not likely.

Jen could see how much work this would be to fix up. Had she been overzealous here?

Probably. But she'd bought this place, and maybe fixing it up into something really beautiful could be a project that would capture Drew's imagination, too. Maybe this could be something he looked back on fondly when he was a grown man—how he and his mom had fixed up the old mansion that became Mountain Springs's first art gallery.

Jen leaned against the counter, and when the center of it sagged, she immediately straightened.

She fiddled with her phone again, and this time she dialed her sister's number. It rang twice before it was picked up, but there was no hello.

"Lisa?" Jen said into the phone.

There was a toddler's laugh and the rustling sound of clothing. A TV show could be heard in the background.

"Lisa?" Jen said louder.

There was another rustling sound and the phone hung up. Jen sighed and dialed again. It rang once, and this time Lisa picked up.

"Hello?" She sounded tired.

"Lisa, hi. It's me."

"Hi, Jen." Lisa sighed—not thrilled to hear from her, it would seem.

"How are you doing?" Jen said, choosing to ignore her sister's tone. "So how did you enjoy the wedding?"

"It was great," Lisa replied. "How come you sat on the opposite side of the dining room from the rest of us?"

There was the old petulance in her sister's tone.

"Blame Aunt Gayle," Jen replied. "She was the one who parked me in Siberia."

"But you stayed."

"Aunt Gayle was trying to help me out. It turns out I was at Angelina Cunningham's table. She's experienced in renovating old buildings."

"Great."

"You were the one who put me onto Angelina to begin with," Jen reminded her sister with a short laugh. "Come on! It was great to talk to her. Do you know her personally?"

"I see her around the lodge, but no, we're not pals," Lisa replied. "And I was also the one who wanted to buy that old mansion."

"But you said you couldn't afford it," Jen said, her pulse speeding up. "We talked about this—"

"I still can't afford it," Lisa said curtly. "I don't have a wealthy ex to pay for it."

"Hey—" Jen pressed her lips together. "I was a big part of my husband's career growth—"

"Of course." But Jen could hear the skepticism in her sister's tone. Lisa had never seen Jen's contributions to her home with Sam. Her sister had told her repeatedly that she was stagnating. But she was tired of these old fights. She and Sam were divorced now—did she and Lisa need to keep arguing about it?

"And I did end up going over to talk with family at the wedding," Jen said, changing the subject. "You'd already left."

"I was paying a sitter by the hour," her sister said.

"I'm just saying…" She fell silent. She wasn't going to be able to say anything right.

"How's Drew?" Lisa asked.

Lisa might not be a big fan of Jen's, but she did love her nephew.

"He's good. He's…getting ready for Christmas. What can I say? I hate this part of divorce—sharing our son."

"It wouldn't be easy. I can sympathize with that."

Except Jen didn't want her sister's sympathy. Jen had always been the competent older sister—the one with the answers. She didn't like being the divorced one trying to figure things out with her son and her ex-husband.

"So…" Jen cast about, trying to find something to say. "How's the writing?"

"Good. I'm getting another short story published—this one is in an anthology for a small press."

"That's really great," Jen said. "Are they paying you something decent?"

"Just stop," Lisa said irritably. "My writing isn't about the money. This is a really respected anthology. It might not have a huge circulation, but it champions diverse authors.

Getting published there is exciting, and it matters, and—" She sighed. "Never mind."

"No, it's great! I'm not raining on your parade, it's just…"

Whatever. This was an old argument. Jen had wanted an education and degrees, and Lisa had gone the starving-artist route. But why she insisted on starving when she could have a decent day job was beyond Jen.

"Bram!" Lisa's voice grew shriller. "No! Give it to me. Bram… Give it…"

"So how is *my* nephew?" Jen asked, changing the subject.

"He's rotten!" Lisa said with a laugh, and she heard Bram squeal, too. "Aren't you? Are you rotten?"

There was a thunderous peal of chimes and Jen startled. It would take a while to get used to this old place. She headed out of the kitchen and through the dining room. The old house had come with some of the furnishings included, such as the old dining room table that could seat twenty—there was no fitting that table anywhere else—some of the bigger couches and a few larger pieces of art. They weren't worth much—if anything they were gaudy eyesores—but they filled up some of the wall space for the time being.

As Jen made her way to the marble-tiled foyer and the front door, she could hear her sister playing with her son over the phone.

"Can I come visit one of these days?" Jen asked her sister as she pulled open the front door.

Nick stood there in an open winter coat, and he held a leather tool belt in one hand, heavy with tools. He looked different in the light of day—a little older, but not in a bad way. His beard was the full kind—dark, with a few strands of silver worked through. He had that competent look about him, and his dark gray eyes locked on to hers with professional reserve. Behind him the snow was coming down in lazy, pirouetting flakes—a few of which had landed on his hair. Jen covered the mouthpiece.

"Hi," she said. "Come in. I'll just be a minute."

"Yeah, take your time," Nick said, and he came inside, closing the door behind him. He scanned the room, his gaze moving from the marble-tiled floor up to the ceiling. He knocked on the wall a couple of times, then gave her an absent smile and moved on into the large sitting room.

"You want to come over here?" Lisa asked skeptically, picking the conversation back up. "You've never liked my place."

"I've never liked your boyfriends," Jen countered. "Very different."

"Hilarious," Lisa said dryly. "I'm not exactly guest ready, Jen…"

"I'm not a guest!" Jen retorted. "I'm your sister. You don't need to clean for me." Lisa's answer was a short laugh, and Jen lowered her voice. "Lisa, I'd like to see you. Okay? I miss you."

"No, you're lonely, and that's something different," Lisa replied.

Nick looked over his shoulder at her, and she felt the heat hit her face. She hadn't actually expected her sister to put up a fight at the prospect of a visit. How long had it been since they'd lived in the same town?

Jen turned away and lowered her voice further. "Seriously?"

"I'm home today, if you want to come by," Lisa said. "But it won't be clean, and I didn't get groceries."

"That's fine. I don't care. I've got to do something here, and then I'll come by."

"Okay. You have my address."

"Yeah, I'll see you later. Bye." Jen hung up before her sister could change her mind, and she gave Nick a tight smile. "My sister," she said. "We have a complicated relationship."

Nick shrugged. "I've got a brother. I get it."

She was grateful for that, and she nodded toward the kitchen. "The counter is in rough shape, and the kitchen sink seems like it's been leaking for a long time. There's a bucket under there to catch drips, but I think the problem is bigger than that."

The problem hanging between her and Lisa was similarly complicated, and it would be even harder to fix than this dilapidated old mansion.

"I'll take a look," Nick said, and he cast her a relaxed smile.

There was something about his easy way of moving that took down her stress a couple of notches. And there was something in his smile that tugged at her in an old familiar way… She knew that feeling—the promise of rescue. That was dangerous. She'd done this before with Sam, but back then she was being rescued from something entirely different... Feelings brought about by handsome men with alluring smiles weren't to be trusted. Maybe fixing something in this house would be enough to make her feel like she was in control again.

NICK SCANNED THE KITCHEN, noting the original cupboards and crown molding. He poked his head into the pantry—clean and empty—and noted the servants' staircase. Old houses like this one could be a Russian doll kind of situation when it came to work that needed to be done. He ran his hand along the counter and he could feel the soft spots where the wood had rotted away beneath the Formica. It had obviously been updated in the sixties or seventies. He headed over to the sink. This was also original, but when he looked beneath, he saw that there had been some significant plumbing updates.

He glanced up and found Jen watching him in tense silence. She had her arms crossed under her breasts and her blond waves tucked behind her ears. The difference between the almost makeup-free woman before him and the dressed-up version he'd met last night was large, but he liked her better like this. She was more accessible, maybe—not that he should even be noticing.

"So walk me through what you want done before Christmas," he said.

"I need a functional kitchen," she said, "and the shower upstairs is too old to even use, I think. It creaks and groans and the water comes out in a dribble."

"I've got an excellent plumber I work with," Nick said. No need to mention that Bert was his best friend. He wasn't working with him because of the friendship alone. "I don't know how extensive the plumbing work would be, so I can't speak for him, but replacing this counter would be easy enough, and we could install a new sink. The plumbing down here has been updated over the years, so that's a start." He turned on the water and then looked under the sink. He felt along the seals and pipes. "Yeah, it's leaking up here at the tap. That's soaked the counter wood and it rotted out. It's going to affect the bottom cupboards, as well, but I don't know how badly until I get the counter off. That said, it's not as big of a problem as it could have been. I might even be able to find a comparable antique sink to fit this spot."

"That would be great." She brightened slightly.

"Should we go check out the bathroom?" he asked.

"Yes. Let's do that." She headed for the pantry and he followed her up the narrow staircase. There wasn't much space to move in, but Jen was a lot smaller than he was, and she jogged up the staircase, the soft scent of her soap meeting him as he came up behind her. When they got to the top, they emerged onto the second-floor hallway. It smelled mustier up here—the combination of dust and wood, and he glanced curiously at the doors, most of which were ajar, daylight flooding from the rooms into the dimmer hallway.

"I think the third floor must have been the servants' quarters back in the day, but it's been redone since," Jen said, leading the way up another narrow flight of stairs. "There are two large bedrooms and a bathroom up here—and that's the bathroom that I'd like to be functional. I have a feeling the old lady who owned this place before me just used the one on the second floor."

The staircase opened up onto a sitting room on the third floor. There was some antique furniture arranged around a faded rug and a monstrous wood-framed TV set in one corner. A newer TV rested on top of it, using the old wood frame as a stand.

"A lot of furniture came with the place?" he asked.

"Yeah—the pieces that were too large to move or use in a modern home, I suppose," she replied.

"Can I take a look around?" Nick asked.

"Be my guest."

He checked out the first bedroom. The windows were gabled, but the ceiling was high enough for comfort. A large wooden wardrobe sat on one side of the room and a bed had been set up—fresh linens and a gray, puffy duvet. There was a chest of drawers with some framed pictures on top—a little boy in one, and a couple in the other. Her son, perhaps? He was curious, but this was her bedroom, and not his business. He moved on.

The second bedroom was smaller with a

bank of gabled windows on one wall. There were a fair number of boxes—some still taped shut, and others hanging open in the process of unpacking, it seemed. Another bed was in pieces.

A bathroom was set between the bedrooms, each having a door that opened onto it. The bathroom itself was spacious enough—two sinks, a large beveled mirror and a claw-foot tub with a large showerhead looming over the top of it. He headed over and turned on the water. As she'd said, the pipes moaned and rattled, then a dribble of water came out of the tap. That rusted and corroded showerhead would need replacing. Still...

"This house is amazing," he murmured.

"I know, isn't it?" A smile flickered over her face. "Can you imagine the history?"

"The people who built this house owned a silver mine on the far side of the lake," Nick said. "They had a disabled daughter they refused to send to a sanitarium. She inherited it all."

"I didn't know that," Jen replied.

"Eventually, the daughter sold it," Nick

said. "I don't know the rest of the house's history, but I do know that much."

Jen met his gaze for a moment. "Did you grow up in Mountain Springs?"

"I moved here for a job at the wood mill when I was twenty. A couple of years later I met my wife who came out here for a job, too, at a local law firm, and we got married and settled down," he replied.

"Your ex-wife's a lawyer?" Jen said.

"Her name's Shari," he said. "Anyway, I met my plumber, Bert, about the same time."

"Bert Wilkins?" she asked.

"Yeah. You know him?" Nick asked.

"Yeah. I used to babysit for him," she said with a short laugh. "His boys were a handful. So much energy."

"Wow... He and I have been friends for years," Nick said with a shake of his head. "I guess it works that way in a place this small."

"What are the boys doing now?" she asked.

"Nathan's in college, John is working up at a lumber mill and Colin just got married last summer," Nick replied.

"Time flies," she said. "That's great. I'm glad they're all doing well."

"How about you?" he asked. "You obviously babysat for Bert, but…"

"I was raised here," she replied. "That's obvious, I guess. We knew the Wilkins family from church. I lived on the other side of the tracks, though. I grew up in the old row houses—and it was a bit nicer then. I feel like I should point that out."

He knew the part of town she was referencing and could guess she'd grown up poor. "There's something about these mountains that pulls you back, isn't there?"

She smiled wistfully. "I didn't come back for the mountains, exactly… But this place has real potential."

He had a feeling that she was talking about business potential, not the kind of sublime awe he felt when he stared up at those jagged mountain peaks and smelled the glacial fresh air.

"So what brought you home, then?" he asked. "Business?"

She shrugged faintly. "A fresh start has to start somewhere. My parents have both passed, and I have family in Mountain Springs—my sister included. I think I need to get those relationships in order again."

"I know that feeling," he admitted.

"Do you?" She looked hopeful.

"My daughter—I'm trying to fix a few things with her, too."

"Yeah...kids aren't easy, are they?"

"Not really," he agreed.

Why was he doing this—opening up this way? He didn't do that with other clients, but there was something about this woman that was prying loose his reservations. This was getting too personal for him.

"You know, there's a local writer who grew up in that same neighborhood across the tracks," he said. "Did you know Lisa Dear?"

Jen paled. "That's my sister."

"Seriously?" Nick looked over at her in surprise. "I know her. She and I met at the dog park."

"Are you two...involved?" Jen asked delicately.

"No." He laughed softly. "It's not like that. We're just friends."

"Oh." She nodded. "Just wondering. It would have affected things."

"Like what?" he asked.

"Um…" She shrugged. "My sister and I tiptoe around each other a little bit."

"Her dog died," he said. "So I don't see her as often anymore. But we have a lot of mutual friends, so we got to know each other. She used to talk about this house, too—"

Jen dropped her gaze. Whatever friendliness had been building between them seemed to pop, and they stood there for a couple of beats in silence. This was supposed to be about her house—not her sister. And obviously, there was some tension between the two women.

Lisa used to talk about buying this old mansion, not that she'd been able to afford it. It looked like both sisters had similar taste in real estate, at the very least.

"Well," he said, clearing his throat. "I can get that sink and counter replaced for you within a few days. I'm not sure how much damage will be underneath there, but we can rebuild the cupboards and replicate what you've got, or we can look at alternatives."

"I'd like to keep it the same—authenticity and all that," she said.

"Great. We can do that. Once we get the counters off, I can tell you what we're dealing with. As for the bathroom, I'll call in my plumber and get him to check it out. We had a cancellation, so we do have a bit of free time to dedicate to this. But come February, we're booked for another two months."

"Okay." She nodded. "I appreciate whatever time you give me right now. I'll be looking for a contractor to help renovate the rest of the house this spring, too."

Was that an invitation to put in a bid? If he wasn't otherwise booked, he'd throw his hat in the ring for this job. He wouldn't pass up a chance to work on this old mansion.

Nick pulled out a pen and paper, then jotted down some estimates and mentally tallied them. "I'm thinking it will take about two weeks, so up to just before Christmas, and I can do it for this much, if there is only moderate damage beneath." He circled the bottom number and passed it over.

Jen looked at it, then nodded. "I don't have time to shop around, so I'm trusting you on this. Angelina assures me that you're honest and fair." She paused. "Are you expecting me to negotiate here?"

"No," he said with a low laugh. "I give the price that I can do the job for. And that's assuming there aren't any other complications. If anything comes up—more damage than I'm anticipating, for example—that will affect that bottom line, I'll talk to you about it and you can decide what you want to do."

"Did you need some time to think about it?" he asked.

"When could you start?" she asked.

"I could start on the kitchen tomorrow. I could have the plumber for an assessment tomorrow or the day after," he replied. "Full disclosure, though, my daughter is coming for Christmas—I'm actually picking her up at the bus station today. I can guarantee that I'll get this work done before Christmas for you, but I'm going to need some flexibility so I can have time with her, as well."

"Fixing that relationship," she said, her voice softening.

"Yeah." He shrugged. "Trying to, at least."

"How old is she, if you don't mind me asking?" Jen asked. "You seem pretty young."

"I'm forty-five and she's twenty-three," he replied with a small smile.

"They're so cute at that age." She shot him a grin, and he chuckled.

"Absolutely adorable. They know everything." And Amelia was more self-assured than most.

"They seem to think so at twelve, too," she said with a shake of her head. "Okay. You have yourself a deal. Thank you."

Nick held out his hand, and she accepted his handshake. Her hand was slim and cool—just like it had felt in his hand last night while they were dancing, and he pushed back the memory. Her cheeks flushed, and she pulled her hand out of his. He wondered if she was remembering the same thing.

"Okay. I'd better head out, then," he said.

"Sure. Thanks again."

He still felt that inexplicable tug toward her. He needed to tamp that down. This couldn't get personal... Besides, he'd heard a few stories about Lisa's sister who'd married some rich guy. He should have connected it sooner.

Nick turned toward the stairs. "I'll be here by eight tomorrow morning to do some measuring and get started."

He could hear Jen's footsteps behind him on the staircase, and when they got back down to the kitchen below, he cast another cursory glance around the room. It wouldn't be too big of a job, and this place was truly beautiful. He was glad to see that it was going to be cared for and wouldn't just crumble into ruins.

Nick headed for the front door, and when he got there, he stepped back into his boots. He had a few things he wanted to do before he picked up his daughter this afternoon—namely, pull out the old Christmas decorations. Amelia used to love Christmas, once upon a time, and so did he. He used to read her Christmas stories as a kid, take her shopping on Main Street, make hot cocoa together with way too many marshmallows. But that was a long time ago...

"See you tomorrow," Nick said. "And, um, say hi to Lisa for me."

"Will do."

As Nick gave Jen a nod of farewell and he stepped out into the swirling December snow, his heart fluttered in anticipation—and this time not for the beautiful woman with the soft blue eyes that made him talk too much in spite of himself. This flutter in his chest was for his daughter. He couldn't wait to see her.

CHAPTER THREE

JEN PULLED INTO the driveway in front of a squat duplex and parked her SUV behind a rusty white hatchback that blended into the snowy driveway. This was it.

As she got out and slammed shut the door, she heard a thump against the window and looked up to see a toddler with his hands against the glass and a huge grin on his face. That would be her nephew, and her heart melted at the sight of him. The last time she'd seen Bram in person, he was a couple of months old. But she had a lot of photos for the time in between. She waved at him.

Bram thumped the window a few more times until Lisa appeared behind him to scoop him up, and they both disappeared. When Jen got to the front door, Lisa pulled it open before she even knocked and stepped back to let her in.

"Hi!" Jen said, and she leaned it to give her sister a one-armed hug. "You look great."

Lisa wore a pair of purple leggings with a matching hip-length sweater. For all of her claims that she wasn't going to clean, the place smelled like bleach and when Jen glanced around, it was neat and tidy.

"Hi, Bram! How are you?" Jen asked, bending down to the toddler's level and giving him a big smile. "I'm your auntie!"

"Come on in," Lisa said, and Jen slipped out of her boots and hung her coat up on a hook next to the door, then followed her sister inside. The duplex was small and older, and a large section of the living room was occupied by colorful plastic toddler toys.

"So how come you moved?" Jen asked. The last time she'd seen her sister, she was living in an apartment on the other side of town.

"This place has a little yard," Lisa replied. "And I wanted Bram to be able to play outside."

Lisa put Bram down in the kitchen. The dishwasher was whirring and there was a pile of dishes in one sink. Bram headed off to a laundry basket and started to pull the clothes out of it piece by piece. He was still a little young to be running out to play, but Jen could sympathize with the thought.

"Do you want some coffee or something?" Lisa asked.

"Sure."

Lisa pulled a canister out of a cupboard and started filling the coffeemaker on the counter.

"So how long are you back for?" Lisa asked.

"Um…" Jen shrugged. "For good, I think."

Lisa smirked. "No, really."

"I'm serious," Jen said. "I mean, it's a little complicated with Sam. He says that as long as I can wing it here financially and Drew is happy, he won't push for custody. And you love that mansion as much as I do!" It sounded pretentious to even say it, somehow, and Jen felt her cheeks heat. "I think it'll be good for Drew to grow up in a smaller place."

"You couldn't wait to get out of Mountain Springs."

"I know, but that was different." She'd been younger then, and desperate to get away from the dingy life here and achieve something better. Besides, people saw her a certain way in Mountain Springs—she was one of the Dear kids, and no one seemed to expect much from them. If she'd gotten a job and helped her parents pay some bills, that would have been enough. But she'd wanted more than that. She'd been so certain that she'd been destined for greatness, if she could just shake this town off her boot.

"Drew is going to grow up in a mansion, so those small-town ideals might be a little distant." Lisa raised an eyebrow. Her sister always did have a way of making Jen's life sound tawdry.

"Hey, you would have bought it!" Jen countered. "So don't act like me buying that place is some moral failing."

"Yeah, look around," Lisa retorted. "I'm swimming in that down payment."

Jen sighed. "Lisa, we were poor when we were kids. And Mom and Dad did their best, but there is no getting around that. Yeah—I wanted out. I don't know why you didn't."

"Because this is my home," Lisa replied.

"Or, this is your source of all that angsty writing," Jen said, attempting to tease.

"At least I know who I am," Lisa replied.

"I know who I am, too," Jen said.

"Mrs. Taylor, the professor's young wife," Lisa said, but her smile looked more natural now. "She's very bright, they say."

"Oh, shut up," Jen sighed. "I'm not Mrs. Taylor anymore, and I'll have to figure things out. I'm sure you'll enjoy that."

"I'm not enjoying your divorce," Lisa replied, sobering. "But I never liked him. Sam was pompous, egotistical and thought he was better than the rest of us."

"Well, I'm more inclined to agree with you now," Jen said.

"So…about the mansion. Who's doing the work on it?" Lisa asked.

"A friend of yours," Jen said. "Nick Bryant."

Lisa raised her eyebrows. "I could have told you about him if you'd asked."

"I know," Jen replied. "And I would have, but Angelina Cunningham was the one to introduce me to him, and he worked on the lodge."

"He's a good guy," Lisa said.

"He comes well recommended," Jen replied.

"No, I mean, he's a sweet guy," Lisa said.

"And he's got a big heart. He's not your type."

"He's working on the house, Lisa," Jen said. "What do you think I'm going to do?"

"I don't know. I'm just saying—he's not someone to use for your own ends."

Jen stared at Lisa, anger simmering. What did her sister think of her, that she was prowling around looking for some naive guy to manipulate into...into what, exactly? But before Jen could say anything, Bram tramped over to where Jen stood, a pair of his mother's underwear in one fist. Jen squatted down and held out her hand.

"Can I have it?" she asked brightly.

"Oh, geez," Lisa said, rolling her eyes. "Bram, those are Mommy's!"

Bram handed them over to Jen, and Jen wadded them up and tossed them to her sister.

Why did it always feel like she and Lisa were on the edge of a major fight? Their relationship had never been an easy one, but when she'd gone off to school and met Samuel, whatever that was left of it seemed to snap.

"I'm not looking for a guy, Lisa," Jen said.

"Good," Lisa replied. "Do this one on your own."

Jen felt her cheeks heat, but she didn't answer her sister. Whatever Lisa thought of her, over time Jen hoped she'd have to see that she was wrong.

"How's Drew doing?" Lisa asked after a few beats of silence.

"He likes his dad's girlfriend," Jen replied, grateful for a change in topic. "So he's doing fine, I guess. It could be worse. He could hate her."

The coffeemaker sputtered to a stop and Lisa poured two mugs and slid one in Jen's direction.

"How is he doing in school?" Lisa asked.

"Okay. He's smart, but he doesn't really apply himself. I wish he would."

"He has to find what he likes first," Lisa said.

And maybe her sister was right. Besides, whether he liked his dad's new girlfriend or not, he'd just gone through his parents' divorce, and that wasn't easy on any of them.

"And how is Sam?" Lisa asked.

"Better than me." Jen felt tears mist her

eyes. "Whatever. He's self-centered and egotistical, just like you said."

"You said he might push for custody," Lisa
said. "Is that a real threat? Does he want
Drew to stay with him?"

Jen frowned. "He hasn't asked for it out-
right. He thinks having Drew for the summer, spring break and every other Christmas
will work well. He's very busy, with his
books and his classes, and other projects..."

Jen could hear it in her voice—she'd always made excuses for Samuel, and she
let her voice trail away, not finishing the
thought.

"I guess that's good, then," Lisa said. "I'm
glad I don't have Bram's dad asking for anything. It's less complicated."

Jen didn't comment. They'd already argued over whether or not Bram deserved to
have his dad in his life, and Jen's opinions
didn't count for a lot.

"So what about you, Lisa?" Jen asked, trying to brighten her tone.

"What about me?" her sister asked.

"Have you ever considered taking some
creative writing classes?" Jen asked. "The
university offers a few online. I think you'd

have to be enrolled in their creative writing program, but a friend of mine started the program and—"

"Jen."

Jen stopped.

"Do you know what I've been doing all this time?" her sister asked, cocking her head to one side.

Working a housekeeping job at Mountain Springs Lodge and dating the wrong kinds of guys, mostly. But Jen didn't say that.

"I've been reading," Lisa went on when Jen hadn't answered. "I've been reading book after book—the classics, the important authors and all the frivolous fiction I can squeeze in. For years, Jen. And when I wasn't reading, I was writing. Story after story, honing my craft. I don't need a class to tell me how to find my voice or how to get published. I already am published, and I'm good at what I do. I don't need a step up, okay?"

"Okay." Jen eyed her sister for a moment. "How many stories have you had published now? It was about fifteen last I counted, right?"

"Forty-one. But if you want to include just

the journals you'd be impressed with, six-teen."

Jen let out a breath. That many? Lisa was right. That did sound like success in its own right, and maybe Lisa had managed to do that her own way without her big sister's advice. How much had they missed out on in each other's lives these past years?

"Can I read some?" Jen asked hesitantly.

"You've read some before," Lisa said with a shrug. "It's more of the same."

"Yeah, but apparently, there are about twenty-five I never even knew about!" Jen said with a short laugh.

"Don't worry about it. I'll give you a few copies I have kicking around," Lisa replied.

But Lisa didn't move from her position, her mug of coffee in front of her and her gaze on Jen.

Bram had a pile of envelopes in one fist, and as Lisa put her mug on the counter and turned to grab a box of animal crackers, Bram dropped the pile of mail at Jen's feet. She bent down to pick it up, then froze when she saw the front of one of the envelopes. It had a red stamp across it: *Past Due*. Another envelope, this one from the electricity company, said *Final Notice*. Jen's heart sped up, and she gathered up the envelopes and tossed them onto the counter, making sure the top one was a plain envelope. If her sister knew she'd seen the others, she'd be embarrassed, and whatever sisterly rapport Jen hoped to reestablish would be officially over.

Lisa handed Bram a few animal crackers and picked up her coffee again.

"What should I get Bram for Christmas?" Jen asked.

"Nothing."

"He's my nephew," Jen said.

"Look, let's not start that. If we do gifts for each other's kids, you're going to spend more than I can afford to spend on Drew, and it's going to get awkward."

"Okay..."

It didn't feel right, not being able to give the little guy a present, but Lisa was going to be sensitive about money right now. Besides, it wasn't like Jen was wallowing in cash. She had a house to renovate before she could even start building her own business.

This was going to be a lonesome Christmas. Somehow, this made Jen think about Uncle Stu. Aunt Gayle might be remarried, but Uncle Stu, her first husband, was still in town. He'd be lonely, too.

"Lisa?" Jen said quietly.

Lisa met her gaze and raised her eyebrows.

"Have you gone to see Uncle Stu since the divorce?" Jen asked.

"I saw him at Easter, at the big egg hunt we always do for the kids."

"Have you visited him?" Jen asked.

"Not personally. We got Gayle in the divorce, I thought."

"Agreed, but who got *him*?" Jen asked. "He's got his own kids who will be in contact and all that, but… That divorce wasn't his fault, you know. I think he tried to be the man his family needed, but he just couldn't do it anymore. I feel bad for him. And I miss him, too."

Lisa smiled faintly. "Yeah, Uncle Stu was great. Tricia is furious with him still, though."

"It would be really hard seeing your parents split up, especially after all those years," Jen acknowledged. "But I feel for him. He and Gayle got married in a different time."

"I agree," Lisa said. "But you always got along with Stu better than I did. You two liked watching old *Star Trek* shows, remember? That was your thing."

"Maybe I'll drop by and visit him," Jen said.

"You should," Lisa agreed. "I don't have a ton of time, quite honestly. I'm working as much as I can, and when I'm not working, I've got a screenplay I wanted to finish so I can enter it into a local contest in the New Year."

Busy. Yes, message received. But Jen just nodded.

"Of course. I get it. Squeeze in a few visits with me, if you can, though, okay?"

Seeing some family that was just as heartbroken as she was—maybe that was the answer this Christmas. Aunt Gayle was remarried, Drew was having Christmas with Sam and Tiffany, and Lisa was secretly broke. Maybe this Christmas could be about raising a glass in solidarity with all the other broken hearts in the family.

It was better than sitting alone.

MOUNTAIN SPRINGS WAS all decked out for Christmas—lights twined around every tree on Main Street, and the streetlights were hung with festive bells. With the snow-covered mountains and the chalet-styled buildings, this little Colorado town could almost be mistaken for somewhere far away. The town boasted some extreme skiing up in the mountain passes, and lots of good food and cozy fireplaces down in the valley. The Mountain Springs bus station stayed continually busy all year round, bringing in the backpacking tourists looking for a mountain experience.

Nick stood waiting as the latest bus emptied of travelers. He scanned the faces, and when Amelia descended the bus stairs, he couldn't help but grin. She was dressed in a pair of black leggings and a complicated-looking wrap. Her makeup was done, her hair pulled back in some sort of bun, and she squinted past the snow flurries as she waited on her suitcase. The driver heaved it out of the luggage compartment in the bottom of the bus, and Nick came forward to grab it for his daughter.

"Oh, hi, Dad." Amelia let him give her an awkward hug, then stood back as he hoisted her suitcase out of the fray.

Nick led the way through the terminal,

and he glanced down at his daughter cautiously. She looked older—a grown woman now. He'd seen her in the spring when he went down to the university to take her out to dinner. She'd canceled other plans in order to see him, but he'd caught her checking the time on her phone a few times while they caught up. Their visits were always short and somewhat uncomfortable.

"You look great, Amelia," he said.

"Thanks." She hitched her shoulders up against the cold and tugged her wrap a little closer. "So...what's the plan here?"

"I thought I'd take you home," he said. "Are you hungry for some lunch?"

"I could eat."

That was something. "Good. I have the fixings for those pizza buns you used to love as a kid. I figured we could have some for old times' sake."

"Sure."

Nick's pickup was parked near the door, and he tossed her suitcase into the back seat beside some of his dog Goldie's chewed-over tennis balls, then opened the door for Amelia to get into the warmth of the vehicle. He headed around to the driver's side and got in, glad to get out of the frigid wind. He looked over at his daughter again as he started the truck.

"I'm glad you're here," he said. "I've really missed you."

"That was a long bus ride," she said in response. "I was stuck next to a talker."

Nick put on his seat belt, then put the truck into Reverse to pull out of the parking space.

"Nothing changes here, does it?" Amelia said, sounding bored.

Nick smiled at that. "Not a lot. Well... there are a few new hotels that went up since you've been here."

But she wasn't talking about local construction, and he knew it. She was talking about the feel of Mountain Springs, the coziness of being nestled into a narrow valley with those looming, jagged mountain peaks all around.

"You haven't met Goldie yet," he said.

"Isn't this the dog that refused to pee outside?" she asked with a low laugh.

"That was last winter. She was still a puppy."

"Right. Does she pee outside now?" she asked.

"Yeah. She's a good dog. You two will get along."

Amelia fell silent, and for a few minutes Nick navigated the intersections that led back toward Oak Ridge Drive where he lived.

"So…how's Ben?" he asked.

"He's fine. He's with his family in Aspen for the holidays," she replied. "But I'm not sure you should get attached."

Nick wasn't attached to that guy. Ben was nice enough, but his daughter didn't seem as happy as she should be with him. Call it a hunch.

"What's going on?" Nick asked.

"I don't know. I guess I'm looking to get serious about more than just my career. I'm ready to get married, settle down, start a family, maybe. And Ben isn't."

"You think you're ready to settle down?" he asked skeptically.

"Yeah. I do." Her tone was curt.

"And Ben doesn't want that?"

"He would…" She didn't elaborate.

"I'm sorry," he said, unsure of what else to say.

"Don't say that like we're already over,"

Amelia said. "We're talking about that stuff. That's all."

And they were spending Christmas apart. Nick knew what that meant, and he felt a pang of pity for his daughter.

"How is school going?" he asked.

"It's good."

"Any favorite classes?" he asked hopefully.

"Dad, come on." As if that was a pitiful question.

Nick sighed. "How's your mom enjoying Europe?"

"Mom and Chris are doing fine," she said. "I kind of wish I was doing Europe with them, but I understand the need for some private time."

Nick fell silent again. Of course he didn't really want to know the details of his ex-wife's new life. His divorce had been incredibly painful, but he was better off now. At least he didn't have someone constantly looking down on him. Not that Shari had meant to. It was just how she saw the world—the details she noticed, the connections she made. She started out as a lawyer in Mountain Springs covering everything from traffic cases to real estate, and now she was a hotshot criminal defense attorney in Denver. Shari loved pedantic detail. The older Amelia got, the more often he'd heard the old, "For crying out loud, Nick! Even our daughter gets it!"

Had Amelia really understood her mother's theories about legal defenses, or had she just enjoyed her mother's approval when she pretended to? He was more inclined to believe the latter.

"So what about you?" Amelia asked. "Any girlfriend I should be aware of?"

"Nope." He chuckled. "It's just me."

"What about that one—" Amelia cast around "—Bev, was it? You were dating for a while, and then you said you two broke up, and then you got back together..."

Bev had been special, but at the end of the day, they'd been too much alike. They bored each other.

"Bev has moved on," he said, casting his daughter a small smile. "She's living with a guy in Denver now."

"Oh..." She eyed him for a moment. "That's too bad, though. I think you're lonely."

"Why do you think that?" He slowed to a stop at an intersection and waited while some pedestrians crossed the street.

"I don't know. I just get the feeling. Like when you dropped in to see me at school."

"I missed *my daughter*," he said curtly. "That isn't a sign of weakness, Amelia. And it was nine months ago."

Had his visit really been that traumatizing? It was *one meal*!

"You should get married again," she said.

Not interested. He was still gun-shy of marriage, and his personal tastes were his own worst enemy.

Nick's house on Oak Ridge Drive was a short ride from downtown, and he glanced across the street at the old mansion before he turned in to his driveway. He parked and hopped out, grabbed Amelia's suitcase and led the way to the front door.

Nick opened the door and the sound of scrambling dog toenails made him smile. He walked inside as Goldie bounded around a corner and barked joyfully at his return.

"This is Goldie," Nick said. "And Goldie, this is Amelia."

Amelia gave him a bland smile, but she

bent down and ruffled the golden retriever's ears.

"Does that old lady still live there?" Amelia asked.

He knew what house she was talking about—the same one that had his attention lately, too.

"She died. There's been a few different owners since. It just sold again," he replied.

"It went up for sale recently, then?" Amelia asked. She pulled off her coat and stepped out of her shoes.

"Yeah. You want slippers or something?" he asked, looking down at her sock feet.

"Dad, I'm fine." She smiled ruefully. "You know that old mansion is a really good investment. If it were to be restored, it would be just stunning."

"It will be," he agreed. "I'm actually doing some renovations for the new owner. I might put in a bid to do those restorations, too, if I've got the time in my schedule."

"You should have *bought* the place, Dad," his daughter said incredulously.

"Another mortgage? I don't know. Life doesn't always turn out the way you anticipate, and I don't want more debt."

"You have to spend money to make it. That's what Chris always says, and that's why it's easier for people who already have money to make more. But if you're smart—"

"Amelia. Thanks for the advice, but it's no longer for sale," he said.

Always a step behind what the women in his life expected of him. He sighed and headed into the kitchen. He was hungry, in spite of it all. And no, he shouldn't have bought that house. He'd considered it, but he didn't flip houses much anymore. His contractor business kept him amply busy. And it would have put him into some serious debt, he'd have to do the work himself to renovate and restore and that could take years. Sure, he could have sold it, then made some money in the flip, but what about the interest paid to the bank in the meantime?

"I'm going to get those pizza buns started," he said over his shoulder, and Goldie followed at his heels.

Pizza buns used to be his specialty. They weren't really pizza. He used shredded cheese, chicken, onions, celery, mayonnaise and tomato, put it on top of buns, and toasted it all in the oven until the cheese was gooey and bubbling.

"Are these our old Christmas decorations?" Amelia's voice floated to him from the other room.

Nick had gotten them down from the attic last night—the old decorations from when she was little. He figured they could put them around the house together, like old times. He grinned.

"Yeah! Remember how much you loved those little singing bears?"

"Dad, this stuff is junk!"

Her words stabbed past his defenses and made him wince, but he ambled back over to see where she stood at the dining room table, sorting through a box of old ornaments.

"They aren't junk," he said. "You loved those."

"Dad..." She held up a chipped ceramic bear holding a music book, its painted mouth open in an O. "We got these at the dollar store."

And she'd played with them for hours, organizing her choir of Christmas bears underneath the tree. He remembered what she used to look like, lying on her stomach in her Christmas flannel pajamas, her hair all in a tangle, playing with those ornaments that she now considered junk.

"So…you don't want to put them up?" he asked hesitantly. He'd displayed them every year on the windowsill, even after the divorce. It didn't feel like Christmas without them. In fact, they'd inspired his gift for her this year…

"What we need is to go shopping for something decent, Dad," she said. "Something a little less kitsch. What you need is something understated and elegant. How are you going to attract a woman if you don't update your decor a little bit?"

He wasn't trying to attract a woman. Besides, Bev had never complained. This year he wanted a Christmas with his daughter. But if those old ornaments didn't hold the same memories for her, maybe they could make some new ones.

"Are you offering to shop with me?" he asked.

"I think I'll have to," she said. "I can't be leaving you unsupervised with this kind of thing." She waggled the bear at him, her eyes twinkling with laughter.

"Okay, as long as you come with me to shop for it all," he said.

"But not tonight. I'm getting together with Taylor, Mike and Vincent. They're in town, too."

Those were friends from her middle school years, just before the divorce. Nick bent down and smoothed a hand over Goldie's head. She looked up at him with those big, brown, loyal eyes.

"Okay, well…there's time," Nick said, and he headed back into the kitchen, Goldie at his heels again, and pulled out a cutting board to chop onions and celery. It wasn't a complete bust. Amelia had shown some interest in the old mansion. Maybe that could be a starting point for them.

"I'm doing some work on that old house across the street tomorrow morning," he called over his shoulder. "Do you want to come see inside?"

"Really?" she called back.

"Yeah! You interested?" Nick tossed Goldie a piece of cold chicken and she caught and swallowed it in one movement.

"What time?" his daughter asked.

"Eight."

"Too early. I'll pass."

That didn't entirely surprise him, but he was still optimistic. She'd shown some interest, at least. Who knew...maybe this Christmas he'd find a way to remind his daughter that she still had a dad who loved her, even if he couldn't compete financially with her stepfather.

They'd buy new Christmas decorations, he'd cook her some of her old favorite meals and he'd find a way to connect with her if it killed him.

CHAPTER FOUR

JEN SPENT THE rest of the visit with Lisa playing with Bram. Her nephew was a strong, rambunctious little boy, and when she looked down into his upturned face, she was reminded of Drew. Drew was fair-haired, where Bram was dark-haired, but there was a family resemblance in the mouth and eyes.

When she was getting ready to go, pulling her coat back on and stepping into her boots, she gave Lisa a smile.

"I've missed you," Jen said.

"Yeah..." Lisa dropped her gaze.

"Lisa, we're all we've got—each other," Jen said. "Without Mom and Dad, we don't have anyone to make us make up anymore. And that was what Mom always did! She'd call me up and tell me that you were mad at me, or she'd tell you that you'd ticked me off... She ran interference between us, and now that she and Dad are gone, we have to do this ourselves. I don't want to keep fighting like we do."

"A little respect would go a long way," Lisa replied.

"I respect you!" Jen retorted.

"You don't really," Lisa argued. "You love me because I'm your sister, but if you met me in a social context, we'd never end up as friends. You think I'm an idiot for not having gone to school, and you look down on the jobs I do to keep body and soul together while I write."

"I might make different choices in your shoes—" Jen said cautiously.

"No, it's more than that," Lisa replied. "You think I'm beneath you."

"I think you're five years younger," Jen qualified.

"We're both grown women," Lisa replied. "Five years doesn't make that big of a difference. So you're right—Mom and Dad aren't here anymore to help us make up, but I'm also really tired of your condescension. I'm not trying to pick a fight. I'm just pointing it out. You're looking down on me for not having as much, but you're spending your ex-husband's money."

"Is this about me buying the mansion?" Jen asked.

"No."

"Are you sure?" Jen met her gaze. "Because Nick mentioned that you were talking about it—"

"Ah." Lisa nodded. "Right. So why exactly are you and Nick discussing me?"

"He put it together that you're my sister," Jen replied. "And he mentioned that you had talked about the mansion, too. So I'm asking you straight—are you mad that I bought it?"

"I was the one who told you about it," Lisa said. "You only knew about the lodge's renovations and all that because I was working there. You left Mountain Springs for your own posh new life, and then you come back and nab the most sought-after property here?"

"Were you thinking of trying to buy it?" Jen asked. With those bills she'd seen, she hardly thought so.

"I had no hope of buying it, but if I had a little more money saved up—" Lisa's face pinked. "You know what? Whatever! You swooped in and bought it without a second thought. With Sam's money."

"That's my divorce settlement money," Jen said. "I deserved that money. I spent fourteen years helping him."

"Yeah. I know."

It felt like the old arguments all over again—even when they were agreeing, it was from opposite sides. Lisa had always been touchy, in Jen's opinion, at least. Lisa refused to take any advice—from their parents when they were alive, or from Jen. Their mother might have been able to get them to talk to each other again, but Lisa had always taken her own path, mostly just for the sake of exasperating her family. There had been plenty of phone calls from Mom asking Jen to see if she could get through to her younger sister, too, that Lisa wasn't aware of. But then there was the car accident that killed their parents, and Jen and Lisa were left alone…or parentless, at least. Jen had been married and had Drew already, and Lisa had a boyfriend of some sort at the time.

"Is this because of what I said about a creative writing degree? That's just me believing in you—"

"That's you trying to 'improve' me," Lisa said. "I'm thirty-three years old. I've got my own way to do things, and I don't want meddling in my life any more than you want it in yours."

Jen nodded. "Okay. Point taken."

"I'm not your problem to fix," Lisa said.

"I know. I'm sorry. I'll cut it out," Jen replied, forcing what she hoped was a reassuring smile.

"Okay." Lisa nodded. "Thanks for coming."

Jen sighed. Did every visit with her sister have to be so intense? Jen made a kissing face and squeezed Bram's cheeks, then headed out through the snow back to her car. Jen couldn't help but think that her sister, for all of her declarations of being just fine, did need help. It appeared that her finances were in trouble, and she was raising a toddler on her own. The boyfriend had left her before Bram's birth, and he'd never pitched in a cent that Jen knew of. If Jen had her way, she'd have Lisa sue the cad for child support, and get her sister back into school. Lisa's housekeeping job paid pretty well, but if those past-due notices were any indication, Lisa wasn't managing her finances very well. Lisa might not like it, but she was still

Jen's little sister. It was hard to stop wanting to rescue her or offer advice.

When Jen got home, she texted Drew to say hi, and she didn't get an immediate response. She missed him. He might think of himself as so very grown up, but he was still a kid, and she still worried when he wasn't with her. This sharing custody was going to take some adjustment for her.

The sun sank behind the mountains early at this time of year, and Jen flicked on the lights, including the chandelier that hung over that mammoth table. Bright warmth sparkled through the crystals, casting fragments of light around the room, and Jen froze, watching the transformation around her.

Once upon a time, this was an elegant dining room with maids to maintain it, and a family to appreciate it, and it was like the ghost of the house was shining through those crystals... The long table was shrouded in sheets, and Jen pulled them off in a puff of dust to reveal the luxurious wood beneath. It could use a polish, and there were a few obvious marks in the surface of the table, but it was still an extraordinary piece of furniture.

This dining room was so lovely, it made Jen want at least one room in this place to feel beautiful and Christmassy. So she set to cleaning up, gathering the sheets in a bundle and collecting some miscellaneous cleaning supplies that looked at least a decade old that had been left in corners and in one ratty cardboard box. At some point someone else had had a similar idea, she mused.

When she'd collected all the leftover odds and ends that could go into the trash, she headed for the front door. She pulled on her coat and stepped into her boots, then went to toss it into the garbage bins at the side of the house.

It was a long walk around the house through the brisk, cold air as she headed toward the covered car park. There would have been a time when the car park was used for guests arriving for a party, and now it simply held the garbage and recycling bins. However, when this old mansion became an art gallery, there would be events again—art shows, maybe even a few weddings or engagement parties... The thought gave her a thrill.

The sun had set, and streetlights illuminated the road, leaving most of the yard in cozy dusk. Jen scanned the front yard. The house was situated quite close to the street, and across from her was Nick's house—a two-story older home that had been renovated and brought back to life. There was a sweeping veranda around the front, and warm light shone from the downstairs window. A light upstairs flicked on, but when she saw Nick come outside with his dog, she could only assume it was his daughter upstairs.

Or a girlfriend? She blushed. She shouldn't be wondering about his relationship status. He was divorced—that was all she really knew for sure. And the rest wasn't her business. Lisa might know, but she didn't dare ask her sister. Lisa would just assume the worst—that Jen was latching on to some unsuspecting man to make her own life easier.

The dog was on a leash, and Nick came down his driveway at a leisurely pace, the dog trotting at his side. He wore a gray winter jacket, open at the neck, and no hat. He had a certain, confident saunter that drew her gaze, and she felt a rush of annoyance. She'd hired this man to do the work on her new house, and now all she could think about was her sister's opinion of her. Nick was Lisa's friend, and Jen was the one coming back onto Lisa's turf... She was about to turn back to the house when Nick waved. She had an excuse now that he'd been the one to wave, she realized, and she angled her steps across the snowy yard, stopping to lean against the stone gate post that loomed next to the driveway. The fence was long gone, and had been since her childhood, but this cement, lion-topped post remained from days gone by.

Nick crossed the road and gave her an easy smile. "It's a nice night."

"It is," she agreed, and she bent down to pet the dog that was wagging her tail, hopeful for attention. "What's her name?"

"This is Goldie."

"She's beautiful," Jen said, smoothing her hand over the warm, silky head, then straightened. "Did your daughter arrive?"

"Yeah, she's inside." He glanced in that direction, and she saw the confidence in his expression falter. "She's talking to her mother on the phone, so I figured I'd give her some privacy."

"You're hiding, then?" she teased.

"Pretty much." A smile tickled his lips. "What are you doing out here?"

"Dumping trash." She shrugged. "I'm clearing out the dining room."

"I noticed that room. It's gorgeous," he said.

"Yeah…"

"Has Lisa come by to see it yet?" he asked.

She shook her head. "Nope. That's still complicated."

Nick smiled faintly. "I'd be crazy to get involved in that."

Jen laughed. "Probably. I was actually thinking about my son. I wonder if Drew is going to see the same thing I do when I look at it with the chandelier lit… I grew up much differently than Drew has."

He met her gaze. "I grew up pretty far from the likes of this, too."

"Where?" she asked.

"On a little acreage outside of town— a two-bedroom farmhouse with a chicken coop out back, and a few horses."

"That sounds really nice, actually." And it made her feel a little over-the-top to be try-ing to give her son a life in an old mansion when she could have chosen something more down-to-earth.

"It was a good way to grow up," he agreed. "But we didn't have a lot of extras. We only came to town for church, school and groceries." He smiled wistfully. "Swore I'd give my own kid more than I had...and I'm not sure it did her any good."

"Is it not going so well?" she asked.

"Oh...as good as it ever does. Her mom— my ex—is a criminal defense lawyer in Denver, and she married a guy with family money, so the spoiling isn't all on me," he said. "But Amelia doesn't seem to remember the same stuff I do from when she was growing up."

"Is that a word to the wise?" Jen asked. "Because Drew doesn't seem to be appreciating an opportunity to grow up in a gorgeous old house, full of history and character... Twelve-year-old boys seem to have different priorities."

"I wouldn't deign to give parenting advice," Nick said with a chuckle. "But from my experience, you do your best to give them the kind of memories you would have wanted, and they still go their own way. They're their own people."

Maybe that was part of what Jen was afraid of. She was doing her best by her son, and it just didn't seem to be enough.

"Is your daughter more like her mom?" Jen asked.

"She's a whole lot like her mom," he replied.

Jen's phone pinged, and she looked down to see a reply text from Drew.

Watching a movie.

"I texted him about an hour ago—saying I miss him and I hope he's having fun, and this is what I get back." She held her phone up to show Nick, and he squinted at the screen, then chuckled.

"First Christmas without him?" he asked.

She nodded. "Yeah...and he's adjusting better than I am."

"Sucks being the one on the outside, especially at Christmas," Nick said.

"Yeah." She sucked in a breath. "But January will be here before we know it, and I'll get my son to myself for a little while."

Nick nodded.

"Tell me it's easier when they're twenty-three," Jen said, trying to lighten the mood.

"Wish I could." He shrugged. "I was a hands-on father when Amelia was little. I did all sorts of stuff with her—went to all her school plays and her piano recitals. I taught her to cook, and to ride a horse."

"So what happened?" Jen asked.

Nick dropped his gaze, then he glanced up again. "I don't have family money to give her everything she wants. She's going to Harvard—paid by her stepdad."

"That stings, I guess," she said.

"Yeah... Well, I guess part of me resents that Chris is doing this. Just giving someone something—handing them something they haven't worked for."

"A quality education isn't spoiling," Jen said.

"She could have gone to the state school," he said.

"But if her grades were good enough—" Jen countered.

Nick looked at her for a moment, and she could almost see his wheels turning. He was drawing a few conclusions, she could feel it.

"You think I'm a snob," she said.

"No…"

Didn't he, though? She could see it in his eyes.

"If you haven't worked for something, you often don't appreciate it," he said.

"Some things can't be worked for at minimum wage," she said with a shake of her head. "How could a girl pay for Harvard alone?"

"It's not Harvard, exactly," he said. "It's everything. Travel. Shopping. Clothes. Gadgets. Anything she wanted, she got. And I stand by it—if you don't work for stuff, you don't appreciate what you have. My daughter doesn't halfway appreciate it."

That was Lisa's opinion of Jen, too. That she'd married a man with a comfortable life, and she hadn't earned it. But Nick was talking about his daughter—this wasn't about her.

Goldie stood up and started pacing in circles, and Nick looked down at his dog with a small smile.

"She wants her walk," he said.

"Of course…" Jen tugged her coat a little closer around herself. "Thanks for the chat—"

"Unless you wanted to come," he said.

Jen hesitated, and then glanced back at the house. In her mind, she could see her sister's judgmental stare, but there was something inviting in Nick's dark gaze, and Jen found herself returning his smile. Was it so terrible to enjoy a handsome man's company? It was just a walk.

"I should probably lock the door," she said.

"Probably," he agreed. "I'll wait."

She felt a little flutter of happiness at that. She was too old to be developing crushes, and she knew it, but Nick Bryant's easy smile was hard to resist.

NICK WASN'T SURE why he'd asked her to come along. Standing out in the cold winter night, expecting to have a pleasant, solitary walk like he did every night, it didn't make sense to complicate it. But maybe he understood the particular brand of loneliness she was feeling—the kind where a parent could feel that confidence and security in that one unquestionable relationship slipping away.

Add to that, he didn't want to be alone with his own regrets just now.

Jen came back from locking the door, tugging a pair of gloves out of the pocket of her red winter coat. A gust of wind ruffled her sandy-blond curls, and his stomach gave a flip. It wasn't often that a woman made him react like that.

They started walking down the street, Goldie leading the way as she sniffed at the snow and sidewalk. Jen came up to just past his shoulder, and he could smell the faint aroma of her delicate perfume. It vaguely reminded him of Christmas baking—spicy and sweet.

"So what will you do this Christmas?" Nick asked.

"I'm going to survive it," she said quietly.

Nick turned to look at her more directly. "Are you doing okay?"

"I am…" She shook her head. "I'm sorry. I didn't mean to get all heavy. I meant to give you a polite answer like, Oh, I'm going to try and see more of my sister, and I want to drop in on my uncle Stu and see how he is…"

"I think I prefer the truth," Nick said.

"Are you sure?" she asked, and he saw a

sad glimmer in her eye. "Because I can be cheery and normal. Faking it might even be good for me."

"Nah," he said with a low laugh. "Normal is highly overrated."

She smiled at that—a more natural one. "If your daughter wasn't here, what would you be doing for the holidays?"

"I'd be…" He paused, thinking. "I'd be working right until the end on Christmas Eve, and I'd come home to my dog and sit in front of the fireplace. I'd call my daughter, and she'd make stilted conversation with me for a few minutes. And I'd be counting down until the twenty-sixth when everyone's sky-high emotional expectations were past."

Jen looked at him in silence.

"That's the honest answer," he added. "I can be cheery and normal, too, if you'd rather."

Jen laughed softly. "Is it weird that the only person I can be honest around right now is my contractor?"

"Yes," he said. "Incredibly. But you're not alone. The only person I can be open with is my client."

"Are you going to tell Lisa what I say?" Jen asked.

He smiled at that. "Nope. Wasn't planning on it. We aren't that close."

"Okay."

"You two have a lot of tension, huh?" he said.

"You could say that," she agreed. "We have a lot to work out between us. It's part of what brought me back."

Goldie stopped to pee beside a shrub, and they waited under a streetlight while she sniffed around.

"Are you regretting the divorce this Christmas?" he asked her.

Jen shook her head. "No. Samuel and I were very much over. I couldn't go another year being his disappointment, and I don't think he wanted to go another year with a wife who was pushing forty."

"We aren't all like that," Nick said. "Personally, I could never date a woman my daughter's age. Besides, I like a woman who has some life experience to match my own."

"That's nice to hear," Jen said with a small smile. "Do you…have that?"

"A girlfriend, you mean?" he asked.

She nodded, her cheeks pinking a little more than they already were in the cold.

"No girlfriend," he said. "I'm tough to nail down."

She smiled at that. "Just making sure I won't have any explaining to do."

"You're safe." He shot her a grin.

"You know, I wouldn't undo the marriage," Jen said, "because it created Drew, and he's the best kid ever. But I should have left Sam earlier. Being with him sucked me dry."

"That's how I felt, too, that first Christmas," he replied. "Everyone thought I'd be regretting it—wanting to beg Shari to take me back. But I really was past the point of no return." He paused, his mind returning to this daughter. "How old were you when you got married?"

"Twenty-four," she said. "Young. Not that twenty-four is too young for everyone, but it was for me."

He nodded. "Yeah…" Amelia was only twenty-three.

"Does it get easier being alone?" she asked.

Their boots crunched over the snowy sidewalk, and he liked the sound of their synchronized footsteps.

"You get used to it," he replied, and when she met his gaze, he felt a smile tickle his lips. What was it about her that made him want to be the tough guy—the one who had it all together? He wasn't either of those things, truthfully. He had feelings—they just lay deep beneath layers of male pride and social conditioning.

"Besides," he added. "I've got Goldie. She's good company."

"I should get a cat," Jen said. "Or a parrot. I've always wanted a parrot that I could teach to talk."

"I knew a guy who had a swearing parrot," Nick said.

"That might not fit into an art gallery," she said with a short laugh. "And I'm in no hurry to broaden Drew's naughty vocabulary."

Nick laughed at that. "But pets do help. They're...soothing."

"And they get you active," she said. "Well, dogs do, at least."

More than active. Sometimes they could drop a man in front of his pretty neighbor on a beautiful winter night.

When they got to the intersection, he could see all the way down the long, sloping drive that led to downtown Mountain Springs. The downtown core was lit up with Christmas lights, the tall tree glowed from the center of a park and they could see people walking around. The mountainside behind them was lit, too, with the chairlift from one of the ski slopes.

"I love this view," he murmured. "Every night I walk out this way after dark, just to see the lights."

"The tourists have no idea that real people live real lives here," Jen said softly.

He glanced down at her. "They're on vacation, escaping their own real lives."

"I suppose." She chuckled. "And they do sustain our economy. I'm going to be hoping to lure them up to an art gallery soon enough."

They turned back the way they'd come and started walking once more. She fell into step beside him, and it felt good to have her there—comforting. But he didn't want that—not really. Jen was the type who naturally sided with Shari and Chris in the spoiling of his daughter...not what he needed!

Beautiful and vulnerable or not, she was the wrong type.

A chill breeze whipped through the spruce trees bringing a sprinkling of snow with it, and they both dropped their heads against the sudden driving cold. Jen stepped closer to him, pressing her arm against his. Was it instinct that made him want to put an arm around her? He had to stop himself from following through on it. Whatever comfort he felt with her couldn't be mistaken for something deeper.

Goldie trotted on ahead, seemingly oblivious to the cold wind, and when she stopped to sniff that same bush again, he tugged on her leash.

"Come on, Goldie," he called. "We're going home."

The dog complied and caught up with them. He should get back inside, anyway. Amelia was probably finished chatting with her mom, and he'd get another chance to try and chip through his daughter's shell.

When they were in front of Jen's house, she looked up at him with a smile. Her cheeks were pink from the cold, as was the tip of her nose.

"Thanks for the walk," she said.

"Yeah." He nodded. "I'll see you in the morning—we need to start tearing out your counter."

"You know where to find me," she said, and then she turned and headed back up her drive toward the house with the lights shining cozily out of those lead-paned windows.

Funny to think of that old mansion being occupied by a woman like her...

Nick crossed the street, Goldie in the lead. When he opened the front door, she bounded inside, her nails clicking and sliding against the tiled floor.

"I'm back!" Nick called, and he shut the door behind him. "Goldie, come here. We have to wipe off your paws. Goldie!"

She came back, and he wiped her snowy paws with a cloth he had set aside for that very reason. When he rose to his feet, he saw his daughter coming down the stairs, dressed in a pair of snug-fitting jeans, a black turtleneck and a slim-fitting puffer coat. Her makeup was done, and she was wearing diamond studs in her ears.

"Are you going somewhere?" he asked.

"Out with some friends," she said.

"I was hoping we could have the evening together," he said.

"Dad, you told me when we arranged this that you'd be working. You can't exactly get hurt feelings when I make a few plans of my own."

"I'm not hurt," he said irritably.

Amelia arched an eyebrow at him, and he felt that old conflicting feeling of wanting to give her a lecture and knowing he was beat.

"Who are you going out with?" he asked.

"Do you ever know who I'm out with when I'm at school?" she asked, shaking her head.

"Humor me, Amelia," he said with a sigh.

"Jane Tripp," she replied. "We're meeting up with some other people who are home for the holidays, too."

"Where?" he asked.

"Seriously?" Amelia demanded. "Dad, I'm twenty-three! You don't get to give me the third degree when I go out for an evening."

"Right." He sighed. "Just be safe."

"I always am." She gave him a quirky little smile. "Thanks to you, I'm a karate blue belt. I'm pretty sure I can handle myself."

Yeah, that was one thing he'd given her—and insisted on paying for. And for what it was worth, Amelia had worked her tail off for it. One day when she beat the crap out of some handsy guy, he wanted her to be able to say it was because of him, not Chris.

"Have a good night. Call me if you need anything," he said.

Some car headlights swung up the drive, and Amelia shot him a sweet smile.

"Good night, Daddy. Don't wait up."

That was a line she'd never used on him before, but it was very likely she'd used it on Chris. She called Chris Dad, too.

Amelia headed out, the door closing solidly behind her, and he looked out the window next to the door to see her hop into the front seat. The momentary light inside the car showed another young woman, and then the door shut and the car started to back out.

She'd be fine. She always had been. It wasn't that he was really worried about her safety tonight, although he always worried a little bit. Hence the karate lessons.

But Amelia was smart...and she was right about him not having the right to be offended. She'd made plans—so had he, for the most part.

Connecting with his daughter was going to take more than a little bit of Christmas cheer and a couple of weeks coexisting in the same house.

He looked toward the couch—Goldie had already hopped up onto her favorite spot, and she looked over at Nick hopefully.

"Yeah, yeah," he muttered. He'd flick through the channels and he and Goldie would while away a winter evening. It could be worse. He could be a guy with a swearing parrot. Goldie suited him better.

CHAPTER FIVE

JEN WOKE UP slowly the next morning, stretching under the warm duvet and blinking her eyes open in the dim morning light. She lay there for a moment, inhaling the old-house smell, musty and a little sweet, like antique books. She looked around the room, boxes stacked on one side, and her own familiar dresser across from her bed, some framed pictures she'd already unpacked on top.

One was of her parents on their wedding day—two teenagers in the seventies looking excited and a little disheveled. Apparently, their wedding day had been a downpour.

The other two photos were of Drew—one when he was a baby and crying, stretching out his arms toward her. He'd been a fussy, clingy baby, and she'd been exhausted during those early years. But somehow, now that it was in the past, she could smile at the memory of her baby who wanted her and only her. Sam had stayed busy, but when he held Drew and the boy had cried for her, he'd taken it personally. She hadn't known how to help Sam through that. Was this part of why Sam had pulled away from the both of them, preferring his professional accomplishments to time with his family?

The last photo was from Drew's first day of kindergarten—standing there grinning so proudly with a backpack that was almost as big as he was. When she dropped him off at the private school she and Sam had chosen, he'd been the child to cry the loudest, so his bravery hadn't exactly lasted. And neither had hers. She'd cried on that drive home, leaving him at school for his first day. But still, she loved that picture of him.

And now he was twelve and tall and needing his father. She suspected that Sam needed Drew just as much, even though he didn't know how to express it. Jen wasn't going to be the most important one in Drew's world anymore. Those days were past—which was how these things worked if you did it right. He was growing up to be a mature, responsible, sweet kid who was forging a solid relationship with his dad. And she couldn't be prouder.

It was a little lonesome, though.

She tossed back the covers and shivered, reaching for her bathrobe. It was time to start the day. Nick would be here in a couple of hours, and the kitchen would start taking shape.

TWO HOURS LATER Jen was dressed in a pair of jeans and a long-sleeved ribbed tee that fit close enough that it wouldn't be snagging anything while she worked today. When Nick knocked on the door, she opened it with a smile.

Nick came inside, put down his tool bag and peeled off his coat. He was wearing a red plaid button-up shirt that brought out a hint of red in his beard, and he looked...warm.

"Good morning," he said.

"Hi." She smiled. "You're prompt."

"Yeah, it's a short commute." His gaze moved over her. "You look nice."

Jen smiled. "Thanks. Just jeans."

"I like jeans," he said, and then he cleared his throat. "Sorry. I need to get back to a professional distance here, don't I? It's possible, I promise."

"No, you don't," she said. "And feel free to tell me that I look nice in jeans. My ego could use it these days."

He chuckled. "It's just me today. My guys are working at another house today, but they'll be here tomorrow."

Just the two of them today. There would be no buffer, and she'd already been finding herself uncomfortably attracted to this man.

"Do you need me to help?" she asked.

One side of his mouth quirked up into a smile. "Do you want to?"

"Sure. I mean…what else am I going to do, watch you work?" Her cheeks heated as soon as the words came out, because it sounded more flirtatious than she meant to sound. Helping him work was probably safer than just watching him anyway.

He shot her a grin. "Let's see if we can get that counter out this morning. I need to see how much damage is underneath."

"Sounds good."

"I'm going to warn you—I'm bossy when I work. You have to do what I say when I say it."

She eyed him. "So the Nick who walks his dog is a different guy than the Nick at work?"

"Well, the Nick who walks his dog is off the clock," he said. "The Nick at work is on a deadline for a very nice woman who needs this work done before Christmas. And he takes that pretty seriously. Besides, it comes down to safety."

He eyed her for a moment, and she saw a sparkle there that made her wonder if he was flirting. It had been a long time since she'd even paid attention to those things, but this man was making her take notice.

"So, how bossy?" she asked, meeting his gaze.

"I guess we'll find out," he said, and there was a hint of a smile at his lips. "Come on, then."

Nick picked up his tool bag and led the way through the dining room toward the kitchen, and Jen followed. It looked like he was taking charge starting now.

"So here's the plan," Nick said. "I'm going to cut the counter here—just before the sink. We'll get the counter off this side, and then we're going to remove the kitchen sink completely."

"Right." It wasn't like she had an opinion on this part of things. "You're the expert."

"What kind of boss will you make when you get this place up and running?" he asked.

Jen felt a smile play at her lips. "I have a feeling I'll be a bit bossy, too," she admitted. "I mean, it won't exactly come down to safety, but this will be personal. This will be my own gallery and it will reflect on me. So yeah, I think I'll expect high performance from my employees."

"I could see you barking out a few orders," he said.

She chuckled. "That intimidates most men, you know."

"I'm remarkably secure in my masculinity," he said, and he leaned a little closer, a smile turning up the corners of his lips.

She couldn't think of a witty comeback with him looking at her like that, so she just shook her head. "If your work isn't amazing, my online review is going to be scathing. I'll say he flirts like crazy and doesn't deliver."

"Lucky for me my work is that good," he

quipped back with a grin. "And for the record, I don't flirt."

Wait, wasn't he flirting now? He was... wasn't he? If she made a fool of herself and her sister heard about this...

"Okay," he amended. "I'm flirting a bit, but I don't normally. You and I have accidentally become friends, which throws me off. I'm normally obnoxiously professional. You can ask any of the women I've worked for in the last decade."

Somehow, she could believe that, and it gave her a little thrill to realize that the attention he was giving her was different.

"And to prove myself less professional than I'm claiming, I was wondering if my daughter could see inside your home sometime today," he said. "I know this sounds really—"

"No problem," she replied.

"You sure?"

"Of course," she said. "I'll be happy to show her around."

"Thanks," he said. "She grew up staring at the outside of this mansion, and she never had the chance to see inside."

"It'll be nice to have someone to show it to, honestly," she admitted.

For the next few minutes she watched as he used an electric handsaw to cut the countertop, and then he used a crowbar to pry it up off the base of drawers and cupboards beneath. As he hoisted the heavy counter, he beckoned her closer.

"See?" he said. "All that wood is rotted right out. You could probably dig it out with a cotton swab."

She smiled at his turn of phrase. "So everything underneath—" The old cabinets were dark with rotted wood along the top, and she felt her stomach sink. "This is more work than we thought."

"Not really," he replied. "I expected as much. We can rebuild some of the cabinets. The doors and drawer fronts are fine, so it'll all look the same. This is structural. I've got a guy who can redo the inside of these cabinets in no time."

Jen nodded. "Okay, that's good."

"Hold on, you're going to need gloves for this," he said, and he pulled off his own work gloves and passed them over. She slid her hands into the warmed depths of them.

"Now I need you to hold this up, if you can. Let me know if you need to put it down. Okay?"

"Yeah," she said. "Sure."

The counter was heavier than she thought, and it was also secured to the top of the cupboards, but Nick worked quickly with his crowbar, the nails coming loose with a squeal. As he pried up more of the cupboard, it became easier to hold. All the same, her muscles trembled under the strain.

"I need a break," she said through gritted teeth.

"Okay," he said, stepping back. "Put it down."

Jen released it and let out a breath. He was a strong man, and she could see the difference in their strength just by how much he could do and make look easy while she was struggling with simply holding something up.

"You sure you still want to help?" he asked.

The thought of heading upstairs and leaving him to work alone was a little depressing. This might be hard work, and he might be moderately bossy, but he was good company, too. And she didn't want to look weak in front of him.

"I'm fine," she said, and she stretched her arms out, then stepped forward to lift the counter again. "Okay, I'm ready."

The last of the counter came up with a jolt, and Nick dropped the crowbar and caught the counter in his strong grip, lifting it from her grasp.

"I've got it," he said brusquely. "Step back."

She did as he said, and he swung the counter past her, and carried it toward the back door.

"Open the door, would you?"

Jen hurried ahead of him and opened it so he could carry the moldering wood outside. He came back in with a rush of cold air.

"Okay—let's do that again with the next section," he said. "You ready?"

As they worked, she couldn't help but notice this man's strength. He hoisted things she couldn't lift more than a few inches, and while he definitely took charge of things, she didn't mind. The morning drifted by, and after a couple of hours of work, they'd removed the rotten cabinetry and all of the counter on the one side. The more they worked, the more torn apart the kitchen seemed to look, and Jen hoped her expressions didn't betray her own uncertainty. Would Nick really have all of this repaired in time for Christmas?

She didn't have a choice but to trust him, but looking over the ragged remains of the bottom cupboards, her stomach sank.

"What's the matter?" Nick asked, stopping at her side, and the heat from his body emanated against her arm. "Freaking out?"

"A bit," she admitted.

"It'll be done," he said, and then headed toward the sink. "And I'm getting this sink out before lunch."

There was something about his easy confidence that was reassuring. Nick got down on the floor and reached under the sink. He scooted back, disappearing underneath, just his lower torso and legs sticking out. She let her gaze move over him—his stomach was flat, and when he shifted positions, she was impressed by how fit he was.

Cut it out, she told herself. He might have been flirting, but there was nothing easy about this guy.

"Jen, I need you to do something for me," Nick said, his voice muffled from under the sink.

"Sure," she said.

"I'm holding on to a piece of pipe here, and I need you to reach in here and hold it for me for a second," he said.

"Right…" Did he realize how much space he was filling up? Because reaching in was going to put her just about on top of him.

"Come on," he said. "Sit next to me, here—" He scooted over a little more. "And reach inside—"

Jen settled herself next to him, and in the process was forced to put a hand on his tight abs.

"You're in shape," she murmured.

"Perk of the job," he replied, and she felt his calloused hand close over hers as he tugged her fingers up to the pipe he needed her to hold. He was close—so close that she could smell that tangy mix of musk and hard work, and it made her breath catch. As she leaned in to reach the pipe, her sleeve caught something. She didn't think much of it, and pushed past, but as she did, there was an eruption of cold water. It sprayed them both, and Nick reached past her and turned a valve to shut the water off.

Jen sat there in wide-eyed shock, water dripping down her face and soaking into her shirt. Nick was drenched, too, his shirt completely sodden and his beard dripping. He scooted back out from under the sink and gave her a level look.

"Sorry..." she breathed.

For a moment they just stared at each other and Nick's expression was frozen. Was that anger she saw flickering beneath the surface, or something else?

"That was the water shut off," he said, his voice low and measured.

"Yeah..." She struggled to her feet, and cast him an embarrassed look. "I didn't mean to do that."

"Don't worry about it," he said, then laughed. "But I could use a towel."

"I'll be back."

Jen shivered and headed up the stairs. Once she got to her bedroom she peeled of her shirt and got another dry one on. She then grabbed a couple of towels and headed back down. When she emerged into the kitchen, she stopped short.

Nick stood with his back to her, his shirt in a wet pile on the floor. His back was strong and muscled, and he stood there with his weight on one leg surveying his work. She cleared her throat, and he turned.

"Thanks," he said.

She tossed him the towel and he patted himself dry, then draped it over his shoulders.

"Tell you what," he said, glancing back at her. "I'm going to head home for lunch and come back in something dry. The sink will wait."

"Yeah, good idea," she said, but it came out a little breathier than she'd intended. "Again, I'm really sorry. I guess that's why I hired you—home renovations aren't my strong suit."

Nick bent down and picked up his wet shirt. He caught her eye for just a moment, and he smiled faintly. "We're all good at something."

"Is there anything I can do while you're gone?" she asked.

"Eat lunch," he said, then cast her a roguish smile and jutted his bearded chin in the direction of the sink. "And whatever you do, don't touch that."

Jen laughed softly. "Hands off. Got it."

Nick grinned, then tossed the towel to her.

"I'll be back in about half an hour," he said.

"Thanks. I'll leave the door unlocked. Just come in when you're back."

"Will do."

Jen shut her eyes, grimacing after he left. What kind of stories was he going to tell about her once his guys arrived to help him finish up the work? She'd just drenched her contractor! And would this get back as far as Lisa?

But Jen was hungry—it was noon, and she'd been working hard all morning. She turned back toward the kitchen where she had some instant ramen in the cupboard that she could microwave. That with some saltines crumbled into it would hit the spot.

And hopefully when Nick returned, they could put this whole embarrassment behind them...

NICK KICKED HIS front door shut behind him and pulled off his winter coat. He felt goose bumps rise as his bare skin met the cool air. Amelia ambled into the foyer from the kitchen and gave her father a startled look.

"What happened to you?" she said.

He opened the laundry room door and tossed his wet shirt onto the floor.

"A knocked valve," he said with a rueful smile.

"Did you just come home like that?" Amelia started to laugh. "Does the owner know about this?"

"The owner was the one who knocked the valve," he retorted.

"And you, like, peeled off your wet shirt and went home?" Amelia chuckled. "Sometimes I think you're a little naive, Dad. You've got the whole hot contractor thing going for you. Mom is going to think this is hilarious!"

Nick closed his eyes for a moment, annoyance surging up inside him. The last thing he needed was Amelia telling her mother this story.

"I'm getting changed, having some lunch and then—" He eyed his daughter thoughtfully. "You want to come see that mansion?"

"I don't know. Would I be interrupting anything?" she laughed.

"Your father is a professional," he retorted. "There's some of the original furniture in it still, and these massive paintings on the walls. It's...like a time capsule. I think you'd like it."

"Yeah?" Amelia paused, considering. "Is it that cool?"

"Yeah, it is," he said. "And the owner is really nice. She'd probably give you a tour. If you want to see it, now's your chance."

"Okay." Amelia shrugged. "I'm making grilled cheese. I can make one for you, if you want."

And suddenly, they were back to old times...in a way. At least his daughter was happy to see him and teasing him a little. And he was touched by her offer to cook. Back when she was ten or eleven, before the divorce, she used to serve him her own made-up concoctions. Spaghetti with ketchup, scrambled eggs wrapped in rice paper, corn on the cob drenched in butter and sprinkled with parmesan cheese. The last one wasn't bad, actually. Having his daughter cook for him again was nice...

"Perfect," he said, shooting Amelia a grin. "Let me just go find some dry clothes."

A half hour later Nick and Amelia were back on Jen's doorstep. Amelia looked around in undisguised awe at the old place. When she was a kid, a crotchety old woman lived in this house, and she wouldn't let anyone on her property, so they hadn't had a chance to look any closer than the sidewalk would allow.

Nick knocked, then opened the door, letting himself in.

"Hello?" he called.

Jen appeared around the corner, and she smiled when she saw Amelia.

"You must be Nick's daughter," she said.

"Yes. I'm Amelia," Amelia replied. "Nice to meet you." She shook hands with Jen. "This house is amazing. I was hoping to get a peek inside, and Dad said you wouldn't mind."

"I don't mind at all," Jen said. "I can give you the tour while your dad gets started, if you want."

"That would be great. Thanks."

"We'll just start on that end," Jen said, pointing toward the other wing of the main floor, the one he knew she wasn't using yet. She gave Nick a smile. "You mind?"

"Nope, carry on," he said. "I'll get to work."

And while Jen had been a help that morning, she was a strange distraction, too. She was pretty, and soft and smelled good…all things he shouldn't be thinking about right now.

Nick stood there for a moment, listening to the creak of their footfalls and the soft murmur of their voices. He missed having a feminine presence around. That was one part of the divorce that he never did get over completely—a woman's scent, her voice, her touch in the decorating. There were a few times he nearly settled down, but those relationships had never felt quite right, not on a heart level, at least.

Nick stepped out of his boots and hung his coat next to his daughter's, then headed into the kitchen. There was plenty of work to finish up before his carpenter arrived tomorrow morning, and he wanted to make sure that he cleared the way for Floyd to get to work right away—no wasted hours hauling out junk.

He'd sketched what the original cupboard layout had been for the section of cabinetry he'd removed, complete with measurements so Floyd could re-create it. But even as he surveyed the kitchen, Nick's mind was already moving forward to the next stages of the job.

He heard the women's steps coming from the back servants' staircase, and their voices filtered down to him. He was putting in some wooden supports around the sink to keep it in one place while he worked.

"We actually studied something similar in law class," his daughter was saying. "There was a watercolor painting that sold for over a million dollars. It was by this super-popular modern artist, maybe fifteen years ago. Anyway, the buyer left with the painting, set it up in her personal gallery and invited her friends to come see it. But unbeknownst to the buyer, the artist had booby-trapped the painting so that when it left the carefully controlled atmosphere in the gallery, it started a chemical reaction that over the next twenty-four hours turned the painting into a black smudge."

"I heard about that—" Jen led the way

back into the kitchen, and turned back toward Amelia. "The artist claimed that the meaning of the work was life's impermanence, and therefore, the painting was just as it was intended."

"But what about the buyer?" Amelia said. "She didn't get what she thought she was buying, and the beauty of the art was ruined. She threatened to sue anyone involved."

"What happened in the end?" Jen asked. "I never did hear."

"It turned out that the big media attention actually drove up the value of the piece, and the buyer sold it to another collector for five hundred thousand dollars more," Amelia replied. "It was quite hush-hush, though. The new buyer didn't want to advertise that he had it—not wanting to get himself robbed. But had the case gone to court, it's hard to say who would have won."

Amelia and Jen were getting along, Nick noticed. More than that—they were downright hitting it off. He rose to his feet.

"Did you hear about that?" Jen asked, looking over at him.

"No, I didn't," he replied.

"It was a big deal, actually," Amelia said.

"It would have set some major legal precedents had it gone to trial, but it got people thinking more deeply about art, freedom of speech, that sort of thing. Did the artist owe the buyer something more or less than she'd created? Were they allowed to question her artistic freedom in creating a piece that ended in a form they didn't like? Did they have any right to insist that her art conform to their expectations?"

Nick turned back to his work. This was like old times—Amelia and Shari used to discuss this sort of stuff all the time, and they'd very happily left him out of it.

"What do you think, Nick?" Jen asked.

Nick looked up. "What's that?"

"What do you think?" she asked. "If you'd bought a piece of art for a million dollars and it turned into a black smear—do you think you'd have a right to sue the artist?"

"I wouldn't spend a million dollars on a piece of art," he replied.

"Fine, Dad," Amelia said. "If you had a billion dollars and a million dollars was pocket change."

"Then I don't know why I'd bother going

to court over pocket change," he said with a small smile.

Amelia sighed. "He's like this. Don't even bother asking him about art or anything."

Jen's glance moved between them, and Nick felt his ears heat. He was tired of being talked down to, especially in front of Jen.

"Really?" Nick straightened. "Don't ask me?"

"Are you giving an honest, thought-out answer?" Amelia countered. "You never do."

Never? That was a strong position to take. Most times, he'd learned to just back out of his daughter's conversations with her mother. They didn't much care what he thought anyway. But he wasn't going to be put into a corner today.

"You want my opinion? You're not going to agree with it, but I'll give it to you," he retorted. "When people buy something, they have an expectation. What is art but someone's vision of beauty? Well, I'm responsible to the people who spend money for my work—"

"You're a contractor, Dad," Amelia said. "This is different."

"Is it?" he snapped. "I create something

beautiful for my clients, and it takes skill, vision and a whole lot of hard work. Do you think this art gallery—everything from the crown moldings, a polished wood floor, the mansion reworked for a new purpose—is any less important than the pieces of art it holds?"

Amelia eyed him, but didn't answer.

"My clients have an expectation, and I don't get to surprise them. They want beauty, and I deliver it. What that artist did was get her name in the news to increase the value associated with her name—and that was a shifty ploy, in my humble opinion."

"Not all art is beautiful," Amelia countered. "Art isn't about beauty alone, Dad. That's where you miss the point."

Corrected, as always.

"But all art makes us feel something," Jen cut in. They both looked over at her, and Jen shrugged. "I know a local Colorado artist who includes a deeply personal, ugly, truthful pencil sketch underneath every single painting he does. He says that art isn't real unless it includes the vulgar, as well."

As usual, the conversation was going to run right past him. And Jen had no idea about their family tensions. She was talking art. They were talking history.

"You mean Scott Hedgeworth?" Amelia asked. "You actually know him?"

"He's a friend—" Jen stopped. "Well, he was connected with my ex-husband. They both raised money for the same scholarship fund. He came for Christmas one year, and he always attended our New Year's Eve parties. He and I hit it off. In fact, he's promised me two original pieces to show in the gallery when it's open."

"You're going to have two original Scott Hedgeworth paintings?" Amelia shook her head. "You know what those are worth?"

"I have a pretty good idea," Jen said with a low laugh.

"Right. Of course," Amelia said. "You'd know! Dad—do you know who Scott Hedgeworth is?"

"Your mom used to be a big fan of his," he replied. So yeah, he'd learned a thing or two about that particular artist.

"My stepdad got my mother a Scott Hedgeworth painting," Amelia said, turning back to Jen. "And even one of his smaller works cost a fortune. But I mean, Chris can afford it."

Nick couldn't help the irritation that simmered at that. Money wasn't the only thing that measured a man, but it certainly did impress his daughter. He turned back to the trusses under the sink, wishing he could tune the rest of this conversation out.

"Which piece is it?" Jen asked.

"It's called Summer Garden," Amelia replied. "In the foreground is a bee hanging off a flower petal, and in the background is a woman with a wheelbarrow."

"I know that one," Jen said. "I saw his sketches when he was just working on it."

This all felt a little too familiar. He didn't begrudge Jen or Amelia enjoying art, but his view of things, his opinions, were very quickly swept aside as uninformed because he didn't have an advanced degree. But some things were simpler than they thought. That artist with the blackened painting wouldn't have made the money she did without the buyer. And having a hidden trick like that... Art or not, that trick was cruel to the woman who forked out the cash. That was integrity. Not that they'd listen to his take on it.

Amelia shot her father a grin, and he realized he'd missed part of their conversation. "Dad, Scott Hedgeworth is one of the most celebrated American painters today. So I know you aren't going to be impressed, but you should be. Mom sure will be! His work's value has been steadily rising over the last decade, and some very serious collectors have been driving up the price of his work… Mom's Hedgeworth piece is already worth about twenty grand more than it was a year ago. It's an investment!"

But Nick wasn't interested in the exciting things that Chris's money could buy. Nick couldn't give his daughter the things that Chris did. He couldn't afford her Ivy League education, or the trips to Africa and Europe, or the paintings done by celebrity artists. What he could offer was a regular old Christmas with ceramic singing bears and some comfort food. None of which his daughter seemed to value anymore.

"Amelia, I get it," Nick said, cutting in. "But maybe you and Jen could continue this conversation out in the dining room. I've got a deadline here and I'm about to start up the saw."

He wanted space to breathe—space away from the pressure that seemed to be pushing in around him. His daughter met his gaze with a drilling stare of her own. She was offended, he could tell. But he wasn't about to explain himself.

"Sure, let me show you some of the art that came with the house," Jen said. "It's not worth anything, but one of them I really like."

Nick watched them wander out of the kitchen and before she disappeared, Jen glanced over her shoulder toward him, her expression troubled.

He rubbed a hand over his forehead. Maybe this was the reality check he needed to make him stop flirting and get serious. Jen was the kind of woman he seemed to fall for—smart, articulate, educated and filled with ideas and ambitions that knocked ordinary guys like him out of the competition. He couldn't keep up in that world, and he already knew it. He'd learned that in the most painful way during his marriage to Shari.

Amelia's laughter filtered back to him.

"It was my fault," he could hear Jen saying. "I knocked a valve or something, and we both got just drenched. I feel like a fool..."

Of course. The story that would outlive this entire trip—but he couldn't help his grudging smile at the memory of Jen looking stunned, her hair dripping wet, hovering over him as they'd stared at each other in shock. Jen was a beautiful woman...that couldn't be denied. And there was something about her mussed up like that, that had appealed to him.

Even though she was all wrong for him, and he'd never cross that line. Maybe it was okay to appreciate her firmly on this side of professional.

Yeah, his daughter would tease him about this for years, but maybe it was worth it for the memory of Jen drenched.

CHAPTER SIX

ONCE AMELIA HAD LEFT, Jen headed back to the kitchen and leaned against the door frame. Nick stood with his back to her, muscular, competent. His saw whined as he sliced through a piece of counter on the other side of the sink. Then the saw stopped, and he pushed his safety glasses to the top of his head.

"She looks like you," Jen said.

Nick turned around. "Yeah, I know. But that brain of hers is from her mother."

Jen chuckled. "And she's going to Harvard, right? You must be proud."

"I am," he replied. "I honestly think a state school would have been better to prepare her for life. But she's got a rich stepdad now, so maybe Harvard will prepare her for what she can expect. What do I know? She's really bright, and she's going places. I can guarantee that."

And yet there was a lot of tension between father and daughter. Jen had seen that plainly. Amelia seemed to want a fight, and Nick looked on the verge of providing one.

"She asked me to tell her when I open the gallery. I mentioned that Scott Hedgeworth will come for a special appearance, and she really wants to meet him."

Jen watched the complicated emotions battle over Nick's face, then he turned away again.

"This is the first time she's come back to Mountain Springs for about five years. And now she's talking about coming back again for some artist. Not for her dad." He turned back again. "Not that I blame her, exactly."

"What happened between you two?" Jen asked. "Or is it none of my business?"

"It's fine," he said, then sighed. "Amelia and Shari—they're different than I am. They love culture, ballet, theater, art... And they love learning. Constantly. They think about things in a more abstract way than I do, and hey, everyone's different. No big deal. Except, they always make a point of calling me out for being uneducated, or beneath them."

Her breath caught. She'd known there was a dynamic there…

"Oh…so that's what was happening here today—the comment about you being a contractor."

"Yep." He gave her a tight smile. "When Shari and I split up, she went to the city and met Chris, and it was like Amelia finally got the dad she always wanted."

Jen winced. "You can't think that—"

"He took over paying for the stuff I said no to," he replied. "And he gives her access to the stuff I can't."

"But you're still her father," she countered.

"Yeah, I am. You know, the funny thing is, she's a big fan of your sister's, too."

"Lisa?" Jen looked at him in surprise. "I didn't think she was that popular yet."

"It's not about popularity. And anyway, I think the fact that Lisa is a bit obscure makes her more appealing to Amelia," he said. "My daughter got me to read a few of her stories."

Jen felt a flutter in her stomach. Nervousness? Maybe. "What did you think?"

Nick looked over at her with a sober expression. "She's good. I like her stories. They're… I don't know…they have some down-to-earth logic to them that appeals to me. We're part of the same group of friends, but I don't really talk to Lisa about that stuff."

"What do you talk about?" Jen asked. Lisa's writing was a pretty big part of her life.

He smiled faintly. "Movies." He turned away again and pulled out his crowbar. "Now, if you could come hold the counter, I'm going to pry it up on this end."

He pulled off his gloves and held them toward her. He was so big and strong, so confident in his work, but underneath it all she could see a deep sadness.

This was one of Lisa's friends, and Jen realized that she was getting a glimpse of not only Nick's life, but also her sister's.

"Sure," Jen said, accepting the gloves.

Sharing time was over, evidently, but she'd seen something a little deeper in Nick today, and she couldn't help but feel sympathy for his pain. Whatever had gone wrong with Amelia over the years, it had broken his heart.

WHEN THE WORKDAY was over and Nick had left for home, Jen walked through the kitchen. The entire counter had been removed, as well as the rotten bottom cupboards that needed replacing. The old sink was held up on support struts, and the pipes beneath had been removed.

Strange how vulnerable a person was when a contractor was working on their kitchen. She couldn't put this back together on her own if she wanted to.

Jen headed up the staircase toward the second floor. She had her computer set up there next to a leather armchair by a window that overlooked the snow-covered flower garden. The sun had set, and when she sank into the chair with her laptop, she could see her own reflection in the window staring back at her.

"I look tired," she murmured aloud.

Strange, she hadn't felt this old when she was helping Nick in the kitchen. A woman could forget something as simple as what she looked like when she was caught up with a good-looking man...and Nick had something about him that drew her in. Those broad shoulders, how muscular he was, his confidence when he worked—it was a powerful combination.

Jen flicked through Facebook and Twitter for a few minutes, catching up on some friends' posts. When she saw a picture of Bram in his high chair that Lisa had posted that morning, she paused.

Lisa said she had some stories online, didn't she? Jen opened a new window and searched for Lisa Dear. There were a lot of hits that had nothing to do with her sister, but on the second page, one result was for *Grain Magazine*, a well-known literary journal.

"Good for you, Lis," Jen murmured, and she clicked on the link.

It was a short story and very well written. Jen scanned it, then her heartbeat sped up. This story wasn't exactly fiction...not all of it. It was about a student who'd married her professor after a lurid affair. The woman thought her poor family was beneath her, and she loved hobnobbing with the educated elite, until one day she realized how empty it all was, but her parents were now dead, and her relationship with her only brother was nonexistent, and she was left with a hollow life that she'd created for herself, feeling like she'd missed out on everything meaningful. The story itself was well-done—everything centered around the imagery of a pampered cat, looking out the window at the wild possibilities outside. It was impressive—definitely worth the space in a celebrated literary journal. But it was also wildly insulting.

Was that what Lisa thought of her—as one of Sam's pets? As a homewrecker? Because she wasn't! Sam had been two months away from his divorce being final when he asked her out. He and his wife had been legally and physically separated for a year at that point.

Jen's heart hammered hard, and she pushed the computer aside and stood up. She picked up her cell phone and dialed her sister's number. It rang four times and went to voice mail. She hung up. This wasn't a voice mail kind of message.

Her phone rang, and she looked down to see it was Lisa calling her back.

"Lis?" Jen said, picking up the phone.

"Sorry, Bram had my phone," her sister replied. "What's up?"

"So, I did as you suggested and searched for your story online," Jen said. "I found it..."

"Which one was it?" Lisa asked.

"'A Cat's Life.'" Jen paused, waiting.

"Right," Lisa said. "I liked that one. It won a writing contest, you know."

"Congratulations," Jen said dryly. "The problem is, it's about me."

"No, it isn't," Lisa retorted. "It's about a woman who marries her professor and goes on to live a miserable existence of denying who she truly is."

"Is that how you see me?" Jen asked.

"It isn't you," Lisa replied. "Yes, it's about a woman who gets married like you did, but—" She sighed. "Jen, all writing is inspired from somewhere."

"Look, I don't really care about your inspiration," Jen replied. "I care about your opinion of me! And from what I can see, you think I'm a shallow gold digger who has no sense of who she is and was nothing more than a glorified pet in her husband's home!"

"That's not what I think."

"It's what you wrote."

"Okay, you know what?" Lisa said, her voice rising. "Yes, I wrote a story about how you got married. I was furious that you married him! He was…not the right kind of guy for you. You know that now, and I knew it all along. He was a jerk. He patted you on the head. He used you like a secretary and insisted that you follow along his life track. And I used a little imagination to see how that might feel from the inside. Forgive me if I got it right!"

"So you think I married him for money?" Jen demanded.

"I *exaggerated*," Lisa said dryly.

"I didn't marry Sam for his money or his position," she said.

"Come on!" Lisa shot back. "He's skinny, balding and has a terrible personality! What made him attractive if not the big house, the Porsche and the way all the undergrads genuflected when he came by?"

"He's successful, yes," Jen snapped. "But I fell in love with *him*."

"And out of love with him," her sister said. "You can't admit he was a mistake? Not even now?"

Jen rubbed a hand over her eyes. "He was a mistake, but my son isn't."

"I never said Drew was." Lisa's voice softened. "Jen, I'm sorry. I honestly didn't think it would even get accepted. It was one of my first that I submitted to a serious journal. I guess there's something that rang true in that story, and everyone loved it. If I could have edited it and changed the main character to be a little less like you, I would have…"

"Whatever," Jen said.

"I don't think you're a gold digger," Lisa said quietly. "I think you got duped by a very self-centered man who used his position and his wealth to blind you, and you lost sight of who you really were. That's what I think."

Was that any better?

Jen sighed. "I was married to him for fourteen years, Lis."

"And you have a beautiful son," Lisa said. "Don't lose sight of that."

"That's why this old house and the art gallery matter so much to me," Jen said quietly. "Because even before I met Sam and even when my marriage was falling apart, I had a passion that was mine alone. And I'm proud of it! I'm proud that I have an eye for art, and I understand that world. It's something that excites me, and makes me feel alive."

"I'm glad," her sister said, but there was something in her voice that sounded off.

"What?" Jen said irritably.

"You had a whole life before you left for college," Lisa said. "You might not have liked it much, but it's a part of you. I think you cut it out of you and moved on. Or tried to."

"You know what?" Jen said. "I'm not going to feel guilty for not wanting to be poor, or for developing new interests, or for wanting some financial security!"

"Then don't," Lisa said. "I'm not trying to make you feel bad about yourself. I'm just pointing out that you created this whole different version of yourself when you left, and it doesn't include your childhood. How would you feel if Drew did that?"

Jen shut her eyes. "I'm doing my best for him. He'll never be hungry like we were, and he'll have opportunities—"

"Do you think Mom and Dad tried any less hard?" Lisa asked.

"I know…"

"You erased them," Lisa said.

"I didn't erase them!" Jen snapped. That was crossing a line. "I was in contact with them every week!"

"You erased what they gave you," Lisa said. "And they really thought that they'd given us a beautiful life. We had a close-knit family, they raised us with faith in humanity and they wanted us to take care of each other."

"I'm trying to help—"

"I'm not talking about you taking care of me," Lisa said with a sigh. "What I'm saying is, you don't have to be so embarrassed by where you came from."

That was something to think about. Who had she offended, Lisa, or her entire family? She'd thought her parents were proud of her—glad she'd gone beyond what they'd been able to provide. But had she hurt their feelings, too?

"I'm tired," Jen said. "I think I'm going to get going."

"I'm not trying to fight," Lisa said tiredly. "I'm just saying what I think."

"Yeah, I know," Jen said. "It's fine. I've got something to think about, too, I suppose. Have a good night, Lis."

Jen hung up the phone, wishing she could have said a whole lot more. But one thing was certain—for all of Jen's mistakes in her sister's eyes, it was Jen's life that had been inspiring enough to write about. That story all the editors loved hadn't been about the cautious sister who stayed at home, had it?

At least Jen had done something worth writing about.

When Jen was a little girl, her grandmother had given her that silver ball of mistletoe. Her grandmother told her that one day she'd find her own true love, and after that, Jen would look at the little ornament and dream of her future happiness. One day she wanted a man to kiss her under mistletoe and make her feel complete. When she'd married Sam, it had been for all those romantic, heart-swept reasons. She'd wanted her own happily-ever-after so badly, and she'd wanted it as far from this mountain town as possible...

So Lisa was wrong—deeply wrong. But so was Jen, because she'd looked to a man to rescue her and complete her, and that had turned out to be the exact wrong choice to make. That ornament was in the box of Christmas decorations, wrapped in a little cloth to keep it from getting scratched. Did she still believe in finding her own true love? She wasn't so sure anymore.

Her phone rang again, and she looked down to see her son's cell phone number, and she felt the anger seeping out of her, replaced with relief. Drew had been so busy with his dad lately that he hadn't been calling as often as she'd hoped.

"Hi, sweetie," she said.

"Hey, Mom," Drew said. "How are you?"

Jen sank back into the chair to chat with her son. Drew was the one who made this entire mess worth it.

THAT EVENING NICK ate a roast beef sandwich over the sink, eyeing the dishes his daughter had left. She'd cooked some pasta for herself—no leftovers. She was ticked off with him, apparently, because no one was that good at cooking pasta portions.

"I didn't know when you'd be back," Amelia said.

"Yeah, no, that's fine." He took another bite and glanced over at the dog's bowl. He saw a noodle in the bottom of her dish. At least Goldie had gotten a treat out of it.

"What was with you today?" Amelia asked. "We were having a perfectly nice conversation before you got all touchy."

"I get tired of the condescension," he replied.

"What did I do?"

Nothing that she hadn't done a thousand times before, and that was the problem. He should have stopped this a whole lot sooner.

"Forget it," he said.

"I'm serious, Dad. What was the problem? What offended you there? We were talking about—" she shrugged "—law and art."

It was hard to nail it down now, after the fact. It had always been that way—hard to argue his point with a lawyer.

"You make it pretty clear that you look down on my profession," he said.

"I don't." She shook her head. "Dad, I'm sorry if I came across a little dismissively, but that doesn't mean I don't value your work."

"You think I'm not as smart as you are, but I'll have you know that there are plenty of different ways to approach a problem," he countered. "If you were ever stuck with a load of lumber, a hammer and a time deadline, you'd be the one who looked like a fool."

"I know, Dad. Everyone is needed in the system," she said.

"No, Amelia," he said quietly. "My point is that a lawyer isn't more important than a contractor. A stock trader isn't more important than the mechanic who fixes his car. It's not just about everyone being needed. It's about knowing that you aren't actually above other people. You've missed that life lesson somehow—and maybe that's my fault. But more money doesn't equal more worth."

"Is this about Chris?" she asked, frowning.

"This is about *our* relationship," he replied with a shake of his head.

Amelia looked at him silently, and he sighed, looking away. Would it make any difference? Probably not. It was too late to parent a twenty-three-year-old pre-law student. He should have had the guts to face his own daughter sooner.

"I'm sorry," she said after a moment.

"It's okay," he said. What else was there to say? He opened a cupboard and pulled down a few boxes of cookies. He'd stocked up for her visit. Sometimes it was better said with food anyway.

"You got the chocolate mint ones I like."

"Of course." Nick met her gaze. "It's Christmas. My little girl is home."

Home. It felt weird to even say. This wasn't her home anymore.

"Thanks." She held the box unopened. "Can I ask you something?"

"Sure."

"Do you want to get married again?" Amelia asked.

"Why do you ask that?" he asked.

"I don't think you're happy," she said. "I think you want more."

"I'm happy, Amelia. Don't worry about me. I've got a pretty good setup," he said.

"Mom moved on, Dad. She's living her best life. You should, too."

That stung, and he cast his daughter an annoyed look as he chewed his last bite of sandwich.

"Amelia, it isn't always so simple," he replied, putting down the can. "But I'm glad to know you'd be supportive if I got serious with someone again."

"You don't need my permission, Dad," she said.

"And I wouldn't ask for it," he replied.

They exchanged a cautious look, and he wondered if other fathers had to stamp out their turf with their kids like this. Or maybe he and his daughter were particularly dysfunctional. Amelia's phone blipped and she pulled it out of her pocket and looked at it. She sighed.

"What?" he asked.

"My plans tonight just fell through."

"Yeah?" Nick felt a spark of optimism at that. "Where were you going?"

"Out with some friends. They've got some family thing that came up, though."

"'Tis the season and all that," he said. "You have a family thing, too."

"Right." She smiled weakly, and for a moment they just looked at each other. Why did this have to be so difficult?

"I was hoping we could spend some time together," he said after a moment of silence.

"That's why you booked yourself solid with work, right?" she asked dryly. "It's okay, Dad. You don't have to force it."

"I'm not forcing it," he said. "Let's watch a Christmas movie."

Amelia glanced at him. "Like what?"

"I don't know. Whatever you'd like."

Amelia shrugged. "Sure. I guess we could watch *Die Hard*."

Yeah, he'd been more in the mood for

something a little cheerier, but Amelia always had been firmly on the side of *Die Hard* counting as Christmassy.

"*Die Hard* it is."

Their morning had been bumpy, but he still wanted to connect with his daughter. She sank into his spot on the couch next to Goldie, and the dog looked up at him with a scandalized look in her dark eyes. Seeing as she'd just eaten his leftovers, he was grateful for a small show of loyalty, at least.

"It's fine, Goldie," he said with a tired smile. "Just for tonight."

And he chose the easy chair, then picked up the remote. Tonight was for his daughter.

THE NEXT DAY Nick's team arrived at the old mansion promptly at eight. There was the carpenter, Floyd, who was only about ten years into the trade and had the instinct when it came to the work, and Nick had seen him work miracles with cupboards in the past. He came with a carpentry apprentice who didn't cost as much to employ, but would be useful as an extra pair of skilled hands, nonetheless. Then there was Bert, who was his best friend and a master plumber.

"I have to tell you," Bert said, lowering his voice. "I'm pretty excited to get my hands on these pipes. This old place is amazing."

"Yeah, I know," Nick agreed. "And if our work impresses her, we have a chance at getting the job for the rest of the renos."

They exchanged a look, and Bert grinned. Bert was tall and lanky with a shaved head to mask his receding hairline. "I'm always impressive. Look at me."

Nick chuckled. "Yeah, yeah."

So Nick worked with his team to measure and cut pieces of wood to re-create the cupboard structure that had rotted out. The work was pretty straightforward, and he liked this stage of things—when everything looked like it was a mess but he could see where all the pieces were going to go. It was a private sense of satisfaction that the work was well underway, and he knew it was going to be great when he was done.

Overhead, he could hear the odd clang of Bert working on the third-floor bathroom, then a shudder through the pipes as water was turned on, some squeaks and moans, another shudder, then silence. Bert would get to the bottom of it—Nick had no doubt.

"So I've got a question here," Floyd said. He held a white-painted cupboard door in one hand, an electric sander in the other.

"What's that?" Nick asked.

"These cupboard doors are solid hardwood," Floyd said. "Beautiful. I mean, whoever painted them white should be shot, but I won't harp on that."

"So what's the problem?" Nick asked.

"I can strip the doors—these bottom ones, at least. Get it back to what it used to be. I might not being able to get them all done before Christmas, but I can sure try."

Floyd rubbed a thumb over a patch of wood he'd revealed on the back of one cupboard door, and Nick recognized the glint in the younger man's eyes. He was hoping that he could get a chance to uncover that wood—just for the sheer pleasure of it. And who knew? Maybe an extra bit of work would give them a step up in getting the bid for renovating the rest of this place.

Nick said, "Let me go see if I can find her."

Nick headed out of the kitchen, and he heard the sander start up again as Floyd turned his attention to the second cupboard. The sound melted into the clang of the plumbing happening on the third floor, and he carried on into the front sitting room. Late-morning light flooded in through the tall windows, reflecting off the prisms in the dining room and making little rainbows over the floor that extended all the way out into the gallery. He paused at the bottom of the central staircase. He could see it already— if he ended up working on this place, at least. He could polish up the old wood, redo some of those fixtures, update the lighting to something with a polished industrial look, and the place would become something new, with the same beautiful bones that made this mansion a landmark.

Nick headed up the stairs and down the hallway, glancing into a couple of bedrooms as he went. At the end of the hallway was the door that led up to the third floor, and as he rounded the corner, he stopped short when he heard Jen's steps on the staircase.

He waited for her to descend, and she started when she saw him.

"Oh…" She hesitated, and in the moment of surprise, he saw something in her gaze that hadn't been there earlier—sadness.

"You okay?" he asked.

"What? Yeah. I'm fine." She tucked her phone into her back pocket.

"You sure?" He softened his voice and when she met him at the bottom of the staircase, she looked up into his face.

"Have you read my sister's stories?" she asked.

"A few."

"Did you read the one about the house cat?"

"The one with the woman who married some rich guy, and—" He stopped, suddenly feeling stupid.

"That's the one." Her cheeks pinked.

"It's not about you, is it?" he asked.

"It would seem so," she replied. "With embellishment, my sister says. But...you know what? That's not me! I don't care if that's the way she sees me. That isn't me!"

"She did talk about you sometimes," Nick said.

"What did she say?" Jen asked.

"She worried, I guess," he replied. "She never liked that guy you married."

"Oh, I know about that!" Jen pulled her phone from her pocket and read aloud, "'She stood in the doorway, watching her professor thumb through her paper, and she wondered if he'd look up. He wasn't so very old, and he wasn't so very married…he didn't wear a ring, at least…'" She stopped. "And for the record, my professor husband might have been my teacher at one point, but I didn't break up his marriage!"

Nick shrugged. "I believe you."

"Does she, though?" Jen's eyes suddenly misted, and Nick was startled at the change in her. She wasn't just annoyed. This was something that stabbed deeper.

"Hey…" He found himself reaching toward her in spite of himself, and he caught her arm with his calloused hand. He tugged her down the last step until she was standing next to him, and he realized in that moment how close she was to him in this narrow staircase.

"It's fine, I just…" And she looked up at him, then the words seemed to evaporate from her lips. Her cheeks pinked further and she dropped her gaze again. "I didn't realize how she saw me."

"Maybe it's just a story," he said.

"There's one too many of them to brush them off that easily," she replied.

"Yeah, I read another one along a similar theme. And part of what I like about Lisa's writing is that she doesn't glorify the wealthy. As you know, I have my own issues with measuring up to a rich guy."

"Do you count me as one of the wealthy?" she asked.

He glanced around. "You bought a mansion, Jen...so along the spectrum, you're closer to it than I am."

"Do you think I have some hollow existence, meaningless and regrettable?" she asked dryly.

"Do you?" he asked.

"No," she replied.

"Good."

Jen eyed him for a moment, her gaze narrowing. "I expected you to lie to me."

"I'm not that guy," he said, and he smiled. "I'm honest to a fault. You can join the lineup of women who hate that about me."

Jen smiled faintly at that. "I might like it."

That would be a first...or maybe it was just the women who needed his professional services who liked that aspect to his personality. They weren't counting on him to say the perfect romantic thing, or to be anything more than a solution to their renovation needs.

There was no space between them for him to step back without walking back a few steps and exiting the stairwell, and she didn't seem inclined to move away, either...

He could see the redness around her eyes from tears, and the fine lines that showed how her eyes crinkled up when she smiled, although she was regarding him soberly now.

Involuntarily, his gaze dropped down to her lips—soft, pink, free of any makeup or lip gloss, and completely natural—and just for a moment he had the uncontrollable thought of tipping her chin upward, and covering those lips with his.

"You...um...were looking for something?" Jen asked.

"Yeah." He cleared his throat. Maybe some space would be better. He led the way back out into the hallway. "I was looking for you, actually. Floyd has discovered that your cupboard doors are all original hardwood, and he wants to know what your plans are for them."

"I hadn't thought about it yet," she replied.

"You might want to start," he said, and

they walked slowly down the hallway together. "He's suggesting stripping them of the paint, eventually, and leaving the natural wood. But that's a personal opinion, and—"

"Nick."

He paused, then their steps both slowed. "Yeah?"

"It matters to me that you don't think that bit I read to you reflects my real life," she said.

Nick pressed his lips together, wondering what the right thing was to say. "I'll tell you something," he said thoughtfully. "You were talking about that artist who has a sketch of something ugly beneath a painting of something beautiful, and I think this is a bit like that. The people who don't know you or your sister personally would gobble up the fact that the author based this on her older sister's marriage—or maybe on her own anger over her older sister's marriage. The readers like layers and complexity. But for you, your sister's story is like the artist who booby-trapped her painting. It went from something beautiful and turned into something else, something painful, and you feel…betrayed. You wanted to be happy for her, and instead, you feel attacked."

Jen blinked up at him. "That's exactly it."

"Can I tell you something else?" he asked, his voice low and gravelly.

"Sure…"

"I don't judge people by their younger sisters' short stories," he said with a small smile.

"Ever had the opportunity before?" she asked, but he saw her smile.

"Well…not until now. But I'm making a stand."

She chuckled. "Thanks."

He nodded toward the staircase. "Let me show you those cupboard doors."

Because that was safer. He knew how to coax beauty out of an old kitchen, but he wasn't sure how to relate to this woman without crossing all sorts of lines. She was already a whole lot more than a client, and he was softening to her in a way that he knew was dangerous for his own emotional equilibrium.

He didn't want to enjoy a flirtation. This Christmas, he just wanted to keep his feet on the ground.

But if he had to be honest with himself, he was still thinking about what it would feel like to kiss her.

CHAPTER SEVEN

THAT EVENING JEN knelt on the kitchen floor in front of a cabinet door that lay in front of her. She'd bought herself a small electric sander that afternoon at Floyd's suggestion, and she moved it slowly over the painted surface, the paint coming off in a floury powder. As he'd instructed, she stopped short of completely cleaning the wood, not wanting to take off too much. The rest would have to be done by hand. She wasn't used to this kind of work, but it was satisfying. And the skill that it took to renovate a home was staggering. Nick really was a talented man, and she had a new appreciation for how easy he managed to make it look.

She was still upset with her sister, and that wasn't going to be easily resolved. It wasn't that she begrudged her sister using some of her life experiences to jump off from—it was that her sister seemed to see the worst in her at every step. Not one story showed a charitable view of Jen. Each one that used a fragment from Jen's life showed her in the worst possible light—a woman out to steal another woman's husband, a heartless shrew with deep regrets, a shallow waif without any idea of what she was missing out on… And if Lisa's stories used a varied approach to these little snippets from Jen's life, Jen might have seen them for the creative outlets that Lisa claimed them to be. But there was no varying treatment of the theme—the character was always the same, completely indifferent to the people around her or her own deeper moral failings.

But Jen *hadn't* stolen Sam from his first wife. His ex was already living with her new beau, and the only thing holding up the paperwork was a disagreement over a vacation property. Jen wouldn't have gone out with him otherwise. In Jen's humble opinion, that kind of overlap was forgivable. But not to Lisa.

What she needed was to understand what she had done to leave her sister so bitter.

Jen used a piece of fine sandpaper to take the last of the paint off a corner by hand.

The wood was warm beneath her touch, and she liked the antique, dusty smell of it. But she'd planned to do more than just work on her kitchen tonight. And she wasn't the only one with heartbreak this Christmas.

She picked up her phone and flipped through her contacts and dialed Uncle Stu.

"Hello?" There was the sound of music in the background, and he sounded relaxed.

"Hi, Uncle Stu, it's Jen. How are you doing?"

"Jen? Hi, there! I'm fine. How are you? I heard all about that big house you bought."

"I was actually wondering if you'd be free for a quick visit," Jen said. "I'm kind of antsy tonight, and I thought I might come by."

"That sounds nice. I've been baking, and there's more than a single man can consume, I can tell you that. Do you know where my apartment is?" Stu asked.

"You'll have to give me the address…"

Stu's apartment was in the tallest building in downtown Mountain Springs—ten stories. It was on a corner, the bottom floor consisting of some picturesque shops on two sides of the building, all of them decked out for Christmas. There was a little restaurant, a coffee shop, a tourist gift shop and a small bookstore. Next to the bookstore was the entrance for the apartments above.

This was the most expensive apartment building in Mountain Springs, and for the most part, it was occupied by wealthy buyers who used the apartments as vacation homes. Uncle Stu had always loved this building, though, so when he and Gayle divorced, he'd bought an apartment on the fourth floor, overlooking the bustling street.

Jen got off the elevator at the fourth floor and by the time she got to her uncle's door, he was standing in the doorway waiting for her. He was dressed in a pair of chinos and a T-shirt, and he accepted her coat and hung it up while she took off her boots. His apartment was warm and cozy.

"It's great to see you," Stu said with a smile. "Come on in."

The apartment was newly renovated, by the looks of it, and neatly furnished. Stu and Gayle had been comfortably well-off, and his decor reflected that. A leather love seat faced a gas fireplace, and a bank of windows overlooked the street. The blinds were open, and Jen could see the flash of headlights moving below. The apartments smelled of spices and recent baking, and the kitchen, which was fully visible in this open-concept space, was clean, with a pile of washed pans in one sink.

"I realized that I hadn't come by to say hi yet," Jen admitted. "With the wedding, and—" She stopped and then winced. "I'm sorry. I know that's probably a sore spot."

"Nah." Stu shook his head. "Gayle and Matt invited me, you know."

"Really?" Maybe that shouldn't surprise her. Gayle and Stu were still connected, but no one knew what that was going to look like now that she'd remarried.

"The invitation was a kind gesture," Stu said. "But I let them have their special day without distracting everyone with the bride's ex."

"That's very mature," Jen said, meaning to joke.

"I better be, by this age," Stu replied but his eyes were sad. "My kids sent me pictures. She was just as beautiful on this wedding day as she was on the day that I married her."

"She was," Jen agreed. "And Matt really loves her."

"He'd better. If he hurts her, deal with him myself," Stu said.

Jen followed her uncle through the apartment and ambled up to the gas fireplace, holding her hands toward its warmth.

"What's it like?" Jen asked. "Seeing Gayle move on, but knowing it's for the best?"

"It hurts like hell," Stu said quietly. "But the right things often do. Our marriage might have worked for me because I was hiding a whole lot, but it wasn't fair to her. I had the kind of love I needed—secretly—and now she can have the kind of love that she needs, too. But she's doing it openly, fairly. I'm happy for her."

"Are you still in contact with... Steven?" she asked.

"No," Stu replied. "That was a clean break. He wasn't ready to come out of the closet, and they moved—you heard that didn't you? His wife blames me, of course. And I haven't heard from him since."

They fell silent, and Jen looked out the bank of windows, down at the street below. There were plenty of tourists walking along, and the light from the shops spilled cheerily onto the sidewalk. So much Christmas cheer for everyone else this year...

"You're a good guy, Stu," Jen said at last.

"That's debatable. I have a daughter who still won't speak to me," he replied.

"You're a good guy," Jen reaffirmed.

Stu gave her a sad smile. "I made brownies and cookies, and…three different kinds of pie. I don't know what I was thinking. It's therapeutic, I guess. Anyway, let me get you a plate, and I need to hear everything that's been going on for you."

For the next few minutes, Jen munched on her uncle's baking and they chatted about how life had unfolded for both of them over the past couple of years. Ironically, Jen had more in common with Stu right now than she did with Aunt Gayle. Aunt Gayle was blissfully happy in her new marriage, while Uncle Stu and Jen were on the fringes.

"I'm a bit stuck with Lisa," Jen admitted. "What do you do when someone you care about thinks the worst of you?"

"I have a lot of people who think the worst of me about now," Stu replied quietly.

"Right," she said. "I'm sorry about that."

"What can you do?" Stu asked with a shrug. "Look, you live your life with as much honesty and integrity as you can in the moment. Sometimes you'll get it right.

Sometimes you won't—I made enough of my own mistakes. I should have come clean with Gayle a very long time ago. But you do the best you can in the present, and then you wait. Some people will see you for who you are, and they'll love you. Other people will see you for who you are, and they'll hate you. There's not a lot you can do about it."

"That's the tough part," Jen said. "Lisa used to know me better than anyone…"

"Yeah," he agreed. "As siblings do."

"I wish she could just be proud of me—see everything I've done and gone through, and think I'm doing okay."

"Are you proud of yourself?" Stu asked.

Jen paused, considering for a moment. "Yeah. I am. I'm still standing, and I think I deserve a medal."

Stu chuckled. "I'm proud of you, too. I never liked Sam much."

"People keep saying that," she said.

"But I always liked you a whole lot," Stu added. "Look, when you do come across people who know you inside and out and still think you're fantastic, you hold them extra close. They don't come along every day. Trust me, I've learned that in very painful ways the last few years."

"Am I supposed to stop caring if my sister even likes me?" Jen asked.

Stu shook his head. "I don't know... I think you'll always care." He pushed himself up from his seat. "Do you want eggnog?"

"Yeah, I do." She smiled. "Thanks."

Funny. She thought she'd need to be comforting Stu this Christmas, but he was turning out to be the one with the wealth of wisdom. It was the kind of thing that came from experiencing the worst, she realized. When a heart was turned inside out, there was a strange peace that came with finding out that life didn't end when it got painful.

Jen would get through this Christmas the old-fashioned way—one foot in front of the other. Maybe she'd earn a bit of the wisdom that Stu had picked up along the way. It never came easy, did it?

THE GARAGE WAS HEATED, but a draft from the closed door still permeated the space. Nick wore old comfy slippers and a sweater over his T-shirt. Inside, Amelia was on her phone chatting with Ben. She sounded...in love.

And what more could he want for his daughter, except he still worried about her. She deserved someone who saw what a treasure she was, too, and if the match wasn't quite the right fit, Amelia deserved a guy who was.

Whether or not Ben was the right fit was Amelia's call to make, and as her dad, he'd support her. That was how this worked. But he still worried. He'd heard enough about Jen before meeting her to know that her marriage had been hopeful and optimistic…and wrong for her. Jen had gotten married at twenty-four, and Amelia was only a year younger. Maybe it wasn't too young to be thinking about marriage and a family of her own. Maybe he was the one who wasn't ready for her to be quite so grown up.

Nick's personal tools hung on the garage wall, every tool in its place. He'd always been particular about his tools, and this space was a private, peaceful respite from the world. He liked the order, the feeling of possibility.

He picked up the carved wooden bear from his workbench. He'd been carving these for a month now in his spare time—a whole bear choir, just like the chipped and faded porcelain ones from Amelia's youth. He wanted to give her a new choir of bears—these ones made with his own hands. He'd paid careful attention to detail. Every bear had its own expression, with big soulful eyes and delicately curling fur. He'd taken his time with them—a few he'd even tossed into the fire and restarted. And now that he knew his daughter didn't share his particular nostalgia, he felt a little stupid.

All that work, and he couldn't give this to her for Christmas. Maybe it had been amateurish and ridiculous to begin with. What would Amelia want for Christmas this year? Shopping money, probably, and here he was trying to foist some carvings onto her.

He ran a work-roughened thumb over the singing mouth of the largest bear, and he felt a pang of sadness. A month ago, when Amelia had confirmed that she was going to spend the holidays with him, he'd made plans to remind her of their good times. He'd turned down friends' invitations to go out for dinner. Bert would come over and hang out in the garage rather than going out for a beer because Nick had been carving these bears. Nick had been so certain that this Christmas he and Amelia would finally reconnect and find that warmth between them again.

He couldn't say that he and Amelia had no warmth, exactly…it was just different. Maybe those sweet times were gone for good. Kids grew up. Heck, parents grew up, too. Maybe this was the new normal, and he should be grateful for the time he got with his daughter.

He put the bear down on the workbench once more. He couldn't bring himself to throw them out—he'd poured his heart into these carvings. Maybe they'd just stay here—remind him of the good old days and let Amelia remember the times that made her happy in her own way.

He heard the front door open and shut, and he headed up the stairs and back into the house. He looked out the window to see his daughter hopping into a car with another young woman, and he lifted his hand in a wave that Amelia didn't see.

A text came in, and he looked down at it.

Going out with a friend, Dad. I grabbed the spare key so I can let myself in when I get back. I'll be late.

He texted back a thumbs-up emoji and returned his phone to his pocket. Goldie came padding up from her spot on the couch where she'd been dozing, and he bent to pet her head.

"Just you and me tonight, girl," he said. "What should we do with ourselves, huh?"

Goldie gazed up at him lovingly. Yeah, he had a life of his own, and he couldn't expect his grown daughter to fill any of the holes for him. She wouldn't want the job anyway.

By eleven, Amelia still wasn't home, so Nick left a light on in the kitchen for when his daughter returned. He headed up to his bedroom and Goldie hopped up on the bed where she always slept and flopped over, watching him as he puttered around the room, putting away some folded laundry.

As he passed his window, the blinds still up, he paused, laundry basket in hand. Across the road, he could see the old mansion—the third floor lit with a cozy glow. The curtains were open there, too. He could see Jen's outline in the window. She was standing motionless, seemingly looking out into the darkness, and he wasn't sure if she

could see him. He was about to turn away—
he was no Peeping Tom, after all—but there
was something about the way she stood that
seemed so solitary.

"Don't be a creep," he muttered to himself, and as he turned, Jen raised a hand in
a wave.

He felt an embarrassed heat rush to his face.
She wouldn't be able to make out that much
detail, he was sure, but he waved back awk-
wardly. She disappeared from the window,
and he let out a sigh. Then his phone blipped.

Nick dropped the laundry basket back into
the corner and scooped up his phone. It was
a text from Jen:

Hi. Sorry to spook you. We have a direct view
into each other's bedrooms.

He chuckled and typed back:

The last owner kept her curtains shut. And I
normally do the same. Didn't mean to spook
you, either.

Nick sank onto his bed and leaned back

against the headboard. He flicked on the TV, as he normally did, just as another text came in.

This is a very big house. I'm not complaining, but I think I'll put in a security system sooner rather than later. Is the neighborhood safe?

Nick smiled faintly.

Yeah, it's safe. But there is nothing wrong with security for a single woman.

Would she answer? Or just say goodnight? He found himself hoping she'd chat a little bit, and he wondered if that was hopelessly naive of him.

She answered:

I agree. Besides, old houses have weird sounds at night. Things creak and groan. I know it's nothing, but I'd feel better knowing it's ghosts and not burglars.

There was a pause. She added:

That was a joke.

He chuckled aloud.

I wasn't sure. Do you believe in ghosts?

She texted back:

Not tonight.

Nick looked over at Goldie, who looked back at him placidly. Was he nuts to be doing this—chatting with a woman he should be keeping an emotional distance from? Probably, but his daughter was right about how solitary he was. And it was nice to chat with her tonight, he had to admit.

I saw my uncle Stu tonight, she added. I feel better having seen him.

So he's doing okay? he asked.

He is. He's got a very mature attitude toward all of this. Not that it makes it any easier, of course.

Of course, he replied. That was an understatement. Have you talked to your sister about her stories?

I tried. Neither of us were at our best.

His feelings about the situation with his daughter were similar.

Maybe I should Google some more of your sister's stories. Maybe I'll learn about your scandalous teenage years.

Har har, she texted back. Actually, feel free. She's a very good writer. Just keep in mind that it's very much fiction.

I know, I know, he replied. Only joking.

For a couple of minutes she didn't reply, and he flicked through some channels, wondering if he'd overstepped. But then his phone pinged again.

You were really insightful today, she texted.

Was I? he asked. He didn't get accused of insight too often.

My sister's writing is her art. I might feel betrayed, but people love her work. I wish she liked me more, but I think I have to let the grudge go.

He smiled faintly.

I don't think that was my point.

What was your point, then?

That even art has limits if you want to have people in your life, he texted back.

LOL! I like how you think.

He grinned at that. He paid attention. He didn't always join the conversation, but he had opinions.

Are you normally up this late? she asked.

No, he texted back. But my daughter is out with friends and she said not to wait up, so...

LOL! So you're going to wait up, aren't you?

Of course.

You're a good dad, she texted.

He felt his throat thicken with emotion that took him by surprise. A good dad? He hadn't felt that way for a very long time now. There was another ping.

I'm turning into a pumpkin. I should say good-night, she texted.

I've got work in the morning, so I'd be smart if I did, too.

Your client must be a real stickler.

Was she joking around, or did she really suspect she was tough to please? It was hard to tell without being able to see her. Texting could be dangerous that way.

Nah, he wrote back. She's the perfect client—smart and with artistic vision. I'm the lucky one in this deal.

He waited for her to answer, but there was a pause that stretched for almost a minute.

His phone blipped and he looked down at her text:

You're a sweet guy. I'd better turn in. Good night, Nick.

He couldn't help but smile at that, and he typed back, Good night.

Then he looked up to see her turn to face the window. She waved, her fingers fluttering, and then the curtain swept shut.

He was starting to feel something for her, even though he knew it was dumb. She was the kind of woman that made him want to open up. But he knew how this ended—she'd enjoy his down-to-earth views until it wasn't a novelty anymore and just became irritating. Right now he was just the beefy contractor. And she was the gorgeous client. So there was sexual tension.

He looked toward the mansion across the street again.

Except, he didn't get the impression that she wanted that from him, either. Mostly, she seemed to want to be his friend, and that might be even more dangerous, because he could very easily fall for her and just sit here in the agony of unreturned feelings.

No, it couldn't end well, regardless. He needed to stay professional.

Nick got comfortable on his bed again and picked up the TV remote. Goldie came closer and lay her head on his lap, and he flicked through the channels, stopping at a home renovation show.

He was only a man, after all, and that was the part that had disappointed his ex-wife the most. He was the exact man she married, and he'd never risen to her hopes of what he could become under her manipulations.

But as a man, Nick wasn't going to even
pretend to sleep until his daughter was safely
home. Whatever. Amelia could complain to
her mother about it later. He was her dad,
whether she liked it or not.

CHAPTER EIGHT

THREE DAYS LATER Jen was happy to see a
note on the bathroom door that read, "It
works. Enjoy." There was still a groan and
a rattle when the water was turned on, but
the bathroom was now fully functional, and
Jen enjoyed her first piping-hot shower from
the depths of that claw-foot tub.

Jen stood under the hot shower, steam bil-
lowing out the top of the shower curtain. The
past few days had been strange between her
and Nick. They'd started texting each other
in the evenings—not for very long, but it had
gotten to feel like a habit already. When he
was working in the house with his team, he
was more cautious and reserved. But there
was something that seemed to tug them together. When they passed each other in a
doorway, his fingers grazed hers. And it
made her heart speed up just to think about
it. Something so small it could seem acciden-

tal, but she knew it wasn't. He was feeling this, too. Something was sparking between them, and while she had been telling herself it was friendship, it felt like more.

And that was bad. This was Lisa's friend, and Jen had only just moved back. With Lisa already thinking that Jen took the easy path by marrying a guy with money, the last thing she needed was Lisa thinking that she was doing that again—fooling around with the guy who could renovate her home.

When people told the story later—when *Drew* told this story later—she wanted to make sure that they could tell the story with pride. She wanted Drew to see his mother building something on her own, not leaning on a man to make it happen. She wanted to prove Lisa wrong, because deep down she had a needling feeling that her sister had a point... She'd loved Sam, but she'd also loved the life he'd offered her.

She'd wanted security, and she'd paid for it! Well, not this time. She was going to earn this on her own.

Jen turned off the water and flung back the curtain. She shivered as the cooler outside air hit her body and she grabbed a towel, wrapping it around herself. There was a big cabinet with doors next to the sink, and she'd already arranged her toiletries inside, leaving a full shelf for Drew. He was old enough now that he'd started quite the collection of hair supplies and body sprays, and she arranged the bottles that had been brought in boxes on the middle shelf, looking at half bottles of gel, teen face cleanser and some temporary hair dyes he'd kept from last Halloween. It all made her feel a bit misty. She missed her son.

Jen dried her hair most of the way, letting her natural curls define the rest of what her hair would do that day with the help of a bit of mousse, then she headed barefoot to her bedroom. She could hear the bass tones of men's voices downstairs as Nick and his team continued working on the cabinets.

Jen got dressed into a cozy, cowl-necked sweater and a pair of leggings, then smoothed some face cream on and did just the basics for her makeup. She was just giving her curls an extra shake to loosen them up when her phone rang. It was Lisa, and Jen sighed.

"Hi, Lis," she said.

"Hi," Lisa said. "How are you doing?"

"Good."

There was a pause. "I've got an evening shift, and I normally swap babysitting with a friend of mine, but she's got the flu, and I'm stuck." Lisa's voice softened. "I've got childcare lined up for the daytime, but tonight I could use a hand…if you were free."

"You're asking me to babysit?" Jen asked, and she couldn't help but smile. Lisa had been so self-sufficient all this time that the request for help surprised her.

"Yeah, I'm asking…" Lisa said. "I mean, I know your place isn't exactly toddler proof, though."

"I'd love to," Jen said. "It's a great chance to hang out with my nephew."

"Is it safe?" Lisa asked uncertainly.

"I've raised a toddler of my own," Jen replied. "And I can keep him safe. That's a guarantee. Besides, the third floor is just fine. And I'll keep my eyes on him the entire time. And maybe my lips just plastered to that squishy face."

"Okay…" Lisa sounded mildly stunned. "I thought this would take more convincing."

"Lisa, I'm nicer than you think," Jen said. "Besides, I think Bram likes me, too."

Lisa laughed. "Okay. Thank you. I'll bring him by your place around five."

"Perfect. See you then," Jen said.

As Jen opened her bedroom door, she heard footsteps on the stairs and Nick appeared at the top of them. He hesitated, then shot her a smile.

"I'm checking on the bathroom," he said. "How's the shower working?"

"Good. It was nice and hot. I can't complain," she replied.

"You mind?" he asked, gesturing toward the room in question.

Jen shrugged, and Nick went into the bathroom and looked around. Jen paused in the doorway, watching him as he felt along seals, stretching to reach. He was a big man, and she couldn't help but notice the bulge of his biceps. Nick tested the taps a couple of times.

"Satisfied?" she asked with a small smile.

"Are you?" he asked, and he caught her gaze. The bathroom suddenly felt smaller with him in the center of it, and his dark gaze moved over her in a warm sweep.

"I definitely am," she replied. "This will be perfect—completely functional. And like I said, the water is nice and hot."

Did that sound like flirting? She hoped not.

Nick nodded. "I always double-check. I'll sign off on Bert's work then, and cut him a check. He's got Christmas plans. Imagine."

"He's one of the lucky ones," Jen said. "What's he doing?"

"He and his wife are going to see their son and daughter-in-law in Denver," Nick said. "He's got a new grandbaby to spoil."

"That does sound nice," she admitted.

Nick dropped his gaze and licked his lips. "I'm not sure if this is really bad form, but... what are you doing tonight for dinner?"

She felt her heart speed up just a little. He was right—it would be a terrible idea. Their veiled flirting was one thing, but...

"I'm babysitting," Jen replied. "Why?"

"Oh... So definitely busy," he said, and some red tinged his cheeks.

"I'm babysitting here," she amended. "So I won't be far away, exactly. In fact, if I left the curtains open, you could probably watch me chase a toddler."

Nick chuckled. "That would be very creepy of me. But I picked up a beef roast, and there is no way my daughter and I are going to finish it. I just thought…maybe you'd like to help me out with that."

"You're cooking, huh?" she said. "That's tempting. But I've already got a two-year-old I'll be wrangling."

"Does he eat beef?" Nick joked.

Jen laughed. "I don't know. Maybe."

"I doubt he'd make much of a dent on my roast, but what if I invited you both?" Nick asked. "Besides, my place might be a bit safer for a toddler. Theoretically. If we watched him really closely. There's fewer loose nails and whatnot—that's for sure."

He had a point, not that she needed a lot of convincing to let him make her a home-made dinner.

"Thanks. I'll double check with Lisa to make sure she's okay with it, but I'd like that," she said, and when she smiled, he gave a quick nod and turned toward the stairs again.

"Okay, so I'll count you in," he said. He glanced over his shoulder once, and the warmth in his gaze belied the casual tone of his words. This felt like a date.

NICK TROTTED BACK down the stairs, and he couldn't help his smile. Whatever was developing between them wasn't wise—he knew that. But his daughter would be there, and so would Lisa's boy, so that would change the dynamic.

He hadn't been planning on asking Jen over, but it had come out of his mouth before he could think better of it. He wanted to see her—simple as that. He was a grown man, and he could keep the rest under control.

The rest of the day, he and Floyd worked on cupboard doors and finishing the insides of the cupboards and drawers. This was all easier work before the new counters were installed. There were a few problems—a large section of wall came away behind the sink, and so they needed to repair the wall behind the cupboards first. But one step at a time the kitchen was coming together, and he was pleased with their work.

Around five, the peal of the doorbell echoed through the house, and he glanced out of the kitchen to see Jen opening the big front door. Her sister was there, and he walked over to say hello.

"How are you doing?" Nick asked, giving Lisa a smile.

"Hanging in there," she replied. "How's my sister treating you?"

She glanced around but didn't venture farther inside.

"She's a taskmaster," he joked. They talked for a couple of minutes, a diaper bag was handed over and then a wide-eyed toddler, who reached back for his mother and started to howl when Lisa kissed his cheek and left.

Jen stood there for a moment, holding the little boy, then she looked up and caught Nick watching her.

"He's mad," Jen said, readjusting the little guy in her arms. "Bram, sweetie, it's okay. Mommy's coming back. You're just going to play with Auntie for a little while. That's all."

Bram sniffled and looked at her, then the tears started again. He wriggled and a boot dropped off his foot. Nick remembered this stage of things—toddlers had their ways of letting their displeasure be known.

"We're pretty much done for the day," Nick said. "We can clear out, and I can get that roast into the oven. You want to come right over?"

"Do you mind?" she asked.

"We made good progress today," he replied. "Besides, Floyd's got a family at home waiting for him, and he makes brownie points with his wife if he gets home a bit early."

Jen smiled wistfully at that. "Far be it from me to mess with a man's brownie points."

"Right?" Nick chuckled. "Just give us a few minutes to clean up."

As promised, Nick and Floyd cleaned up in record time. Nick picked up the diaper bag for Jen and waited while she wrangled the little guy back into his coat and boots. Then Nick held her coat for her, and as she slid her arm into the sleeve, pausing to readjust Bram in her grasp, he caught the soft scent of her perfume.

"Thanks," she murmured, shrugging the coat up onto her shoulders, and her blond curls brushed over the back of his hand, raising a shiver on his arm.

"Yeah, no problem…" He let go of the coat and reached for the door. Did she know how she made him feel, or was he successful in hiding it? As long as his daughter was around, that would douse whatever was sparking here and they could go back to a regular friendship, because being friends was the only relationship that would actually last between them.

They headed across the street to his place, and when he unlocked the door and let Jen inside, he could tell that his daughter wasn't back yet. And he couldn't help the tingle of relief that they were alone for a few more minutes. The house was silent, and he flicked on some lights to welcome them. Goldie came bounding down the stairs toward him.

"Come on in," Nick said. "I've got some crackers around here somewhere. I mean, they aren't Goldfish, but if the kid likes sage and oregano, we might be in business."

He bent down to give Goldie's ears a rub.

Jen laughed. "Let's give those crackers a try."

"Goggie!" Bram said, and he squirmed to be let down. He reached for a handful of Goldie's tail, and she looked around and gave the toddler's face a lick.

"Goldie, go to the couch," Nick commanded.

Goldie hesitated.

"Hey! Now."

She sauntered over to her spot on the couch, and Nick grabbed the remote and turned the TV on. It didn't take him long to find the cartoon channel, and Bram's gaze immediately glued to the screen.

"There we go... Magic," Nick said, shooting Jen a grin. "You okay with that?"

"Perfectly. He looks happy," Jen replied.

Nick grabbed the box of crackers from the cupboard and handed them over to Jen.

"As promised," he said.

Jen shook a few into her hand and brought them over to Bram.

"You do realize we'll have to vacuum up after him," she said over her shoulder. "Handing crackers to a toddler is...adventurous."

"Don't worry about it. That's what Goldie's for," he replied with a chuckle. "She'll find every last crumb, I can guarantee it."

As if to prove him right, Goldie leaned over and delicately removed a single cracker from Bram's stash with her front teeth and gulped it back.

"Hey—" Nick said. "Those are his. I'll get you a chewie."

Once Goldie had her chewie treat, he

washed his hands and got to work on the roast. It had been marinating for the past couple of days, and he flicked on the oven and set to work. When he got the roast in, he turned back to find Jen watching him.

"So this is what it's like in here," she said.

"You were wondering?" he asked with a half smile.

She blushed. "I'm curious about everything." Her gaze moved over to the smart artificial tree at the far side of the living room. "Like that."

He followed her over and watched as her gaze moved over the ornaments.

"You're the kind of person who puts memories on their tree," she said.

"Yeah, I guess so," he replied. "Most of these are from when Amelia was in elementary school."

"Those little bears are cute," she said.

He looked down at the ceramic bear choir and shrugged. "Yeah, Amelia used to love those. She'd make them sing the songs she was learning in school for the Christmas concert. I used to look forward to bringing those bears out every year, because it would make her eyes light up." He felt his throat tightening with unbidden emotion and he took a step back. "You know how it is."

"I do," she agreed softly. "For my son, it was the Christmas tree. I always get him a new ornament every year that goes along with his interests. One year it was a Spiderman ornament. One year it was a Monopoly game ornament... You know, whatever tickles his fancy that year. And he loves going through them all and putting them all up."

"Are you going to do a tree this year?" Nick asked. "Or is it just too much with the move and everything?"

"It is too much, but I promised Drew I would. He's worried I won't have a proper Christmas if I don't put a tree up."

"He might have a point," Nick said.

"The silly kid doesn't realize I won't have a proper Christmas without *him*." She blinked tears back. "Sorry. I'm still getting used to this whole shared custody thing. I'm not sure I'll ever be used to it."

"It's not easy," he admitted. "And I'm not exactly the guy to give advice about how to make it work. I never did get a handle on parenting this way."

Jen met his gaze then nodded. "Most people just tell me to tough it out. They say I'll get used to it, and I should find stuff I like to fill my time. And I get it—that's probably very sound advice. But I don't want to find hobbies. I don't want to miss him less... I just—" She sighed. "I don't want to be a part-time mom."

"I got pushed aside," Nick admitted. "I was always the brawn, and Shari was the brain. Our daughter was more like her mom—and maybe that was just inevitable because she's a girl. When we were married, I could be the dose of testosterone in the home, and it was generally okay. They'd tease me and roll their eyes and call me a silly man, but it was still okay. But when Shari and I split, I was no longer the dose of testosterone—I became some kind of stranger..." He paused, winced. "I'm not saying that'll happen to you."

"You can't promise it won't," she murmured. "Your daughter didn't miss you?"

"At first, she seemed to, but I couldn't keep up with her life. Her mom married a guy with a lot of money, and he was able to give her anything she wanted. She didn't have to ask me for anything anymore, and Chris was...this is going to sound mean, but... Chris wasn't quite as strong a dose of testosterone."

Jen laughed softly. "He was more interested in...their stuff."

"Art. Books. Theater. Lectures. The whole thing. And don't get me wrong, he's a better match for Shari in every way. I'm fine with that. Shari and I didn't work out. But he was also a better match as a father figure for my daughter in every way, and I haven't gotten over that."

"She's still yours," Jen said quietly.

"Yeah." That was a fact, but he wasn't sure it was one that Amelia cared much about. "You know...she's got this boyfriend..."

"Yeah?" Jen said.

"His name is Ben. They've been on again off again for a couple of years now, and my daughter is now saying that she wants marriage."

"With Ben," Jen clarified.

"Yeah." He sighed. "I don't want her to make your mistake."

Jen froze.

"I mean—" He winced. "That might have come out wrong."

"What mistake?" she said.

"Marrying really young to a rich guy who didn't appreciate you?" he said.

"Marrying for money," Jen said. "Is that what you think I did?"

"I didn't mean it like that," he said. He'd stepped in it this time, but he couldn't stop now. He'd better explain himself. "But yeah—a rich guy who won't see the value in my daughter…a guy who's never been man enough to commit to her, but has all the money and resources to control her if he decided to—that scares me."

"Sam didn't control me," she said.

"That's good. I'm not sure if Ben would or not, but when your little girl is looking to tie herself to a man in marriage, you want to know she'll be okay, and if she's not, that you can do something for her."

"Right…" Her cheeks colored.

"I wasn't meaning—" The front door opened, and Nick turned to see Amelia come inside, and the words died on his lips. Goldie leaped down from the couch and raced to meet her. Amelia had a shopping bag in one hand, and she lifted it up to keep it free from Goldie.

He glanced back at Jen, and she shrugged. Apology accepted? He could only hope.

"Hi, Amelia," he called. "Glad you're back."

"I picked up some ornaments—" Amelia stopped when she saw Jen. "Oh! I didn't realize you had a guest, Dad. I'm sure I can find something to do—"

"It's fine," Nick interrupted. "This isn't a date, it's a neighborly visit."

"Right." Amelia gave a slow smile, then shot a grin at Jen. "I'm taking my father in hand, by the way. Those old, sad ornaments are about to be replaced. I picked up some stuff that's color coordinated and understated. I'll make something of him yet."

Nick looked around the living room—the Christmas tree, the little choir of bears on the windowsill, and Bram sitting on the couch staring at Amelia in undisguised curiosity. Was this really such a sad room? He hadn't thought so. Amelia used to come barreling down those stairs to answer the phone when her friends would call, and she'd lie on her stomach in front of the Christmas tree trying to guess what was in her presents.

"Need help?" Jen asked quietly.

He didn't need help, but he could sure use the company. He smiled. "Thanks. I've got another peeler here somewhere, too."

Jen joined him at the counter, and when he passed her the peeler, her soft fingers lingered over his.

"Your daughter loves you," Jen said.

And maybe she did, but she also felt the need to change him. Just like her mother had. He was tired of being cleaned up and dusted off. Maybe he just wanted to decorate with those old chipped bears and be the guy he'd always been.

As he reached for a potato and started to peel, Nick glanced down at Jen.

"I married young," she said softly. "I'll admit that. And he was a bad choice."

Nick glanced over to see his daughter squatting down to talk to Bram, one hand on Goldie's head. This was his little girl, all grown up, and he did want to protect her. But the wealthy guys out there wouldn't be intimidated by some contractor.

What if Ben was just another guy who

thought he deserved the world and wanted his wife to get on board?

But it was comforting that Jen seemed to understand his anxiety.

PERCITA ATKING 211

thought he deserved the world and wanted
his wife to go on beauty...
But it was comforting that Jen seemed to
judges had the anxiety

CHAPTER NINE

THE REST OF the evening flowed pleasantly,
all conversation about marriage mistakes
over. They had dinner, and the roast was
delicious. Not only was it great to have a
proper sit-down meal, but Nick was a good
cook, too. There were mashed potatoes on
the side, and steamed peas. Bram made a
mess of himself eating the potatoes by hand-
fuls, and Amelia was upbeat and talkative
on all sorts of subjects from politics to art
to celebrity gossip.

Jen kept an eye on the clock, and when
it was getting close to Bram's bedtime, she
made her excuses and started gathering up
Bram's things.

She'd enjoyed the evening, but having
Nick's daughter here made the tone different.
It also reminded her of exactly what people
seemed to think of her now that she was divorced. When she was still married to Sam,

she had the defense that they were happy. But having divorced him, she couldn't stand by that any longer, and having Nick mention his worries about his daughter in relation to her own choices had stung. If she let herself flirt back with him, was he going to think the same thing her sister did—that she was just looking for a way to make her life easier?

"I'll help you carry everything back," Nick said.

Jen glanced around herself at the diaper bag, and Bram's coat and boots. Bram stood there rubbing his eyes and gave a slow yawn.

"Thanks," Jen said. "I could use the help."

"Come on, Goldie," Nick called. "Walk time."

Goldie bounded for the door, and Jen shot Amelia a smile.

"It was really nice seeing you again," Jen said. "Take care."

"You, too!" Amelia said.

Amelia was smart and interesting. Jen had a feeling that whomever Amelia married wouldn't be able to push her around too easily. But she didn't seem to have a lot of consideration for her father's feelings. Maybe

Nick was right and state school might have been better for her, character wise.

They headed out into the cold night together, Bram's little head against Jen's shoulder as they walked back through the evening dark. Nick was at her side, and when she came to an icy part on his drive, his strong hand came under her elbow to steady her.

"It's been a long time since I've carried a kid this size," Jen said.

"Even longer for me," Nick said.

"Does it still feel like yesterday?"

Nick smiled faintly. "Yeah, it does."

Even when Drew was little, Sam hadn't been this attentive, and she glanced up at Nick. He was strong and solid, and she liked the look of his beard shining in the light of the streetlamp. He was just so…male, and she liked it. Dammit—was she softening at the thought of rescue again? She'd better stop that.

There was something about this man that made her feel that much more feminine, though. Maybe it was the sheer size of him. He was right about being a source of testosterone—he oozed it. She shivered, and it wasn't because of the cold. Then she fixed her gaze ahead of her. The last thing she needed was for Nick to notice her eyeing him like that.

They crossed the street, and as they got onto Jen's property, Goldie trotted happily ahead of them, her tail wagging. Jen had left some lights on, and the house glowed softly in the darkness, the snow that bowed the tree branches glittering in the moonlight.

"So what do you do when you aren't working?" Jen asked, glancing toward him.

"I walk my dog," he said, then smiled ruefully. "Honestly? I work a lot. When I'm not working, I tend to watch some TV, walk Goldie, sometimes I go out for dinner with a few friends. Bert and I have been buddies for ages. He's good at dragging me out. I'm not a real exciting guy."

"There's nothing wrong with a calm life," she said.

"I agree. I'm not apologizing."

"So how come you're still single?" she asked. "I know a few women personally who'd happily settle into a calm life with someone like you."

He glanced at her and raised an eyebrow. She felt the heat hit her cheeks.

"I'm not suggesting myself. You know what I mean," she said.

He chuckled. "I'm just… You really want to know?"

"Yes, I want to know," she said.

"I'm attracted to the wrong kind of woman," he said. "I know a lot of guys who get married a second time, and it's just the same thing all over again. They just keep doing the same things. I don't want to repeat my mistakes."

"That sounds wise," she replied. "I think I'd rather not repeat mine, either."

"Where did you go wrong?" he asked.

"I think you probably have a few opinions about that already," she said.

"That shouldn't matter," he said. "You'd know better."

"I let my heart lead," she said. "And I know that sounds like a ridiculous complaint, because falling in love with someone is all about heart, but I let myself get caught up in what I hoped would be our life together, and…it got away from me."

"No one warned you?" Nick asked. "No one pointed out that there might be unforeseen complications there?"

Jen's mind went back to her wedding—the planning, the excitement. Her parents had been very excited about the wedding. They saw Sam as a sign of success for the entire family—a connection they could be proud of. Sam made her feel safe and secure and important because he was older than she was and established... It was Lisa who'd been the vocal one.

"My sister tried," Jen said. "But she was a teenager at the time, and I didn't take her seriously. How about you?"

"Nope," he replied with a rueful smile. "Every single person in my life told me that I couldn't do better. She was more than I deserved."

Jen winced. "Ouch. But I kind of got the same thing. He was miles above me, and I was lucky to have nabbed him—that's what people told me. But for all the judgment about who I married and why, you and I might have made the very same mistake."

Nick gave her a look of surprise, and then a slow smile moved over his face. "You have a point."

They came up the steps before the door, and they came to a stop. Jen hitched Bram a little higher in her arms. He was asleep now, and she could feel the warmth of his baby breath against her neck.

"Don't you ever get tired of trying to figure out all of your mistakes?" Jen asked. "Defending yourself?"

"Yeah, I do," he said with a nod, and he met her gaze. A smile twitched at one side of his mouth. "I've got my daughter here trying to get me to move on, and I guess it has me digging it all up again."

"What if we didn't?" Jen asked.

"Didn't dig it up?" he asked uncertainly.

"Exactly," she said. "What if we just left it alone and enjoyed Christmas? I get it—people think I'm going to find a man to solve my problems again. I'm determined not to. I have my self-respect. And you feel like you have to explain yourself. But what kind of gift to yourself would that be to not dig up all those old mistakes? You've got your daughter reminding you of everything, and I've got my sister doing the exact same thing. And I'm sick of it! I'm not leaping into any new relationship, but I'm also tired of beating myself up about the last one."

"You have a good point," he said.

"I mean, look at us, Nick. We're successful people. You run your own business and you're very good at it. You're the one who did the work on the Mountain Springs Lodge renovation, and that's really something. That lodge is featured in travel magazines now because of your talent."

"I am pretty proud of that," he said with a slow smile. "And you're doing rather well, yourself. You're opening a gallery."

"It's a dream come true for me," she replied. "I think we deserve to just enjoy what we've worked for, don't you?"

"All right," he said, the smile warming his gaze. "Let's make a pact—we just enjoy the holidays."

"And we hold each other accountable," she said. "No beating ourselves up. Let's just have Christmas."

"Deal." He met her gaze, and Bram wriggled in her arms, moaning softly.

Jen reached into her coat pocket for her keys, and they slipped from her fingers into the snow.

"Here," Nick said, and he scooped them up, then unlocked the door for her. He pushed it open and let her go inside first.

Jen carried Bram to a large divan—one of the pieces of furniture from the last owner— and laid him down, coat and boots still on him. He settled and slept on. When she looked up, she saw Nick put the diaper bag down and he cast her a smile. Goldie sat obediently at his feet.

"Thank you," she said, crossing the room toward him again. She undid her jacket and loosened her scarf. "It was nice of you to help me get home."

Nick nodded and he put his hand on the door handle again, but his gaze stayed on her face.

"It's no problem," he said softly. "We're neighbors."

"Right." Neighbors—but when his gaze moved over her face like that, she wasn't feeling neighborly...

"I, um—" he started, but then his gaze moved down to her lips, and for just a moment she felt like the room around them had suddenly dimmed, and it was just the two of them standing on the marble tiles, and all she seemed able to focus on was the way his lips looked with the bristle of his beard.

"I should get going," he said after a few

beats of silence. He leaned down to give Goldie's head a stroke, then pulled open the door and let a puff of frigid air inside.

"See you," she said, and her voice sounded breathy in her own ears.

His dark gaze met hers, and she held her breath. He leaned closer, and the bristle of his beard and the softness of his lips brushed across her cheek. Then Nick stepped outside with Goldie at his heels, and he pulled the door shut behind him, leaving Jen alone in the foyer, goose bumps forming on her arms.

She shut her eyes and released a slow breath.

That didn't actually count as a kiss goodnight, but it did make a smile tug at her lips, and her fingers touched the spot where his beard had tickled her skin. That flutter in her chest was something she shouldn't let get out of hand, either. Nick was a man who could very easily sweep her off her feet... and she wasn't doing that again. Lisa would have no cause to question this accomplishment—and neither would she.

Her phone blipped and she looked down to see a text from her son.

Hi, Mom. What are you up to?

There was an awful lot that had happened tonight that she'd never tell Drew about, but she was glad for the distraction.

I'm babysitting your cousin, Bram. He's really cute. Hold on, I'll send you a picture.

She headed over to where Bram was sleeping and took a picture of the sleeping toddler.

Life wasn't over. Tomorrow she'd get a tree. Drew would definitely like that. There was still plenty to enjoy this Christmas. She just had to keep her feet on the ground.

THE NEXT MORNING Jen drove her black SUV to Dickerson's Nursery. It was on the far side of town, and up the mountain about five miles, following a twisting road. The nursery serviced most of Mountain Springs all year long—with the greenhouse and Christmas trees in the winter, and with plants and shrubbery in the summer. But as she drove, her mind kept drifting back to that kiss on her cheek.

It was innocent...probably. Right? It was

just a polite gesture. Except, she and Nick had had a connection lately. She'd assumed up until now that he wasn't feeling what she was—here she was, nearly forty and newly divorced. She wasn't at her most confident. Divorced men had it easier—they were snapped up in no time. Look at Sam! So she'd been thinking that her attraction to Nick was a bit silly, or at the very least very safe in that it wouldn't be returned.

So he kissed her on the cheek. What was she worrying about? They were both adults. Maybe it was just a slightly awkward moment and Nick was currently regretting it. They weren't dating—they were friends. Surprisingly good friends in this short period of time. And she shouldn't make more of a friendly buss than was intended. She'd get a Christmas tree and put all of this behind her. When Drew arrived, things would feel more normal again.

Jen parked and looked at the familiar sign, a little faded and in need of a new coat of paint. She got out of her vehicle and locked it, then headed toward the front gate that was decorated with oversize red-and-green Christmas tree baubles, capped with snow.

A brisk wind whipped a chilly dusting of snowflakes off the surrounding trees and into Jen's face, and she ducked her head against the cold.

The trees were all cut down and tied with twine, leaning against the fence that surrounded the sales lot. The sales hut was right next to the entrance, and it was in the style of a little log cabin with big, bright windows. There was some canned Christmas music being played over the loudspeaker—"Here Comes Santa Claus"—and Jen did feel cheerier already. Maybe her son was right about getting a tree. She wound her way around the lot, looking at the different trees from the tiny tabletop variety all the way up to the massive spruce trees. She realized that if she got a regular six-foot tree, it would be dwarfed by the massive front room. Unless she wanted to drag a Christmas tree up to the third floor…which she didn't.

A family with three little kids came past her, the kids babbling with excitement and the couple holding hands. Jen watched them for a moment, feeling wistful. That was the life she'd wanted—and the life she'd had for a little while.

But then her gaze moved past the little family and landed on a woman she recognized. It was Renata, from the Second Chance Dinner Club. She stood next to a tree, a thick scarf and faux fur coat wrapped around her. She looked warm and the browns of her coat set off her rosy face and short chestnut hair. A burly man with a full, wiry beard was talking to her—tall, broad, a little hefty and wearing a red plaid jacket. Renata's face was flushed and her eyes sparkled when she looked up at him. He took out a pad of paper, wrote something on it and handed it over. She reached out to take the slip of paper, and he didn't release it right away, leaning in to say something else that made her blush deeper. She dropped her gaze, said something, and he let go of the slip of paper, chuckling.

"Okay, well, give me a call." His voice carried over to where Jen stood as he turned.

Jen couldn't help but grin—that looked like Renata had just been asked out. Romantic complications were great fun in other people's lives.

Renata spotted Jen, and Jen waved and headed in her direction.

"What was that?" Jen asked. "It looked like he just gave you his number?"

"Um…" Renata shrugged. "Yeah, he did."

"Do you know him?" Jen asked.

"Yeah, that's Sebastian Dickerson. He took over for his uncle after he retired, so he's running the nursery now."

"Right." Jen shot the shorter woman a smile. "And, he looks interested in you…as more than a customer."

"Oh…he's been asking me out for a couple of months now," Renata said with a breathy laugh.

"You've been hanging around the nursery?" Jen joked.

"No!" Renata rolled her eyes. "Seb's mom is at the assisted living facility where I work, so I see him there."

"Are you going to go out with him?" Jen asked.

Renata shook her head. "I don't think I'm ready. I've got enough on my plate dealing with Ivan—my ex—right now. But it's just been hectic, especially this Christmas, and I don't think adding a boyfriend into the mix is going to make it easier."

"Yeah, I could see that," Jen agreed. "How long have you been divorced?"

"Three and a half years," Renata replied.

That was a whole lot better than Jen's brand-new divorce. Was Jen going to be unsteady on her feet for another three or four years, too? She hoped not.

"Has Ivan been dating?" Jen asked, sobering. "I mean, I remember you said he was cheating on you, but..."

"Yeah, he's gone through a couple of girlfriends," Renata said, and her eyes turned sad. "But I'm the one with the kids most of the time, so..."

"Is Seb a good guy?" Jen asked.

Renata brightened. "Yeah, he really is. He's...he's a big teddy bear. He's really sweet."

"No pressure, but it must be nice to have someone asking you out."

It was nice having a guy cook her dinner, too, and having him walk her back home... Maybe a little too nice.

Renata sighed. "It is and it isn't. I like Seb—a lot. It's just that I'm afraid of falling for a guy and having it turn out like it did with Ivan." Renata blushed and shook her head. "This is where it stops. I'm not interested in another relationship. I've got the kids to worry about."

Renata glanced over her shoulder again, and Jen followed her gaze toward the little sales hut. Seb stood there with his arms crossed over his chest. He had that lumberjack kind of look about him, and his blue eyes were locked on Renata. When she caught him, he dropped his gaze as if trying to find something he'd dropped. If Renata was vulnerable, maybe Seb was a little bit, too.

"Did Angelina text you yet?" Renata asked.

"I had the notifications turned off because I was driving," Jen said. "Let me check."

She pulled her phone out of her purse and saw the text.

"She wants to do dinner tomorrow evening?" Jen asked.

"There was a cancelation at the lodge restaurant, and Angelina said she hated to waste a table. Besides, at this time of year, we can all use a little moral support," Renata replied.

"Won't the others be busy with family?" Jen asked.

"Family is why we need the support!" Renata said with a laugh. "My family includes three kids who are fighting with their father right now, and an ex-husband who keeps leaning on me to fix his relationship issues with his kids. I don't know about you, but I need a dinner out with a few women who understand what it's like to be single over the holidays."

"Yeah, I could use it, too," Jen agreed.

"I should go pay for my tree," Renata said. "Seb said he'd help me get it tied onto the roof of my car, so..."

"Right." Jen couldn't help but smile at that. "Enjoy."

Renata rolled her eyes. "See you tomorrow night."

Jen turned back to the Christmas trees and looked up at their aromatic branches. She glanced over her shoulder once to see Renata and Seb heading out of the lot together, a tree over Seb's shoulder. Life went on—wasn't that what she'd been noticing since she'd arrived in Mountain Springs? Life continued, even after a woman's life was torn apart and her heart was left in tatters. But the life that continued wasn't quite what she'd imagined, either.

She and Lisa still weren't connecting all that easily, and the moral support she'd found in her hometown was coming from relative strangers instead of the family she'd hoped to be counting on.

Funny how things turned out.

Jen stopped in front of an eight-foot spruce. It was huge, and it would be absolutely breathtaking once she decorated it... but it was too much of everything—too much Christmas, too much celebration, too much confidence in her new position here in town. She felt like she should be starting out with something smaller.

"How big of a tree are you looking for?" someone asked. She turned to see a young man standing behind her.

"I'm not sure. I've got a pretty big space to fill," Jen admitted.

"If you've got the space, this one will be amazing," he replied. "I chopped it down myself. It's got perfect shape, and it's really full. How high are your ceilings?"

So Jen bought a Christmas tree—a massive Christmas tree that she was assured would be truly gorgeous. She didn't doubt it. But who would be sitting in front of it this holiday?

Just Jen, with her tattered heart and ambitious hopes for the old mansion. Maybe she was hoping the old house that had represented prosperity and success to her as a little girl could somehow transform her into a glossier, braver, more idealized version of herself. Because that mansion demanded more than some ordinary little tree in a corner. It wanted a huge, glittery display of Christmas joy right in the center windows. And that house demanded more of Jen, too.

She was crazy for buying this tree, wasn't she? And maybe she was a little crazy having dumped her divorce settlement into an emotional purchase the size and shape of her childhood heart.

CHAPTER TEN

NICK MOVED THE electric sander slowly over a cupboard door. He'd taken them off their hinges, and they lay on top of wooden supports as he worked on them, gently removing layers of white paint from the hardwood.

His mind wasn't on the job, though. He'd been thinking about last night, and the impulsive kiss on Jen's cheek. If he'd just helped her across the street and left, there would be no problem. But he'd done something that changed their balance—he'd definitively crossed the line between friends and something more—whatever this was. He wasn't normally like this. He could keep his head and heart separated pretty successfully, but when it came to Jen, something seemed to draw him in. It wasn't just that she was in a similar situation—divorced and with some very good reasons to stay single for the time being—but she was different, interesting and too much like his ex-wife.

Jen might look very different than his ex, and her personality might be a lot different, too, but she was the same type—successful, educated and driven. Jen was the kind of woman who wouldn't be satisfied with a man like him for long. Maybe Jen wouldn't be quite so cruel as Shari had been, but she'd still be unhappy.

Yet, he'd kissed her…chastely enough, but still. In the moment it had felt right, and he hadn't wanted to just walk away and let the evening fade. He'd wanted to do something—seal it somehow.

He turned off his sander just in time to hear the front door open. He headed through the dining room and saw Jen toss her purse on a side table.

"Hi!" she said. "Do you think I could borrow you for a minute?"

"Yeah, you bet." He brushed his hands off and crossed the front room. "How big of a tree did you get?"

"Well…" Jen smiled uncertainly. "Eight feet, the guy said. And it's supposed to be a wide one, too."

Nick followed her out the front door without bothering to put on a coat. The tree that was tied to the top of her SUV hung over the front and the back, and he let out a low whistle.

"That's a tree!" he said.

"Anything less felt…like not enough for the house, you know?" she said, and she looked a little pained as if she was rethinking that.

"You said you wanted to just enjoy Christmas, right?" he said. "This is a good start."

It took a couple of minutes to untie the tree, and then he rolled it off the top of the vehicle so as not to scratch the paint. Jen took the lighter end, and they started toward the house, but after a couple of yards, she stopped.

"Sorry, I need to rest for a second," she said, putting her end down and rubbing her hands together. She braced herself then lifted it again.

This was a big tree, and it was a bit unwieldy, but it wasn't too heavy for him alone. He carried lumber and large pieces of equipment on a regular basis, building up his physique. He was tall and muscular, but his bulk came from hard work. He didn't like seeing her struggle under the weight of it.

"Jen, I can do it," he said.

"What?" She turned, and he felt an unexpected rush of tenderness toward her. Nothing seemed easy for her right now—her gallery, her divorce, her son…this tree.

"Let go," he said.

"Are you sure?" she asked. "It's really heavy."

"It's fine," he said. "Let go."

Jen released the tree, and he readjusted his grip toward the center of the trunk before hoisting it once more. It was easier to carry it alone, and he felt better not watching her struggle. Jen hurried ahead to open the door for him, and he carried it through and into the entryway.

"Where do you want it?" he asked.

Jen shut the door behind them. "I was hoping to put it in the front window. I've got the stand set up there already."

In years past the old lady used to have a massive tree in the exact same spot, sparkling with lights that illuminated the entire space. It was a nice thought to have a tree there again.

Nick carried the spruce over. The stand

looked like it would be big enough to support this tree. He moved the stand with his foot, and then hefted the tree upright and angled the stump down into it.

"I'm going to need you to hold this—" he said, and Jen hurried to his side and grabbed the tree by the twine that held its branches in.

For the next few minutes they adjusted the tree until it was straight, and then he screwed in the supports that would keep it upright.

"That should do it," he said, and he stood back up again. The tree loomed high above the top of the windows.

"It's huge, isn't it?" Jen said.

Nick pulled a knife from his belt and cut the twine. The boughs sprang outward in a rush, the smell of pine and a powdering of snow launching into the room. It was beautifully shaped. He pulled the twine out of the branches and stepped back, glancing over at Jen. Her gaze moved up the length of it and a smile broke over her face.

"I like it," she said.

He felt an unexplainable rush of satisfaction at her expression. He had nothing to do with this tree, besides carrying it in, but seeing her look that pleased warmed him.

"It's great," he agreed. "Nice pick."

"I tend to reach for too much," she said. "I think, why not me? Why can't I do it? And it doesn't always work…"

"Jen…" he said quietly.

She looked over at him, and her gaze had turned melancholy.

"This is a beautiful tree. It's not too much. And neither is this house. I think it all fits you, if you ask the guy who's renovating your kitchen."

"I don't know if you have the time," Jen said, casting him a hesitant look. "But if you wanted to help me decorate…"

Nick could feel the smile tugging at his lips. "Sure. Contrary to popular belief around here, I really do like Christmas."

She met his smile with a relieved one of her own. "It's hard enough having Christmas alone without decorating the tree alone, too, you know? I think I wanted to avoid that."

Jen pulled a string of lights out of a cardboard box.

"It's not so bad," he said. "I've gotten used to it."

She glanced over and met his gaze. "How's it going with Amelia?"

"We had a talk," he said. "I'm not sure how good it was, but… I left it too long, you know? I should have tangled with her sooner."

"She's intimidating, though," Jen said.

"Do you think?" he asked.

"They're young and convinced they're right. And we're—"

"Not old," he interrupted with a low laugh.

"Definitely not," she agreed, but she laughed, too. "But I remember being a kid and seeing people our age and thinking they were ancient."

"That goes both ways," he replied. "I see young adults my daughter's age, and they don't look so grown up to me. Just big kids, you know?"

Jen smiled. "I really do. I want to make sure they eat and encourage them to make good choices. There's nothing cool left about me anymore."

Nick laughed. "Amelia thinks you're cool."

"Amelia hasn't seen the mom side of me."

Nick didn't talk parenting stuff too often, and there was a thirsty part of his heart that missed this...having his daughter around to butt heads with, and support, and be proud of. He missed being an active dad, and somehow, Jen seemed to bring that out in him.

Nick watched as Jen nestled the first string of lights into the bottom boughs of the tree, looping them around. That string of lights ended, and Jen grabbed another one, and they continued the process. After plugging in the third, Nick took the lights from her fingers, and for just a moment they stopped and their eyes met. His breath caught, and he was the first to look away.

"Hold on," he said. "I'll grab a ladder."

Nick handed back the lights, and for just a moment, he closed his fingers down over hers. She could tug free if she wanted, but she didn't move. Her lips parted, and she sucked in a quick breath. What was it about her that made him want to toss all logic aside? He let go with a rueful little smile and headed back to the kitchen where his tools and supplies were. A minute later he came back with a short ladder and set it up in front of the tree.

Jen had opened a box of ornaments. She pulled out something swaddled in white cloth. He leaned over to take a closer look as she unwrapped something silver.

"Mistletoe?" he said.

"It always goes on the tree first," she replied, and her cheeks pinked. "I've had this since I was a little girl. My grandma gave it to me with the condition that I didn't kiss anyone under it until I was much older."

Nick reached out and took her hand, lifting it higher so he could get a closer look at the little silver ball of carved leaves she held. A bell inside it tinkled softly.

"How old did you have to be to kiss someone under it?" he asked, and he caught her gaze.

"Oh, I don't know," she said with a breathy laugh. "At least forty."

The rest of the room seemed to fade away, and all the reasons why he should stop this seemed to drain out of his head.

"How come it goes on first?" he whispered.

"I don't know… I've always done it that way. When I was little, I used to dream of the man I'd kiss under the mistletoe," she said, her voice soft.

"Lucky guy," he breathed.

"I've never kissed anyone under it," she said, and her gaze flicked up to meet his. "For whatever reason, it just never happened. Sam wasn't really that into Christmas, and boyfriends before him… I don't know."

Never… That thought was both a little sad and irresistible. He stepped closer and he pulled her hand against his chest, putting his palm over her fingers. He could feel the little ornament in her hand resting against his shirt, and his heart sped up as he looked down at her.

"What if I kissed you under it?" he asked softly.

"Pity?" she asked, teasing.

"Far from it," he said, his voice lowered. "More like weakness."

He should stop—right? He should pull back…but he couldn't quite bring himself to do it. Instead, he leaned closer, his mouth hovering over hers, and he felt the whisper of her breath against his lips.

"I'm going to blame this on the mistletoe," he murmured, and lowered his lips to hers.

Jen leaned into him, her hands pressed against his chest, and she let out a soft sigh. He kissed her gently at first, but then she tipped her face upward and he deepened the kiss. Nothing else seemed to matter—just the feeling of this woman leaning against him and the softness of her lips under his...

The very small part of his brain that still clung to the vestiges of his logic knew that he'd regret this.

Nick pulled back and shut his eyes for a moment.

"How wrong was that?" he murmured.

"I don't know..."

He opened his eyes and looked down at her plumped lips. Kissing her cheek had been stepping over the line...this kiss sailed right past it. Whatever—this could all be part of the same mistake...

And he slid his arms around her waist and tugged her back against him. If he was going to regret a kiss, he might as well make it one to remember.

NICK'S LIPS MOVED slowly over Jen's, and she found herself responding to him, kissing him back. There was a faint voice in the back of her head telling her she should probably stop this, but it faded when Nick's hand moved up to her cheek and his rough fingers touched her face ever so gently. He was strong—his chest under her fingertips was muscled and firm. This was crazy, and she knew it, but here in his arms, the warmth of his body emanating against her, his beard tickling her face, she couldn't bring herself to pull back.

They'd been dancing around whatever attraction was stewing between them, and she'd assumed they'd simply continue that dance... His hands moved over her back, tugging her closer, and she leaned into his embrace. She couldn't seem to pull together two coherent thoughts, and so she stopped trying, and she exhaled a soft sigh.

Nick pulled back, his lips still hovering over hers, and when she opened her eyes she found his dark gaze searching hers.

"Do I need to apologize for that?" he murmured.

"Nope," she said, and she smiled, then straightened, tugging out of his arms. He let them drop at his sides. The air was colder on her own. The mistletoe ornament hung off one of her fingers, and she looked down at it, feeling the heat come to her cheeks.

"Call it a mistletoe kiss, and we never have to speak of it again," he said, and she could hear playfulness in his voice. Would he rather not talk about it? She turned and hung the silver ball on the tree, safely out of reach. But when she looked over at him again, she could see that same glimmer of intensity in his gaze.

"So do you kiss all of your clients if they're within reach of mistletoe?" she asked.

"No," he replied, his voice low. "I told you before I'm hard to nail down." He dropped his gaze. "I haven't kissed anyone in a couple of years, truthfully. Mistletoe or not."

"Oh..." She felt the breath squeeze out of her lungs.

"I didn't mean for it to come out like that," he said. "I'm just saying, I'm not some kind of player. That was definitely out of bounds. I probably do owe you an apology."

Except, she'd liked it. She'd imagined being kissed over the years, looking at her little silver ball of mistletoe. Nick's kiss had felt...perfect. Remembering the feeling of his hands moving over her back, the brush of his beard over her face and the softness of his lips gave her a shiver. By itself, it could be a rather sweet memory—a mistletoe kiss at long last. But kisses had a way of getting out of hand—she knew that much.

"It's okay. I think…we've been trying to avoid that," she admitted.

"You, too?" he asked softly.

"Me, too." She glanced up at him.

"Listen, I should probably be clear," he said. "I'm not looking for a relationship, and I don't know if that seemed like I was trying to start something up… And I know I sound like a jerk. Trust me, I'm hearing it come out of my own mouth." He pressed his lips together, irritated. "I'm just trying to say that I'm not the kind of guy who fools around. I just… I've been thinking about doing that for a few days now."

"It's because we got to be friends," she said.

"That might be it." He didn't look convinced, though. "But I haven't kissed any friends recently, either, so…"

She smiled at his dry wit. "Good to know. I feel special."

"You should." He smiled back, and his dark gaze met hers. "But I'll keep it under control."

She couldn't help but feel a little disappointed—even though she wasn't looking for a man.

"I don't want a relationship, either," she said. "My divorce is really fresh, and you're my sister's friend, and..."

"You think I'll kiss and tell?" he asked.

"I don't know," she said. "Maybe I just want to have this time be about me alone—building something for my son and me. I'm not looking to complicate it. I want to look back on this and not feel..."

He dropped his gaze. "Right. I get it."

"I don't want to feel like I found some man to fix it for me again, okay?" she said, the words coming out in a rush. "I have enough regrets about that in my first marriage."

He nodded. "So...let's chalk that one up to mistletoe and let ourselves off the hook."

"A very handy excuse," she replied, and a smile toyed at her lips.

Her phone rang, and Jen was glad for the distraction. She looked around for the handset and found it in her purse by the door. She fished it out and picked up the call halfway through the fourth ring. The number was Sam's. She sighed and instinctively tried to straighten her hair before she picked up.

"Hello?" she said, doing her best to sound normal.

"Hi, Jen. How are you doing?" Sam said.

She shut her eyes, pushing back all those conflicting feelings that seemed to surround her ex these days. "I'm great," she lied. "Merry Christmas."

"Yeah, yeah, Merry Christmas to you, too," Sam said. "That's actually why I called."

"Oh?" She let her gaze flicker toward Nick. He was fiddling with the lights again on the tree. "What's going on?"

"Something's come up, and I can't have Drew here for Christmas, after all."

Jen froze, her mind skipping ahead. He was canceling Christmas with Drew? This was going to crush their son.

"What's come up?" she asked, turning away from Nick and the Christmas tree, her heart speeding up.

"What...you have other plans?" Sam asked.

"Sam, I'm thrilled to have my son with me for Christmas—that's not the point. Drew is going to be so upset. What happened?" she pressed.

"Tiffany's grandmother issued a last-minute invitation for the holidays, and Tiffany thinks it's really important that she be there. Apparently, her grandmother has some announcement she wants to make about her will."

"So let Tiffany go," Jen said flatly. "Why do you need to be there?"

"Moral support," he replied, his tone cooling. "She and I are in a relationship, Jen. I know that might be hard for you to come to terms with, but this is real."

Jen clenched her teeth, attempting to get her rising anger under control. "I fully accept the validity of your new relationship with a twenty-two-year-old. I do. I support it and wish you only happiness in your future with her. I hope she's very, very patient." She sucked in a steadying breath. "But you're dumping your son for a girlfriend's grandmother's last-minute snap of her fingers."

"You sound upset," Sam said archly.

"Never mind." There was no winning with Sam. He'd only cast her as a petulant child, no matter how close she was to forty—it was his superpower. "How are we going to do this?"

"I'm putting Drew on a bus to Mountain Springs day after tomorrow just before Tiffany and I drive out," Sam said. "I'm going to make the most of my last couple of days with him."

"Good. I'm glad you're doing that," Jen said.

"He'll arrive—" there was a pause "—hold on, I'm just checking the email... He'll arrive at ten in the morning on Thursday. The ride is only a couple of hours."

"I'll be there to pick him up," she replied.

"Thanks, Jen. And I'm sorry if I'm messing up any plans you have..." The warmth in his tone was back.

"Drew trumps any other plans I might have," Jen said tersely. "He always has and he always will. Can I talk to him?"

"Sure...hold on."

Jen looked over to find Nick watching her, his expression concerned.

"Drew will be here for Christmas," she said, by explanation.

"Mom?"

Jen turned away again. "Hi, sweetie. So I hear I get you for Christmas, after all."

"Yeah... I guess."

"I'm thrilled, son. It'll be fun," Jen said. "I got the tree—it's massive. You'll approve. I'm just decorating it now."

"Okay..."

"Drew, I know you're disappointed," Jen said, lowering her voice. "But it's going to be a wonderful Christmas, I promise. Besides, I'm thrilled I get to have you with me. It was going to be pretty lonely for me."

"Okay..." Drew sighed. "Dad needs his phone back."

"Call me later on video and I'll show you the tree," she said, trying to sound cheery. "You're going to love it."

How many times did she have to reassure him that he'd love this Christmas in order for her to convince herself?

"I'll call you later," Drew said. "Bye, Mom."

He hung up first, and Jen looked over at Nick again. He was watching her with a sympathetic look.

"Your ex has other plans?" he asked.

"His twenty-two-year-old girlfriend felt the need to schmooze with her grandmother before the old lady makes an announcement about her will," Jen replied, then she sighed. "I sound bitter, don't I?"

"I don't even know these people, and I'm disgusted," he replied. "Drew's upset?"

"Definitely," she said with a sigh. "But it's okay. I get my son for Christmas—I'm not going to complain about that."

"And there's the tree," Nick said with a faint smile.

"It's a great tree," she said, and she felt some of the tension slip away. "I'm glad I got the big one now. Drew really is going to love it."

"When does he arrive?" Nick asked.

"Thursday morning," she replied. "Sam says he wants to spend some quality time with him before he leaves...for what that's worth."

Nick nodded. "I'm sorry."

"At least I'll have Drew, right?" she said.

They fell silent, and Jen's gaze moved toward the box of ornaments, her emotions jostling inside her. A phone call from her ex had a way of changing the mood fast. She wanted Drew at home with her, but she also knew how much this would hurt her son.

"Do you want to do this alone, after all?" Nick asked quietly.

Jen looked up, and she met his inquiring gaze, then nodded, feeling tears prick her eyes. "Actually, I do. If you don't mind. I can take it from here, if I can use the ladder."

This was her tree—and it was time to own this. She couldn't lean on Nick for emotional support. Wasn't that what she'd done with Sam? She'd looked to him to give her a home, to give her a purpose. Not this time.

"No problem," he replied. "Are you okay?"

"I'm fine," she said. "I'm just trying to figure it all out."

"I'm in there if you want to talk," he said, hooking his thumb toward the kitchen.

"Thanks," she said. He was a sweet guy, but she had to stop this.

Nick closed the distance between them and pressed his lips against her forehead in a brief kiss. She wished it didn't feel as nice as it did. Then he turned toward the dining room, his boots echoing through the room. A moment later she heard the whir of a sander starting up. Nick was handsome, sweet, and strangely sensitive. He seemed to know she'd want her space. He was just the kind of man who could sweep her right off her feet and turn off her brain. A long time ago, when she was young and dreaming of mistletoe kisses, he was the kind of guy who would have filled her fantasies. But this wasn't about romance or moving on... this was about standing tall and building her own life for once, apart from a man. This next step post-divorce had to be by herself.

Jen sighed and looked up at the tree. She didn't have enough decorations to fill it up, but if she spread them out, it might be okay. She reached into the box of ornaments and pulled out Drew's first Christmas ornament in the shape of a teddy bear.

Jen hung the ornament and reached for another—this one was a felt candy cane that Drew had made in elementary school. Maybe this oversize tree in this oversize house would be just what Drew needed, too, while they all pretended they were doing better than they were.

CHAPTER ELEVEN

THAT EVENING THE streets had all been freshly plowed, so Jen's drive to Mountain Springs Lodge was a peaceful one. Through open curtains, TVs flickered and Christmas trees twinkled. She saw people as they wandered past the windows or sat on couches… These were families doing what families did, and it made her even more lonely for the family she used to have.

Not that she wanted to get back together with Sam. That relationship was over, but Lisa was right about her dive into a marriage in hopes that it would give her something she'd been longing for. She'd wanted a family of her own—a husband, some kids, a pet or two. She'd wanted that secure feeling of being at the center of a loving home that could give her a sense of identity.

Except, Sam and his goals had stayed the center of her identity…and the money she used to buy this place had come from Sam's pockets. But making it a success—that would be hers alone, and she wouldn't relinquish that sense of accomplishment to anyone. This restart didn't have to be her own.

But a fresh start didn't have to be solitary, did it? She might be overly cautious right now...it was possible, at least. Would it be so terrible to see how things went with Nick?

He was sweet, handsome, sensitive, and he seemed to be feeling something for her, too.

It was something to think about.

When she arrived at Mountain Springs Lodge, Jen found parking near the door. She wore a black pantsuit tonight—it was cold, and a long woolen coat on top.

When she got inside, she took off her coat after all—and looked around the now-familiar Christmas decorations—the Christmas tree in the fireside room, the wreaths and checked it, then on the wooden walls...

"Jen, you made it!"

She turned to see Belle come to the lodge. Belle took off a faux fur-lined wrap and held it over one arm as she met her way to Jen. She was dressed in a dress, with a gray dress that looked like it ma

…then made their way …you …dining room where they spotted Angelina and Renata at a window-side table. Soft Christmas music played through the dining room, mingling with the murmur of people visiting while they dined. Jen could feel her nerves relaxing already. Renata was right—with all the pressure of Christmas, it was a good idea to spend an evening with women who understood what she was going through.

When they slid into their seats, everyone said hello and there were a few minutes of idlechitchat while they perused the menu. …en ordered the red wine beef ragout with a …she said with goat cheese, and her …vored … the very thought… …one … …ask wh…

want to say that out loud. There was a certain amount of intimidation that came with a woman who had an advanced degree, too.

"I've…um…agreed to a date," Renata said.

All eyes turned to her, and she looked around uncomfortably.

"With who?" Belle asked, leaning forward. "Is this with that guy whose mother is in your old folks' home?"

"Seb. Yeah…" Renata's cheeks pinked. "I saw him again when I got my Christmas tree—in fact, Jen was there."

"He did seem pretty smitten," Jen confirmed with a grin. "I saw him give her his number."

"I guess he didn't trust I'd call him, so he asked for mine while we were getting the tree tied to the roof of the truck, and he called me later on and suggested we get a coffee," Renata said.

"This is great!" Angelina said with a grin. "I'm glad you finally agreed. I mean, how many times has he asked you out?"

"I don't know…" Renata shrugged.

"At least twice after he visited his mother," Belle said. "And then there was that time that we all agreed he'd asked you out but you thought he was just making conversation about your weekend plans—"

"And what about the time she saw him at the gas station and he bought her a chocolate bar because it was cold out?" Angelina added.

"That wasn't asking me out!" Renata said with a laugh.

"No, it was just so sweet," Belle replied with a grin. "He's a nice guy, Renata! I'm glad you finally said yes."

Renata winced. "I'm thinking of canceling."

"No!" Jen hadn't meant to chime in, but Seb did seem like a nice guy. And more important still, Jen had seen the way Renata had looked at him, too.

"I don't know…" Renata shrugged faintly. "I'm gun-shy. Things went so, so badly with Ivan."

They fell silent, then one by one they nodded. Jen could understand Renata's fear all too well. And having heard about her ex's horrible treatment of her, who could blame her for being scared? Was a safe, single life such a terrible thing? Except when they were young, how many of them had dreamed of being safe and single? Jen hadn't. She'd dreamed of love and a family, and the beauty and excitement that only came with a bit of risk.

But there were good guys out there, too, and Jen thought she'd met one of them in Nick.

"I get it, Renata," Belle said softly. "But how is it fair that Ivan moved on, and you don't get a chance to have a good guy once in your life?"

"Isn't that the way it is, though?" Angelina asked. "For the most part, at least. The one who ruins the marriage waltzes off and has no problem starting over. I agree. It's hardly fair."

"I see the way Seb looks at me," Renata said. "And I think...he's not going to stay like this. Look at me! I've had four children. Things sag that never used to. I've gray and fine lines forming... I'm not exactly some prize anymore."

"Oh, shut your mouth!" Belle exclaimed. "You're gorgeous! You're curvy. You're smart, compassionate, funny. You've got life experience, Renata. Do you know how many gorgeous, spoiled idiots there are out there? Do you want to face life with some shallow kid who has no idea what it's all about yet? If Ivan does, let him. He has no depth or character anyway. But you have everything a man could want, and everything that could keep him enthralled with you forever. Don't question your worth because one moron thought he was worthy of a mistress on the side. He's the one with the problem, not you."

"But Seb's a *man*," Renata countered. "Ultimately, they all want women like you, Belle."

"Seb seems to have eyes only for you," Belle said. "If your gut tells you not to date him, then don't. I think we'd all agree with that. Seb isn't going to complete you, and you don't need a man to be happy. Right? But if this is just you feeling like you aren't enough to keep a man's attention…"

The waiter came back with their drink order, and a second waiter came with the food. For the next few minutes they ate. The food was amazing, as it always seemed to be at Mountain Springs Lodge, and Jen listened as Belle asked Renata questions about

Seb and gently teased her about her ability to make men fall in love with her.

"What about you?" Angelina asked, turning to Jen. "How are the renovations going? Tell me everything!"

"I had to get a tree—I mean, I wanted to get one. And while I was looking at some sensible five- or six-foot trees, I realized that it would just be swallowed up in that house! I ended up getting an eight-foot tree, and it's the right size for the space, but I have to say, I could add another two trees in that front room, and it wouldn't be too much..."

"You hired Nick, right?" Angelina asked. "How's his work? A good contractor should make this easier on you, not harder. In my experience with Nick, he's a good one, but if he isn't the right fit—"

"He's great." Jen felt some heat hit her cheeks, and if Angelina noticed, she didn't let on. "He's very skilled. I have no complaints. I guess I'm just realizing how big of a project this is—money-wise, work-wise..."

"I got like that with this place." Angelina looked up, her gaze moving over the ceiling and toward the window. Then she shrugged. "But one step at a time, it comes together. And when you can see what you imagined come to life in front of you, it's pretty amazing."

"I think it would be," Jen agreed. "But I've got a habit of jumping in enthusiastically before I've thought things through. I did it with Sam—I should have seen that we wouldn't work from the start. I did it with this mansion—I mean, it came on the market, and I offered a low price on instinct, nothing else! I hadn't even had an inspection done yet! They took my offer, and here I am."

"At least you're willing to take a leap," Angelina said. "That was one of the things Gayle mentioned about you more than once—you don't let life pass you by."

But she might have been able to avoid a few heartbreaks if she'd leaped a little less enthusiastically.

"Look," Angelina said, lowering her voice. "If you decide you want out of this purchase, I'll buy the mansion from you for fifteen percent more than you paid. That should cover the cost of renovations right now."

Jen's eyebrows rose. "Really?"

"This is not pressure for you to sell. There's no time limit to the offer," Angelina qualified. "I'm just saying, if you decide you do want to sell the place, don't sell it to someone else. I want to buy it."

"I'll keep that in mind," Jen said. But she didn't want to sell. She wanted to make a success of the place, and she still thought she could do that.

"I think we need to talk about Belle's neighbor," Renata said, drawing Jen's attention back to the table conversation.

Belle blushed, and the women laughed.

"We need a bottle of wine first," Belle said. "And I also need you all to promise you aren't going to make fun of me. I have no skill whatsoever in dating! I'm horrible at it, and I don't tend to have Renata's artless way with making men fall in love with me, either, or her ample bust, might I add."

They all laughed.

"I require a guy to ask me out," Belle went on, "because if the tables turn, I make a fool of myself…"

Jen couldn't help but chuckle as Belle launched into tales of her dating woes. Jen wasn't alone—dating, starting over, taking risks both financial and personal…it was scary. But tonight they could buoy each other up in the knowledge that every last one of them was intimidated by something. And that was comforting.

NICK STOOD BESIDE his Christmas tree, looking over the ornaments he'd collected over the years. This year there were the new color-coordinated ones his daughter had picked up for him, and he fingered a delicate glass snowflake. He had to admit, he liked them. Amelia had good taste, even if he fought it.

But looking at his own Christmas tree sparked more recent memories with Jen in front of her tree. He'd meant that kiss—every heart-pounding second of it. He might not be able to offer a future, but that didn't mean he didn't want to. Jen was extraordinary, but she'd need a different guy, someone who could keep up with her, match her in the part of life that mattered most to her. And he needed to stop falling for the wrong woman. Because he was jeopardizing everything by kissing her—his reputation, his chance at working with Jen Taylor on any other project in the future… All for a moment that had felt too perfect.

But now, standing in front of his tree—a fake one, no real spruce tree in his living room—he couldn't let himself off the hook. What did a perfect moment matter if it wasn't going to be more than that? His feelings had gotten entangled with this woman, and he had nothing to offer! What did that make him? He couldn't toy with a newly divorced woman's emotions, and he felt like a bad guy for having kissed her. Sure, in the moment, it had been about giving in to his feelings, but in the long-term? He didn't come out of this looking very good.

"What's the matter, Dad?"

Nick turned to see Amelia coming down the stairs.

"Nothing. Why?"

Amelia came up next to him and gave him a curious look.

"You look grim. Do you hate the new ornaments that much? If you let me dispose of a few things in here—"

"No disposing," he said. "And I don't hate them. They're nice. You chose them."

Amelia gave him an apologetic look. "I'm not going to be able to stay for Christmas, Dad."

Her words sank in and he looked at her uncertainly. "What?"

"I was talking to Ben—and his family

asked if I'd join them in Aspen for Christmas and the week following, and... I said I would."

Nick felt a flood of disappointment. "But you were supposed to spend Christmas with me."

"This is important. This is...my future. Ben's ready for me to meet his family and get to know them a little bit. It's a big step forward for us, and I said I'd go."

"So this Ben—" Nick swallowed. "He's willing to commit more permanently now?"

"Maybe. I think we're getting there," she replied. "We want the same thing. We want to build something together, make a name for ourselves."

"A power couple," he said.

"The only way to go." Amelia smiled softly.

"So what changed his mind about spending Christmas with you?" Nick asked.

"The thought of losing me, I think," she said.

"And it never occurred to him to come here and meet *your* family?" he asked.

Amelia didn't answer, and the pink in her cheeks suggested that option hadn't occurred to her, either.

"So you've got to go win his family over first," Nick concluded. He didn't like that.

This guy was already asking Amelia to jump through hoops.

"I'm not worried about that. I'm smart, I'm getting a Harvard pre-law degree, mothers like me. Come on, Dad," she said. "I'm sure they're very nice. Besides, I'm only getting in the way with you and Jen across the street."

"You aren't in the way of anything," he countered.

"You sure about that?" Amelia shot him a grin. "She'd be good for you. She'd also be good for me, if you decided to settle down with her—if that factors in at all."

Amelia was teasing now, softening him up the way she used to years ago, but he knew that there was a hint of truth in the joke. Jen would fit in with his daughter very well, and that didn't give him the reassurance that Amelia intended.

"No, it doesn't," he said with a small smile. "I guess you've made your plans. When do you leave?"

"I'll take a bus there—it's the most direct way. They aren't arriving until Christmas Eve, so I thought I'd leave Christmas Eve morning," she said. "It gives you and me a little more time together anyway. Right?"

His daughter was throwing him a bone, much like the one Drew's dad had tossed to him. But what could Nick say? His daughter was a grown woman, and she had every right to choose where she spent her Christmas. Maybe she'd end up marrying this guy, after all.

"Then do me a favor," he said. Since she was willing to make this up to him a little bit.

"Sure, Dad."

"Come with me to work on the house tomorrow. I want to show you what I do. Give you a feel for it, before you start a career in law and marry into finance and never touch a hammer again."

Amelia chuckled. "All right. It might be fun. Besides, it's another chance to see inside the mansion. Twist my arm."

This would be good for both of them. Nick was tired of apologizing for who he was and what he did for a living. He was tired of not feeling like he was enough for his own daughter. It was time to show her what he did—up close and personal.

"We're getting up early, then," Nick said with a grin. "Set an alarm, or Goldie will stick a cold nose on your face."

CHAPTER TWELVE

JEN STOOD IN the bus station, her coat tugged around her as she watched for Drew's bus from Denver. It was running late, no surprise at this time of year with the snow in the mountains.

The station wasn't heated well. With the constantly opening doors to the platform outside, cold air kept whipping through. She took a sip of the coffee she'd bought at the little kiosk in the corner. It wasn't great, but it was hot. She'd picked up a hot chocolate for Drew, too.

That morning Nick had arrived at eight as usual, but this time he brought his daughter with him. That had made it a whole lot easier to keep their chemistry under control. Amelia had wanted another tour of the mansion, and Jen had obliged. They'd gone all the way up to the attic, which wasn't heated at all. Freezing though it was, Jen had enjoyed looking around at a few old items that had been abandoned there—an old, beaten-up gramophone, a couple of antique traveling trunks that were empty and a few crates of local newspapers from the thirties and forties. The entire house was a historical gold mine, and she deeply hoped her son would appreciate it.

She'd been noticing how Nick related to his daughter that morning. There was a bit of a distance between them, but he was trying. He'd been putting her to work with some sanding—nothing too strenuous—and Jen had overheard him pointing out some of his previous work, the new counters, the new sink, and explaining how making the improvements blend into the original style was more important than doing something modern and new.

He seemed like a good dad...except she knew he'd parented from a distance. His daughter had done most of her growing up with her mom in Denver, and he didn't seem like the kind of father who preferred it that way. That distance between Denver and Mountain Springs seemed to be difficult for split parenting—for the parents and the kid. Amelia had missed out on her father's influence in her life.

A bus pulled up to the platform—*180 from Denver*. She moved forward to the window so she could watch for Drew. She was excited to see him. It had been two weeks now, and that felt like too long.

Drew was the third person off the bus, right behind an elderly couple, and he paused, looking around with a slightly nervous expression. She waved through the window and then went to the door. Drew visibly relaxed when he saw her and grabbed the suitcase the bus driver hauled out for him.

Drew looked taller, and just a little bit older—or was she only imagining that?

"Hi, sweetie," she said, handing him the takeout cup and leaning in to give him a squeeze. "I missed you. I brought you hot chocolate. Thought you might like it."

"Oh, yeah. Thanks." Drew took the hot chocolate, and she took his suitcase so that he could drink it.

"When was the last time you were in Mountain Springs?" Jen asked him. "I think it was when Bram was born, wasn't it?"

"Yeah, I guess." Drew took a sip of the hot chocolate. "I didn't like it much."

"What are you talking about?" she asked. "I took you skiing."

"I still didn't like it here," he replied.

So he was determined to have a bad attitude already. She gave her son a sidelong look, then led the way to the SUV. Once they were inside and she started the vehicle, she looked over at Drew.

"You're upset," she said.

"No."

"Of course you are," she said. "You were really looking forward to Christmas with your dad, and having him change his mind on you probably really hurt your feelings."

"Tiffany could have gone to see her grandma without us," Drew said. "Or I could have gone along."

"That's true," she agreed. "But Tiffany is just a girlfriend, sweetie. She's not...permanent."

"They were talking about her moving in," Drew said. "She's permanent."

"Okay, but she's not moved in yet, is she?" And Sam was moving on that quickly? Did Jen even want to know this? Maybe it was easier for men, especially someone of his reputation. And what was she expecting? He'd been nearly divorced from his first wife when she met him. Sam wasn't the kind of man who stayed single long.

"No, she's not moved in yet. But she's got some clothes and stuff there. And she stays the night a lot."

"Okay, so the moving in is still in the talking stages. It's complicated when people are starting new relationships. It's not like being married and settled."

And kids were a big complication, whether they deserved to be or not.

"I'm his son!" Drew said, staring angrily out the window. "I'm supposed to be part of stuff. And Dad just dumped me. He's busy with Tiffany now, and I'm supposed to be okay with that. He said I'm being a baby about it, and you'll do the same thing when you meet someone."

"That isn't true," she said. But a boyfriend would complicate things, divide her attention. "And I don't have a boyfriend."

"I've got friends at school who have stepparents," he said. "I'm not an idiot. I know how this works."

"You're twelve, and you know very little of how the world works," she retorted.

"Well, Dad said that this was grown-up stuff, and that I needed to come back to be with you, like I'm some kind of baby," Drew said.

Jen winced. "Spending time with your mom doesn't make you a baby. I'm your mother. I take care of you. We're a family."

"Yeah, and Dad's my father. He's supposed to do that, too," Drew shot back.

What could she say? Should she defend Sam for acting like his son didn't matter? Or was she supposed to tell Drew how she really felt about the situation? That didn't seem healthy. Drew needed parental support, not to be stuck in the middle of an argument. Drew hadn't chosen this divorce, but he was the one splitting his time between parents and feeling like he'd just been punted out of his father's Christmas.

"Drew, we get to have Christmas together," she said, reaching over to pat his knee. "And I, for one, am happy about that. So let's just enjoy it!"

Drew didn't answer, and Jen pulled out of the parking spot and headed back to the road.

"You're going to love the house," she said as she pulled into traffic. "It's this beautiful old mansion that's almost a hundred years old. The videos you saw just don't do it justice. You'll see what I mean. And that's where we're going to be living."

"What's my room like?" he asked.

"It's on the third floor. There's a bathroom between my bedroom and yours, so you get a bit of privacy. It's not a very big room, but it has a great view out over the front yard. It makes you feel like you could be some fancy person from the nineteen twenties."

"But we aren't rich," he said.

"No, we aren't," she agreed. "I'm just saying—" Jen sighed. He wasn't willing to be cajoled, either.

"Did your dad let you open your presents early?" she asked instead.

"Yeah. He got me a laptop for school, and an Xbox."

Sam hadn't mentioned the new Xbox to her, and she felt a wave of annoyance. She didn't want Drew burying himself in video games. He was the kind of kid who could just sink into it and forget talking about his feelings all together.

"That's nice," she said, trying to sound brighter than she felt.

"Can I set the Xbox up when we get home?" he asked.

"Not right away," she replied. "I want to show you around first. Besides, we're going to have some time limits for that Xbox. Heads up."

Drew went silent again, and she glanced over at him, noting the irritable look on his face. The snow crunched under her tires as she pulled to a stop at an intersection, then eased forward again.

"You know, when I was a little girl, your Aunt Lisa and I used to love when we drove past that old mansion—"

"Yeah, you told me this story before," Drew said, then glanced toward her with a sliver of caution. "No offense."

"You know what, Drew?" Jen said, her patience at an end. "I'm going to need you to drop the attitude, okay? This isn't easy for me, either, but I'm doing my best! You're right—things are different. Your dad and I are divorced. We live in different cities. Dad is moving on with some twenty-two-year-old who could just about be your sibling—"

"I like Tiffany fine!" Drew retorted.

"Well, great. I'm glad," she snapped. "But this is going to be your life here in Mountain Springs. You're going to be attending school here. *I'm* here! So maybe you could stop being so negative and look at the bright side!"

Because he certainly seemed capable of doing that with Tiffany.

Drew sank into a sullen silence for the rest of the drive back to the house, and a certain heaviness swelled in Jen's chest. She'd been so looking forward to seeing her son today, but he obviously wasn't happy about being here with her. Sam had already warned her that if Drew wasn't content in Mountain Springs, then he'd go for custody.

What if Drew decided he wanted to live with his dad during the school year, instead? What if she ended up being the parent who got him on holidays and some weekends? That thought was enough to make her heart stop. She glanced over at Drew. He looked tired, and deeply sad. She'd been hoping he'd be as happy to see her as she was to see him, but being a mom and being a growing boy were two very different experiences. She was forced to wonder, was moving back to Mountain Springs a mistake?

Jen pulled into the drive and up to the main doors, shooting Drew a smile as he leaned forward to get a better view of the mansion.

"Keep in mind that we'll have to get the brick pressure-washed this spring, and we can have this drive repaved. It's pretty cracked right now. And we're going to renovate the inside completely—I have a man who's working on the kitchen right now. I'd actually kind of hoped to have it spruced up a little more before you saw it—"

"This is a dump," Drew said softly. There was no more attitude in his tone now, just quiet honesty that stung.

"What?" she said. "No, Drew. This is a historic site! This mansion has been here for..." The words faded on her tongue...*for almost a hundred years.*

Drew didn't seem to care about the history. He wasn't seeing what she used to see as a little girl who grew up in a row house and saw this old house as the epitome of grandeur. He'd grown up within walking distance of the University of Denver in a beautiful new house with a three-car garage. When he saw this old mansion, he wasn't thinking the same things.

"Come inside and have a look around," she said. "Come on. You'll see. This is going to be amazing."

But she didn't feel quite so confident anymore. She'd been counting on his first impression being one of amazement that this was going to be his new life. And if he couldn't see the beauty on the outside of this mansion, she wasn't so sure he'd see it on the inside, either.

Jen sighed, then pushed open her door and hopped out.

"Grab your suitcase," she added.

Because maybe she'd babied Drew just a little too much, and there was no way she was going to carry Drew's bag while listening to him insult the home she'd bought for them. It was one or the other. Not both.

Great. And she'd been so hoping that he'd love it, too.

NICK HANDED HIS daughter a piece of sandpaper. She sat at the brand-new counter, perched on a stepladder and with a cupboard door in front of her. Winter sunlight dappled the snowy yard outside the kitchen windows, and cold seeped in from the same place. These windows were at least thirty years old, and the amount of heat that would escape through them was astronomical. He made a mental note to mention it to Jen.

"And just smooth over the edges," he said. "Gently. You don't want to take off more than just the last of the paint or you'll dull the detail in the carving beneath and there's no getting it back."

"Dad, maybe you should do this," she said.

"Why?" he asked. "You're doing fine."

"Right." She cast him a pained look. "I'm not really a...construction kind of woman, Dad."

Nick rolled his eyes. "Come on. This is good for you."

"How, exactly, is this good for me?" she muttered, applying the sandpaper as he'd shown her.

"It's good to know how to use a few tools, Amelia," he replied. "How do you expect to get things done around your own home if you don't know the basics?"

"I don't think refinishing antique cupboards is actually considered a basic," she replied.

"But using sandpaper is," he said and chuckled. "Besides, you'll probably be renting your own place soon enough, won't you?"

"Chris thinks I should buy," she said. "And he'll give me a pretty hefty down payment to get me started."

Of course Chris would. Chris handed her money, but Nick was trying to give his daughter something different—an ability to do a few things herself. Money came and went, and it could be used up faster than Amelia probably appreciated. She was allowed to be good at more than one thing—academics were great, but there was more than book work out in the world.

"Are you waiting to buy until you're working as a lawyer, then?" Nick asked.

"That's the plan," she replied, leaning over the cupboard door and following Nick's instructions. "Until I'm done school, I'll be living on campus anyway. And if things get more serious with Ben…"

"Just for simplicity, let's leave Ben out of it," Nick said. "When you buy a place that's yours, you're going to need to know how to do some of this stuff."

"I'll hire someone," she replied.

"And how will you know if they're messing it up or not?" he asked.

Amelia looked up at him. "I'll get you to come take a look?"

Nick grinned in spite of himself.

"I'll be happy to," he said. Happier than she probably realized.

He heard the front door open and shut. There was the sound of muted voices and Nick glanced over at his daughter.

"That would be Jen," he said. "Keep on that. I'll be back."

He ignored the exasperated look his daughter cast in his direction and headed out through the dining room. Jen was just hanging her coat up, and he saw a tall, blond-headed boy standing next to her. He was only a couple of inches shorter than Jen, and his expression was unimpressed.

"Hi," Nick said.

"Hi, Nick," Jen said with a tired smile. "Drew, meet Nick Bryant. He's the contractor working on the kitchen right now."

"Hello," Drew said sullenly. "So where's my room?"

Nick saw a flash of irritation in Jen's gaze, and then she shrugged. "Up those stairs, and then up another flight. Third floor. You'll find it, I'm sure."

"You aren't going to show me?" Drew asked.

"I'm confident in your ability to climb stairs," she said dryly. "Your stuff is in there, so you'll know which one is yours. And come back down once you've found it. I want to show you some things down here first."

"Fine," he muttered.

"Don't forget your suitcase." She pushed the suitcase toward him.

Drew picked up the suitcase and headed on up, Jen watching him go with a grim expression on her face.

"I take it he's upset about his dad," Nick said.

"That's an understatement." She sighed, then stepped up to the staircase and raised her voice. "You can use the bathroom on the third floor, Drew! Don't use any bathrooms on the second floor!"

"I wasn't going to!" Drew's voice filtered back down.

Jen rolled her eyes and came back to where Nick was standing. "He's taking it out on me."

"What's he upset about?" he asked.

"His father booting him out days before Christmas," she replied. "And he's determined to hate it here."

"Give him time."

"It's all I can do, I guess." Jen cast him a tired look, and he had the urge to put an arm around her. Instead, he leaned over and nudged her with the side of his arm.

"It'll be fine," he said.

She didn't answer, but she also didn't look so sure. Instead, she leaned toward him, too, resting against him. He eased his arm around her shoulders and for a moment they stood there like that, Jen at his side, and his hand holding her solidly against him. He wanted to help, if he could, but he knew that figuring out her son was her job. Still, if he could help her feel a little stronger in the process, he'd feel like he'd done well.

"Parenting is hard," she said after a moment.

"Yep," he agreed. "Really hard."

Jen looked up at him, her sandy-blond curls falling around her face, and those brown eyes meeting his, and for just a second, he had an image of what it would be like to face all of this stuff together, just like this. With an arm around her and the certainty that it would be easier with a partner in it.

Drew's footsteps sounded on the stairs, and Nick pressed a quiet kiss on the top of her head, then dropped his hand. He wasn't sure why he'd kissed her again. It had just felt natural between them, and he'd wanted to show her that he cared. Jen took a step to the side, but he noticed that her cheeks had pinked.

"I'll let you show him around," Nick said, and he gave Jen a smile. "Don't let a kid question your good taste."

"That's probably sound advice," she said, then Drew appeared on the stairs.

"Come on, son," Jen said. "Let me show you the main floor."

Nick headed back to the kitchen. Jen would sort things out with her son. He remembered being about the same age, and he'd been a pain in the butt, too. It was perfectly natural. Still, he glanced once over his shoulder to see Jen by the Christmas tree, her hands on her hips and a smile on her face.

As Nick went back in the kitchen, he saw his daughter sitting where he'd left her, but the sandpaper was on the counter, and she was on her phone texting.

"It that Ben?" he asked.

"Yep," she said absently, the soft click as she typed not slowing down.

"Right…" He sighed. "Look, Amelia, if you were working a job, would you stop to text?"

"I'm not working a job," she said, looking up. "I'm visiting my father. And if I wanted to send someone a quick a message, yeah, I would stop and do that. My employer doesn't own every second of my time. I'm a human being with relationships that exist outside of work."

What was he going to do, make up for the past ten years with one day of proper work?

"Gotcha," he said. There was no point in arguing with her.

"There are new ideas about management these days. If employees are treated with respect, they work harder and produce at a higher level." Her tone was a little too patronizing for his liking, and Nick shot his daughter an annoyed look.

"Now you think I don't respect my employees?" he said. "Have you managed a team before? Have you had the outcome of a project be entirely your responsibility?"

She caught the sarcasm in his tone. "So that's why I'm here—the job? Really?"

"My point is that the real world is a whole lot different than you think right now. There's theory, and then there's application," he said.

She looked back down at her phone again. This was always how it had been—Shari and Amelia treating him like he was a rung lower than they were. She finished typing and dropped her phone back in her pocket.

"It's been nice to see you in action and everything, but I think I'll go, Dad."

Nick met his daughter's drilling gaze. For just a second, meeting his daughter's ire-filled stare, it wasn't her mother he saw in her stubborn stance. Sure, she looked like her mother, but the set of her jaw, the tilt of her head—it was like looking in a mirror. Was the battle against his own DNA?

Nick watched as Amelia headed out of the kitchen just as Jen and Drew were coming in.

"I'm heading out," Amelia said with forced cheerfulness. "Nice to see you, Jen."

"Oh, you, too!" Jen called after her. "See you!"

Drew ambled into the kitchen, looking around.

"This would have been where the servants cooked for the family," Jen said. "If you see that staircase over there, that leads up to the second floor. It's a servants' staircase, so they could move around the house without bothering the family."

"Do we get servants?" Drew asked dully.

"Nope," Jen said. "Anyway, take a look at what Nick has been doing. He's been fixing up the sink and counters. He's also redoing the cupboards to look more the way they did originally."

"Huh," Drew said.

"And when I turn the bottom floor into an art gallery, I'll close off the kitchen so that the only access is by this back staircase, which will lead up to our living area," Jen went on.

"More paintings and stuff," Drew said.

"Yeah…" Jen's enthusiasm seemed to wane a little. "Paintings and stuff."

"Did you want to help me out with some of this?" Nick asked. "I can show you how to use a power sander so you can work on your own house. It's a matter of pride."

Drew's eyes lit up momentarily, then he seemed to change his mind.

"No, thanks. I don't think I'll be here too long," Drew said.

Nick saw Jen's eyes widen as the barb hit home. Drew was trying to hurt her, and he'd finally succeeded. He had the urge to bark at the kid, tell him to apologize—but he wasn't part of this.

"Upstairs," Jen said, her voice low and trembling. *"Now."*

Drew seemed to hear the threat in her tone, because in a split second he went from attitude-plus to looking a little scared.

"Sorry, Mom," he muttered.

"I said *now*," she said. "Let's go."

Drew turned toward the staircase, and Jen followed him, their footsteps thudding through the walls until they faded away. Nick stood there, feeling hollowed out. Nick and

Jen were both meeting their matches today in their own children. Amelia was ditching him for Ben's family, just like Sam was doing to Drew. But Drew was just a kid...

Nick was tired, sad, but not quite ready to give up. When he finished work today, he was going to have a word with his daughter, and this time she was going to hear him out.

CHAPTER THIRTEEN

JEN MARCHED DREW up to the second floor and down the hall, past the multiple bedrooms and toward the far end. Drew looked into the rooms as he passed.

"This isn't a tour," Jen said. "We're going to talk. Keep walking."

They arrived at an old library at the far end of the second floor—a few books had been left behind, and the built-in wooden shelves were covered in dust. A few boxes of her own books sat piled next to the corner windows, the cardboard boxes bathed in watery winter sunlight. A cold fireplace loomed on one end of the room, the flue shut, but a finger of cold air still managed to make it through.

Drew looked around himself for a moment, then cast her an annoyed scowl.

"Now." Jen crossed her arms over her chest. "I've had just about enough of this. I know you're upset. I know this divorce was terrible for you—it was terrible for *all* of us! And I'm not bouncing back as fast as your father did, either. But when you say things just to hurt me—"

"I'm not," Drew cut in. "I'm not saying stuff to hurt your feelings. I'm saying what I mean."

Her heart fluttered at that. "You said you didn't intend to stay here very long," Jen said. "What did you mean by that?"

Drew looked away, his expression stony, and Jen rubbed her hands over her face.

"Drew…" Jen softened her voice. "You really don't want to live with me? You want to live with your dad during the school year?"

The very thought made her heart squeeze in her chest, and she longed to just order him to behave himself. But this went deeper. He was old enough to choose where he wanted to live now, and she'd assumed that because she'd been the one to do most of his raising, that he'd prefer her for the school year. Maybe Sam assumed it, too.

"I don't want to leave you," Drew said, tears welling in his eyes. "But I was supposed to see Dad this Christmas, and now I can't!"

"I didn't cancel that on you," Jen said. "You know that!"

"I know, but I still can't see him, or my friends from school. And if we live here, then I can't see my cousins, either. Or my aunts and uncles."

"You've got an aunt and a cousin here, too," Jen said. "And you've got your great-aunt Gayle and her new husband, and Uncle Stu... Besides, Denver isn't that far away. We'll work this out. You'll see your dad a lot, I promise. I'll make sure of it."

"How come you couldn't just stay married?" Drew asked miserably.

"Because—" She sighed. "Drew, sometimes there are problems that are bigger than all of us. Your dad and I...we both changed, I guess. Or I did. Your father wanted me to keep being the person I was when we first got married, but I couldn't do that. I do wish it could have been different, son. I didn't want this to be how it turned out, either."

"So if you can't stay married, how come you can't at least live in the same city?" he countered. "I've got friends whose parents got divorced, and they live like three blocks apart, and the kids can see both their parents all the time. You could do that."

Yes, she could have stayed in Denver. She could have kept doing what she'd been doing the past fourteen years, and she could have watched Sam move on with a woman less than half his age and been the bitter ex-wife with a ringside seat.

"This was a chance for us to get to know my side of the family better, too," Jen said. "We should have done that earlier, but it's better a bit late than never. And this old mansion, it's a chance to start something really special. This art gallery is a dream come true, son."

"Yeah, for you," he said. "Not me."

Jen met her son's anguished gaze. He'd lost so much in their divorce, and she couldn't fix it for him. Add on to that a father who prioritized his girlfriend over him, and Drew was really struggling. Her heart ached for him, but she couldn't change any of it. All she could offer was this second chance at a meaningful life, and promise that she'd help him to see his dad as often as possible.

"Can't you give Mountain Springs a chance?" Jen pleaded.

"I never asked for this," he said.

"Okay, but here's the thing. Sometimes in life we get blindsided by bad stuff—like your parents getting a divorce—and we're furious about it. There will always be something you didn't choose. But then there are times in life when we trip over amazing things that we never expected, either. And we have to be able to enjoy that when it comes."

Drew was silent.

"I love you, son," she said, and her voice shook. "To the moon and back."

"I love you, too, Mom," he said.

Jen sucked in a breath. "Will you stay with me here in Mountain Springs for the rest of the school year?"

Drew's lips wobbled. "I guess I have to."

"You don't have to," she said, the words catching in her throat.

Jen wrapped her arms around her son and gave him a hug and a kiss on his forehead. He was almost as tall as she was now, and before she knew it, she'd be making him bend down if she wanted to kiss him on his forehead.

"I'll stay," he whispered.

"We'll be okay. I promise," she said.

Drew blinked back tears and looked around the room again. He wasn't seeing what Jen saw in this old house. He was seeing loneliness, a sort of prison that kept him from the life he'd known in Denver.

What would she do if her son changed his mind and asked to live with his dad? Would she stay in Mountain Springs? Her heart sped up at the very thought—not a chance! She'd sell this place to Angelina and head back to Denver. She'd build a life that let her be close to her son. Her ambitions were nothing without Drew in them with her. She was a mom first.

Had she made a mistake chasing after her own belated dreams all the way in Mountain Springs? The marriage might not have lasted, but having a child together changed everything. They had an obligation to their son, even if Sam wasn't manning up quite yet.

"We'll talk about it more," Jen said. "You know I'm always here to talk, right?"

"Yeah..." Drew swallowed. "But if I really hate it, can we move back?"

There was something in her son's voice, a level of pleading she'd never heard from him before. Plus, he was asking her to move back with him. He didn't want to leave her behind. This wasn't a complaint; it was a desperate hope. He was asking if his happiness mattered, if it factored into her plans. Because his Christmas hadn't mattered when Sam's plans changed...

Sam might not be the father he should be right now, but he was Drew's dad, and Drew needed him. Desperately. He needed both of them. Jen could blame Sam for not doing well enough in his role, or she could step up and do what her son needed and give him two parents in the same city.

"If you're miserable, I won't be happy, either," Jen said. "You can count on that, son."

But oh, how she hoped he could be happy.

"Okay." Drew nodded.

Jen sighed. "Look, you were really rude before. Nick is a nice man who made sure that you had a hot, functioning shower up here and redid the kitchen so we'd be comfortable while we started fixing this place up. He's been working really hard, and he didn't deserve that attitude."

"Sorry," Drew muttered. "I didn't mean to."

"You owe him an apology," she said. "I raised you better than that."

"Okay. I'll apologize," Drew said.

He was a good kid, and she couldn't blame him for not knowing how to navigate all of this, or for feeling out of control. But she also had a life to put together for the two of them. Would it be here in Mountain Springs, or would it be in Denver? She'd been so certain that this was the second chance she wanted, but if it came at the expense of Drew's emotional needs, it wouldn't be worth it.

But she'd been softening to the idea of getting to know know Nick on a more romantic level. He was a nice guy, and genuinely nice guys didn't come around that often.

Still, her son had to come first.

When they got back downstairs, Jen nudged her son in the direction of the kitchen toward the sound of that electric sander. Drew headed into the room and when Nick looked up and turned off the sander, Drew glanced back at her.

"Drew wanted to say something," Jen prompted him.

"I'm sorry I was rude before," Drew said.

"That's okay," Nick said. "You've got a lot going on, huh?"

"I guess so," Drew agreed.

"I get it," Nick said, and he gave him a sympathetic smile. "Hang in there."

"You can go explore a bit if you want, Drew," Jen said. "There's a lot of rooms, and some old stuff was left behind."

"Okay…" Drew sighed. "I'll go look around. Can I set up my Xbox?"

"Sure," she said. "If you can figure it out."

"I know how to do it," Drew replied.

Drew disappeared out of the kitchen again, and Jen met Nick's questioning gaze.

"You okay?" Nick asked softly.

"Not really," she admitted. "But a mom can't show weakness."

Except with an Xbox, maybe. What was she supposed to do, take away every last thing her son loved?

Nick pulled off his gloves and dropped them onto the counter, then came over to where she stood.

"Come here," he murmured, and he caught her hand, tugging her toward him. She hesitated for a second, and then allowed herself to be pulled into his strong arms. He felt so solid and strong, and she leaned her cheek against his shoulder. He smelled good—like wood dust and something slightly musky—and she let out a long breath as his arms tightened around her. What was it about this man's arms that managed to drain all her inhibitions away? It wasn't just attraction, because this was something different—just the comfort of feeling him against her, his heartbeat thudding reassuringly against her chest—that made tears prickle in her eyes.

"Drew's so upset…" Jen whispered.

"Yeah, I know." His voice was a soft growl next to her ear. "But he seems like a good kid."

"I know. But am I doing it right? Or am I making this harder on him?"

"You bought him a mansion. My heart bleeds," he said, humor tingeing his voice.

Nick had a way of making all of this sound so reasonable, and she missed having someone who could do this for her—help her worries settle and put stuff back into perspective. Jen wrapped her arms around Nick's waist, and she felt his hand smooth over her hair, then his cheek rest on top of her head.

"Why do I feel like I'm messing up, then?" she asked quietly.

"I don't think you're messing up anything," he said. "For what it's worth."

She appreciated that, but he hadn't heard the misery in Drew's voice earlier. Nick didn't know that it was within her power to fix this for her son...if that was what Drew really needed. She *could* move back to Denver, even though it would be a personal disappointment. The thing that was holding her here was her own desire to make good in the town where she'd grown up poor. And her hopes to connect with her sister again... *Was* this what was best for Drew?

Nick pulled back just a little and touched her chin with his finger, bringing her lips up to his. His kiss was soft and tender, and she let her eyes flutter shut, enjoying his touch. Then she straightened and took a step back, and he let his hand slide down her arm until he caught her fingers. His warm, rough grip felt so comforting, and she didn't want to let go.

"How far past professional have we gone?" Jen asked with a rueful smile.

"Miles," he replied, and his eyes twinkled. "Sorry."

"I like it this way," she said. "I think we might be complicating things, though."

"There's nothing complicated," he said. "I work on your kitchen and we..."

"Share a few kisses?" she asked.

"Maybe," he replied. "And we talk. We open up. We...get to know each other better."

"You could make a nuclear bomb sound reasonable," she said.

A grin spread over his face. "This isn't a nuclear bomb. It's just two people who are feeling something."

"What are you feeling?" she whispered.

She met his gaze, but then she heard Drew's footsteps on the stairs, and she tugged her hand free. He quickly released her and when she looked back at him, he was watching her with a tender look in his dark eyes. What *was* he feeling? And did she really want it confirmed?

"Mom?" Drew's voice met her before he came around the corner. "Can you help with the Xbox?"

She glanced back at Nick, and he'd picked up his sander again. His gaze lingered on her for a moment, and then he turned the power tool on. He was right. They'd sailed right past professional, and they were miles past neighborly. But whatever it was that was stewing between them couldn't keep going like this. It was moving quickly, and she had a feeling this could careen right out of control without much more encouragement.

Jen was too impetuous in romance—a mistake she couldn't be repeating now that she had a son to protect. Besides, she might not be staying in Mountain Springs, after all... It wasn't only her heart on the line anymore.

"Come on," Jen said. "Show me the instructions. It should be like your old one, right?"

And she followed her son out of the kitchen and toward the stairs. Her ideas about what might be best for Drew had started to change...

NICK SHOULDN'T HAVE kissed her again. He knew that! But there had been something about having her there in his arms—so warm and soft, and she'd felt almost defeated in the way she'd leaned against him.

He'd never been a woman's comfort in parenting—not like this. Shari had always been so certain she knew what was right for their daughter. She'd never come to him for comfort when it came to Amelia, and she'd certainly not been there for him. So to have Jen in his arms, her whole body pulsing with the beat of her heart, it had felt good in a way he'd not anticipated.

And yet, he knew what he was dealing with here...and he knew how this ended. He wanted to be Jen's answer, but he wouldn't be, any more than he'd been Shari's. What he had to offer—strong arms and broad shoulders—were great in painful times, but they weren't enough for the long-term. Not for a woman like Jen.

By the time he got home again that night, he was in a bad mood. Jen had been busy with Drew and she'd avoided him that day. He was frustrated with himself for not being strong enough to hold himself back. Jen was the one in an emotionally vulnerable situation, and she probably thought he'd taken advantage of that by now. He could see how it looked.

"What's with you?" Amelia asked when he came inside.

He bent down and gave Goldie a pet, then looked up to find his daughter eyeing him over the top of her phone.

"Nothing," he said. "Although, I was hoping to have a talk with you."

"So I'm the reason you've got a face like a fist right now?" she said.

"What? No." He sighed, trying to let his frustration go. "I'm ticked off about something else. But I do need to talk to you."

"I'm heading out for dinner," she replied. "Terrance is picking me up in a few minutes."

So she'd head out again, and he'd lose track of what he wanted to say to her, and by the time she returned, the moment would be past. She was playing his game now—he'd always turned to work when he and Shari fought. No, they needed to talk now.

"This won't take that long," Nick said. "Have a seat."

Amelia sighed and headed for the couch. He peeled off his coat and hung it up before he followed her over. He sank into the seat kitty-corner to her.

"You don't respect me," he said.

"Dad, I'm an adult," she replied. "I'm not a little girl anymore. So our relationship isn't going to be the same. You can't use me for free labor, or give me a life lesson about hard work. Those days are past."

"Yeah, I know," he said. "And I'm sorry about that. I'm a bit out of practice here, but this is about something deeper. You've never really respected me. I was cut from a different cloth than you and your mother, so to speak, and I feel like when your mother started losing respect for me, so did you."

Amelia shook her head. "We're all good at different things—"

"Don't give me that, because I've been dealing with this for a decade, Amelia," he said. "But that's not your fault. It's mine. I should have fought harder. I thought that being reasonable was better for you—for us. I don't think that was right. You got this idea that your father was some simple guy and your mother was the brilliant one. And because it didn't work between your mother and me on a romantic level anymore, I think you started to see me the way she did."

"Dad..."

"Amelia, would you just have an honest conversation with me for once?" he demanded.

"I don't think you want honesty," she shot back. "You won't like it."

"I'm damn sure I won't, but it's better than this overly polite banter of ours that I've been putting up with."

"Overly polite?" Amelia retorted. "Dad, at least we're talking! Where have you been the last ten years? You've had your own life! While I grew up, started dating, got my license, started looking at colleges, where were *you*?"

Nick hadn't been a part of her college search. Amelia's grades had been high enough that she had her choice of schools, but Nick couldn't pay for her Ivy League education, and he wasn't about to trail behind them as Chris was the man of the situation. But that wasn't her fault, either.

"You feel abandoned," he said.

"I don't just feel abandoned—I was abandoned!" she snapped. "You didn't just divorce Mom, you divorced both of us!"

"I did no such thing!" he retorted. "Any time I came to visit you in the city, you had very little interest in a dinner with your dad, because you had a stepdad who could buy more for you. And when I tried to talk to you on the phone, you had friends you'd rather chat with. When you came to see me for a couple of weeks in the summer, you moped around the entire time and said how much you hated being out here. Now, you were a kid—and you were going through a lot. But I didn't cut you off, Amelia. You cut me off!"

"I had no choice in your divorce!" she shot back. "And Mom moved me to Denver. Chris was there. What was I supposed to do? Yeah, he bought me stuff you couldn't. But he also taught me how to drive, and he was the one who picked me up from a party that got out of hand. And then, when my ex dumped me and wouldn't let me get my bookbag from his place, it was Chris who drove over and intimidated him into giving it back."

Chris had been there for her, and Nick didn't want to remove his daughter's supporters from her life. That would be incredibly selfish of him. He was glad that Chris loved Amelia like his own daughter, but it didn't change the fact that *he* was her father. And he'd never stopped trying.

"He was a dad to you," Nick said, swallowing. "And I'm glad. I wanted you to have a good relationship with your stepfather. I just didn't want to be swept to the side. The one thing I've noticed this visit—you're an awful lot like me, too."

"You think?" Amelia smiled faintly.

"Oh, definitely. You've got my stubborn streak," he said.

Amelia was silent for a moment.

"It wasn't easy for me, either," Amelia said quietly. "Mom had a new husband, and she was caught up in him. They were all in love and planning trips and smiling at me a little too brightly."

"You could have spent more time with me," he said.

"During the school year?" She shook her head. "I wasn't the only one with a stepdad, and at least mine had the money to try and buy my affection."

"Did it work?" he asked quietly.

"It didn't hurt." She smiled faintly. "Chris was there for me, Dad, but he was still my stepfather. And Mom had to really put in effort to make him happy. She lost weight and started worrying about makeup more, and stuff."

"I thought they were happy," he said.

"They are. But it's different," Amelia replied. "I know I pushed you away a lot, and Mom didn't make it easy on you, but there were times when I daydreamed about you just showing up and taking me away from there."

"Really?" He felt his throat tighten with emotion.

"Of course, there are court-dictated rules to these things. You couldn't do that. I guess I just missed you." Amelia's phone pinged twice and she looked down at it for a moment. "That's Ben."

"I missed you, too, Amelia," Nick said. He missed her still. Then he added, "Go on and call him. I know you've got plans to make. I'm glad we got to talk."

Time was whipping by, years evaporating, and before he knew it, he'd have a married daughter with kids of her own. Before he knew it, he'd have grown old.

"Hey, Dad?" Amelia said, standing up.

"Yeah?"

"I love you, too." Tears misted her eyes,

then she turned toward the front door and put her phone to her ear. Apparently, she'd talk on the phone while waiting for her friend. He watched her pull on her coat and step into her boots, and for the life of him, it was like watching her at ten, just a girl with honey-blond hair and a fierce heart.

The door clicked shut behind her and he smoothed his hand over his beard. He'd messed this up a very long time ago, and he wasn't sure he'd ever get it right again. But he'd keep trying—if nothing else, even as a grown woman with a life of her own, she'd never be able to say that her father gave up on her.

CHAPTER FOURTEEN

THE NEXT EVENING Lisa offered to take Drew out for some KFC, and then back to her place to watch a movie on Netflix. Lisa was looking forward to some time with her nephew, and Jen was grateful her sister wanted to make the effort.

"Come on, Drew!" Jen called up the stairs. "Your aunt is here!"

Lisa came inside, and Bram ran for the staircase and sat down to run his car along the bottom step. His little boots left a trail of melting snow behind him.

"I'm sorry for the mess," Lisa said.

"Don't worry about it," Jen said. "It's winter. And I'm glad you're taking Drew out for a little bit. He's been really upset about leaving his friends and cousins behind in Denver, and it'll be good to remind him that he's still got family out here."

"How's he holding up?" her sister asked.

"He checked out the house a bit and then sat himself down in front of the Xbox his dad gave him for Christmas," Jen said. "I'm just glad to get him away from the games for a bit—give him some real life to explore."

Lisa looked at her with a small smile. "Are you saying you need my help?"

"Yes," Jen said. "I am."

"Do you want to show me around?" Lisa asked.

Jen shot her sister a smile. Was Lisa going to be happy for her about this mansion? It would be nice to have her sister be proud of something she did for a change. "Sure."

Nick came up just then, and he and Lisa exchanged hellos. Nick and Lisa were relaxed and cordial, but when Nick's gaze flicked over to Jen, his expression softened just a little more, and she couldn't help but like that.

"Care to come on the grand tour?" Lisa asked him. "I'd like to see your work. I've never actually seen you in action, you know."

"What's it like?" Nick asked Jen jokingly. "Impressive?"

"Actually, yeah," Jen replied, but she wasn't joking. She turned to her sister. "Really, you have to see what he's done. Do you want to start in the kitchen?"

"Have you talked to Sam?" Lisa asked, slipping out of her boots and scooping Bram into her arms. Then she winced. "Sorry— that might be private."

"It's fine," Jen said. "Nick knows the broad strokes. I tried connecting with Sam. I texted. I called. No answer. He told me he had plans with his girlfriend's family, so I guess he'd turned everything off to focus on that."

"Ironic," Lisa said. "He won't do it for his son."

"Don't say that in front of Drew," Jen said.

"I'm not." Lisa rolled her eyes. "I'm saying it to you."

The sisters' gazes met. "Is it my job to make him a better father?"

"Male perspective?" Lisa said, looking over at Nick.

"I'm not sure. I should have an opinion here," Nick said.

"Actually, I want to hear what you think," Jen said.

Standing there, the three of them—well, the four of them including Bram who had a fistful of Lisa's hair in his chubby hand—felt rather nice, actually. Jen hadn't been sure what it would be like to have her sister and Nick in the same room with her. She hadn't imagined that she'd get along with her sister's group of friends, but maybe she'd been wrong about that.

"I guess it comes down to what Drew needs," Nick said. "He might need you to help him navigate that. And that might include giving Sam a nudge when he needs it."

"I don't think so," Lisa interjected. "I don't think she can make Sam into a better father. He's got all the reason in the world to focus on his son, but he's going to carry on just like he always has. He never listened to Jen anyway. In fact, I'm going to predict that he marries this Tiffany, or someone just as young, and that he'll have another child or two. And he'll be exactly the same with them."

"You think?" Jen asked. "Is that going to turn into another short story?"

"It might." A small smile tickled Lisa's lips. "How many times do you have bitter kids from the first marriage watching a self-centered parent move on with another family? It's cliché for a reason. Sam's not unique."

Jen glanced over at Nick and he shrugged. "She's got a point."

Since when had her sister gotten so wise? Was it all just from watching Jen mess things up? Or maybe it was from a few mistakes of her own. All the same, Lisa seemed to understand the world in a different way from Jen. And Lisa seemed to be right these days.

They started the tour of the house, and Nick pointed out his plans for the kitchen, showed Lisa some sketches of what it would look like once complete. He was proud of his work, and Lisa looked impressed.

Jen led the way through the main floor, and then up the stairs to the second floor.

"This library is amazing," Nick said when they paused there. He ran his hand over a dusty shelf. "These shelves could all be refinished, and you could even find a library ladder to roll along those tracks up there."

"Yeah?" Jen looked around. "Maybe that can be next on the list after the gallery."

Drew came down the stairs and met them in the hallway.

"Can you talk to Drew?" Jen asked quietly. "Encourage him a bit?"

"Of course," Lisa replied. "What are aunties for?"

Jen felt a wave of gratitude. Maybe she wasn't quite so on her own out here, after all...for as long as she stayed. Could Lisa and Bram, Gayle and Matt, and Uncle Stu be enough for Drew? Could Nick and Amelia? It was strange to be including Nick in her support network, but if she and Drew stayed, she could see Nick becoming a bigger part of her life...

All the same, she couldn't confuse what Drew needed and what she needed. They were very different lists.

As they came down the stairs, Drew reached out and touched Bram's hand, and the toddler stared at his older cousin in wonder. Jen could see the family resemblance between the two boys. Bram looked an awful lot like Drew had at that age, and she wondered if there was any recognition between them—that sense of family.

"Is that Bram?" Drew asked.

"That's him," Lisa said.

"Hey, buddy," Drew said, and ruffled his

little cousin's hair, then he looked up at Lisa shyly. "Hi, Aunt Lisa."

"You've grown about two feet since I saw you last," Lisa said with a grin. "Holy smokes. What does your mother feed you?"

Drew didn't seem to know how to answer that, but he grinned back all the same. When they got back down to the door, Jen gave her son a squeeze.

"All right, you have fun," Jen said. "I'll come by and get you around ten, okay?"

"Okay," Drew said. "Bye, Mom."

"See you, Nick," Lisa said with a smile. "Don't let my sister work you too hard."

"She's not as scary as you think," Nick said with a laugh.

As Jen watched her sister, son and nephew head out into the dark evening, she wondered how big of a mistake it was to keep her son so devotedly in Denver. At the time, she'd thought she was giving him a better life with better people. At least Sam seemed to think so. She saw the error of her ways now. There wasn't a "better" family—there was just one big mess of family, and picking out the "more successful" ones for Drew to spend time with had only succeeded in cutting him off from people who could love and support him when life went left. Jen had been the one to do her son wrong in that respect.

Jen shut the front door and as she turned, she saw Nick standing by the dining room entry, his tool bag in one hand. He gave her a hesitant smile.

"On your own this evening?" he asked.

"It looks that way," she replied.

Jen moved away from the door, closer to the Christmas tree with its twinkling lights that sparkled off the sparse ornaments. This tree was beautiful, and she was glad now that she'd listened to Drew and gotten the eight-foot one. It filled up the yawning space on these cold nights, and made it feel like a home instead of a gallery. And funny how a chat with her sister and Nick made things feel easier to handle. She had more people who cared than she'd realized.

"You and your sister are getting along better?" he said.

"She's got a perspective I didn't appreciate before," Jen said. "And she might be better at anticipating what my ex-husband will do than I am."

Nick smiled at that.

"How is it going with Amelia?" Jen asked.

"Well…she's leaving on Christmas Eve to spend the holidays with her boyfriend," he said. He put down his tool bag and came closer to the tree. "She might end up marrying this guy. Looks like they're seriously thinking about it, at least."

"For real?" she turned to look at him. "She won't be here for Christmas?"

"She's got plans," he said. "What can I say?"

Nick dropped his gaze. She knew what this Christmas with his daughter had meant to him.

"Oh, Nick…"

"I'm not sure I can repair this with her, at least not over one holiday," he said, and his voice sounded tight. "I don't think it's going to be that easy of a fix."

"Are you going home to see her tonight, then?" Jen asked.

"She's out tonight with a few friends," he replied. "It's highly possible that she's avoiding me."

"I'm sorry. At least with a twelve-year-old he's still reliant on me for all his transportation."

He smiled faintly. "Well...it's my own doing."

He hoisted his tool belt and started toward the door.

"I was thinking of going for a drive tonight," she said. "I haven't been back to the row houses I grew up in for years. I'm not even sure if they're still there."

Nick turned back.

"A little nostalgic?" he asked.

"Yeah." She met his gaze, and she realized that she didn't really want to make that drive alone. Whatever had sparked between her and Nick might not be wise, but it was real. "Did you want to come?"

"No, thanks. You have a good time, though. I don't need a pity invite."

Was that what he thought—that she felt sorry for him?

"It's not pity," she said. "It's...friendship."

He paused and looked at her uncertainly. "Jen, we're well past friendship."

She caught her breath, and her heart sped up at the rumble in his voice. Yes, they were well past friendship, but where had they landed? All she knew was that she would deeply enjoy his company tonight.

"Then come because you want to," she said quietly.

He was silent for a moment, then he tipped his head to one side. "I do want to."

Jen smiled. "We could grab some takeout on our way."

"Deal," he said, and he smiled back. "But dinner's on me."

She wanted to go back and see the row house where she grew up, the place that had formed her for better or for worse. She wanted to face the home she'd run away from and make some peace with it. It was time to stop running. When she left again, she'd be walking with her shoulders square.

NICK SWUNG BY Toby's Burgers, which had been family run for the past fifty years and served the best bacon double cheeseburger in the county. They each ordered a burger and fries, and he added an extra order of onion rings on top of that. They ate in the car in the parking lot, and when they were done eating, Nick put his truck into gear and headed back to the main road.

There was a soft dusting of snow coming down from the sky, but not enough to impede visibility much or slow down traffic. A brisk wind whipped through the valley, sweeping the dry snow off the roads and piling it into the banks on the side.

"Do you know where you're going?" Jen asked.

"Pretty sure," he replied. "The old row houses across the street from the YMCA that they shut down a few years back."

"That's the place," she said. "I didn't know the YMCA got shut down."

"Yeah, it's all boarded up," he said. "I'm not sure what they'll do with the building now. I've been expecting them to tear it down."

He'd been expecting them to tear down the old dilapidated row houses, too. But that was where Jen had grown up. It was strange to think about her as a child on that lonely stretch. It made Lisa's angst make a little more sense, too.

Jen turned toward the window, watching the buildings aglow in Christmas lights sweeping past them. What was she thinking? He glanced over at her, watching the play of light as they moved over her features. She was beautiful, and he couldn't help but notice it more and more. She was the kind of beautiful that got deeper and more defined with age, and the kind that could turn his life upside down without her ever even trying.

"Do you have happy memories growing up there?" Nick asked.

She slowly shook her head. "No."

"I thought if you wanted to revisit the place—" he started.

"Don't get me wrong, my parents were great," she said, "but we were poor. Dad had an accident when I was about five or six that really hurt his back and he went on disability. Mom worked part-time, but she never did make very much. So we lived where we could afford."

"It was hard," he hazarded.

"Really hard," she replied. "My sister and I had to walk to school, and there were these other kids who lived in the trailer park about a block away and they were really rough. They used to follow after us and torment us. I remember being scared a lot."

"That's awful."

"But I didn't want to worry my parents,"

she went on. "Dad got a few surgeries on his back, but they cost a lot. They were always trying to scrape up some money from somewhere. The thing is, when I got into University of Denver, I was ready to leave this town in the dust. I didn't want to come back for anything. We were broke, we were always struggling and I was constantly trying to protect my parents from more worry. When I left for school, I had no intention of ever returning."

"Not even to see your folks?" he asked.

"I did come back to visit a few times," she admitted. "But mostly I'd call and talk to my parents on the phone. They'd come to the city to see me more often. And I'd show them around the college and they were so happy for me. I'd achieved more than they'd managed and they were proud."

"Then you got married," he surmised.

"Right after I graduated. And then, it was different. I didn't have to worry anymore, and I could send my mom money from time to time. I wasn't worried about being safe or about how to pay for things. We were…comfortable. Finally. It was all I'd ever wanted."

Just to be safe and have enough…the

thought was a heart-wrenching one, and he looked over at her again. She looked back, then shrugged weakly.

"Sorry if that's too much information," she said.

"No, it's nice to know, actually. No one should have to live afraid of their own safety or unsure of how they'll afford the necessities."

"I never wanted to again," she said. "And my sister interpreted that as being a gold digger, I think. It wasn't that. I wasn't marrying Sam for money, but I might have been looking for rescue. And that wasn't healthy. Did Lisa ever mention this?"

"Not really. I knew she had a sister, but she did more eye rolling than explaining."

The falling snow began to wane, and Nick signaled a turn down the road that led to their destination. There were a few cars parked on either side, and a newer subdivision had been built in the past ten years, growing up around the older structures.

"I can see why that old mansion meant so much to you both," he said. "Growing up here, and seeing that old house…it would leave an impression."

"My dad used to drive us past it," she said. "It was on the way to some babysitting job I had, and I used to stare at it. He told me that some people lived better than others, but at the end of the day, it was family that made life sweet."

And then her parents had died, leaving her with a sister who thought she'd sold out and a spattering of extended family. Nick was a dad who'd hoped his daughter would have all the good things in life, too, so he felt like he could understand what her dad might have been thinking. A man wanted the best for his daughter, but he didn't want to lose her in the process...

Nick pulled to a stop when they reached the row houses. It was dark already, but still early in the evening. Most of the houses were aglow from within, TVs flickering in front windows, people passing in front of closed curtains, their shadows betraying their presence. There were a few cars parked along the side of the road, and a couple of trucks.

"Which one was yours?" he asked.

"Number seven." She nodded toward it. There wasn't any space to park in front of it, so he stayed where he was. The heat pumped into the cab, and he reached over to take her hand, twining her fingers through his.

"They did their best," Jen said quietly. "You know that mistletoe ornament?"

"Yeah."

"I used to look at it and dream of my future, but it was only after my parents passed away in a car accident that I really treasured it. I was twenty-seven, and Drew was just a baby. Lisa would have been twenty-two." She looked over at him and sighed. "It wasn't that Lisa expected me to move home after my parents died, but she did want me to come around more often. Looking back on it, I realize how young she was—twenty-two isn't all that old, is it? Anyway, I wanted her to move out to Denver to be closer to me, but she wouldn't budge."

"You were both already set on your paths," he said.

"Maybe," she agreed. "Or we were both too stubborn to realize we needed each other." Her gaze moved ahead to her old house, and he saw her eyes grow teary. "I never did thank my parents for all their sacrifice and dedication to us. I took a lot of it for granted, and I put my energy into doing better. Being better. I wonder now how that made my parents feel. Did I do to my parents what your daughter is doing to you?"

Nick paused, and he sighed. "Maybe."

She nodded and dropped her gaze. "I think so, too. And I wish I hadn't. I can't go back and make it better, and now that I'm here in Mountain Springs again, the things I want to fix are too far in the past to make right."

She was trying to tell him something, and in his gut he felt the direction this was going.

"This place is still a part of you," he said. Wasn't it?

"It is," she agreed. "It always will be, but this is my hometown. It isn't Drew's."

Nick frowned. "He'll make memories here, too."

Jen looked at him, and he could see the sadness in her eyes.

"I raised him in Denver," she said, slowly shaking her head. "That's the life he knows. His dad is out there, his family on Sam's side. And you know what? I had my parents growing up, and they were what made me resilient. If I raise Drew away from his father, it will let Sam off easy, and Drew will be the one to suffer."

"Jen—" Nick tugged at her fingers so that she looked up at him. "Are you thinking about leaving?"

She was silent for a moment, her brow furrowing. Her breath was shallow, and when she looked toward him again, tears welled in her eyes. "I think I have to."

"Why?" He wanted to fix this, to give her a reason to stay, because if she left— He didn't even want to think about how that would feel right now.

"Sam isn't a great father on his own," Jen said quietly. "I'm not taking responsibility for his shortfalls. But my son needs his father, and if we stay out here, Drew won't have one—at least not a decent relationship with him."

"And watching me with my daughter— didn't help, I guess," he said quietly.

"I think I saw what could happen," she admitted. "You were just as hurt as your daughter in that arrangement."

Great. Jen was making the hard choice and putting her son first—avoiding his regrets— and that meant she couldn't stay. The irony was like a punch to the stomach.

"What will you do?" he asked. "You've bought the mansion..."

"Angelina offered to take if off my hands if I decided not to stay," she replied. "It would be a quick sale."

"Okay..." He felt his chest constrict. "So... this is it?"

"Nick, I'm a mom!" Tears welled in Jen's eyes, and she seemed to be searching for something in his face. "The right thing is seldom the easy thing. I have a child. My obligations don't stop with a divorce. You know that as well as I do. This can't be about me. Drew's dad is already putting a new girlfriend ahead of him, and my son needs to be the top priority for his mom right now. Maybe even the only priority. He *needs* that."

Nick nodded slowly, sadness welling up inside him.

"I get it," he said. "You're a better woman than most, Jen. And I've only just gotten to know you—" The words choked off.

A Christmas tree was lit through the windows of one of the row houses, and Nick looked toward it. Just another home with a family inside, celebrating the holidays, and he envied them. He was imagining a little family inside—a husband, a wife, a couple of kids. They'd be thinking about their own Christmas, and probably how they'd afford it, and they'd have no idea that they had more than he did, a man who was financially comfortable with only a dog for company most of the time.

"I wish you could stay," he said, his voice tight with emotion. "The thing is, I have feelings for you, and I tried not to. I really did. But the thought of you leaving now—" He dropped his gaze down to their entwined fingers.

"Yeah…" she breathed.

"Yeah, what?" he pressed, and his breath caught in his chest.

"It'll be hard for me, too," she whispered. "Really hard. I'll be giving up more than the gallery. I'll be giving up—" She took a breath and stopped.

"Giving up…" he prompted.

"You!" she breathed. "I'd be giving up you…"

Nick leaned toward her and covered her lips with his, smothering the rest of her words. She fell into his kiss and he felt like he would melt, with Jen's hair brushing his shoulder and the soft scent of her filling him up. She kissed him back with a wistful longing, and when he pulled back and looked down into her dewy eyes, his heart was full of emotions that both overwhelmed him and scared him, too. But he knew what this was.

"I love you, Jen," he whispered.

He hadn't meant to say it, but once the words were out, he knew they were true. He loved her, and he'd never meant to get his heart involved. He looked down at her, waiting for her to say something, but she didn't, and his heart thudded to a stop.

But he couldn't take it back.

CHAPTER FIFTEEN

JEN BLINKED UP at Nick, and she knew that she felt the same way. She'd been avoiding it, trying to call it something else, but she'd done it again—fallen too fast and too hard. But she couldn't do this! Her son needed at least one parent focused on him right now. He needed stability...and he needed that stability in Denver. What did it matter what she felt for Nick? It wouldn't work! She had other obligations—her heart would never be her own to hand over again.

"Jen?" he whispered.

"I love you, too," she said, and she felt tears prick her eyes.

"Good—" His lips brushed hers again, and she leaned into his embrace. His kisses, the tickle of his beard, the way his breath warmed her face... It felt so right and so safe, even though it was impossible.

She pulled back. "I can't do this, Nick.

I think it was good for me to come back, maybe make a few connections with my past again, but I have to do the right thing. I can't put my heart ahead of my son's." Her breath caught in her throat.

"You're a good mom," he said. "But what about what you need? I don't think that should be just tossed aside."

"I need my son in my life, and if he's miserable, my ex is going for custody," she said.

"Then fight it," he said.

"I don't have the emotional energy to take on a custody battle!" she said. "Is that what you're really asking me to do?"

He shook his head. "No, of course not…"

"What I need doesn't matter right now. I can worry about myself later," she said. "Drew needs stability, and he needs family."

"But you do, too," he said.

"I'll make my peace with the rest of my stuff later," she said. "It'll have to wait."

Just like she'd done before—running to Denver, marrying Sam, putting her own past aside in order to move forward. She could see the pattern even now, but this wasn't about her own inclinations anymore. This was about what Drew needed.

"We're two people who fell in love with each other, and as of a week ago," she added, "neither of us were in a place for a relationship. What changed, exactly?"

Nick sighed and he leaned back in his seat. He looked down at her, his heart shining through his eyes, and she could see the jumble of emotions there.

"I want to be enough for you," he said quietly. "But you're right. Nothing has really changed—except our feelings. You're amazing—beautiful, smart, sexy... You're very easy to fall in love with, but I'm not quite so easy to be with for a woman like you..."

"Like me?" she asked.

"I've done this before, too," he said, his voice low. "You're educated, you have money behind you now, you've got ambitions for an art gallery and you think about the world differently than I do. If there's one thing I've learned over the years, it's that getting older only makes me more of what I am. I'm not going to improve. This is it—and I'm not a smooth, educated guy. I won't talk political theory with you, or the deeper meaning in art. I work with my hands, and I fix stuff. And yeah, I create beauty, but I'm the kind of guy that women like you hire. You might even appreciate my uncomplicated way of seeing things when you're feeling off balance. But not for the long haul."

Women like her.

"I hired you because I was told you were the best," she said. "I'm not some rich woman all high above you. I grew up there—" She pointed at the row houses, her finger shaking.

"Yeah, but you're a step above me now, Jen." He met her gaze and shrugged. "It's not about social status…or maybe it is. Right now we're aiming at different worlds. If we followed our feelings, you'd start getting frustrated with me. Because a big, tough lug like me can be comforting when everything is falling down around you, but when that tough lug just keeps on the same way he's always been, a woman with more adventure in her future starts to feel antsy. It's nice to be comforted, but that doesn't last forever. I've learned that the hard way."

"You don't think you'd make me happy," she said.

"Do you?" he asked.

How could she know that? Right now, for

today, and tomorrow, and maybe even for a year, yes, she could be blissfully happy in this man's arms. But what if Drew was miserable? What if he was determined to go live with his dad? Boys didn't always warm up to the men their mothers dated. It was hard for them, and Drew had been through a lot lately. He'd already felt the sting of his dad putting his girlfriend first. She knew for a fact that she couldn't be happy while her son wasn't.

"Look." Nick reached for her hand again when she hadn't answered. "You've got to do what you know is right for you. I can't talk you out of it, even if I want to. Because no matter how well I argue it, or how much you want to believe me, you know what you need. And we can't talk our way out of that."

She knew what she wanted, but she'd followed her hopes before and been stung by it. What did she need? She needed her son in her life, as an absolute minimum, and she needed a respectable path on her own while she got her balance after this divorce. She needed family. And she needed to be able to look back in this transition in her life and be proud of herself, be confident in what she'd created. She didn't want to need a man to make her feel whole.

"I need to do this on my own," Jen said, her voice choked with tears. "And that's all I'm really certain of right now."

"That's fair," he said quietly.

Jen turned her gaze toward the row houses—number seven just up ahead. Not much had changed—a few porches had been painted over the years, but that was about it. There were the same chain-link fences surrounding tiny yards piled with snow. A few plastic light-up Frosties stood in the yards. There must have been a sale at the hardware store.

And staring at that familiar street, she could see a girl in her mind's eye—blond hair, a coat that was a size too small—marching down that snowy sidewalk, her heart reaching for a life beyond this one.

Jen had come home looking for something she'd left behind, but maybe it wasn't something here, after all. Maybe she'd just needed to say goodbye.

"Should I take you home?" Nick asked.

"Please." She wiped a tear from her cheek. "I'm sorry, Nick."

"Don't be," he said. "I wanted to come tonight, and I'm glad I did."

Still? Even after they realized that whatever this was couldn't happen between them? She looked over at him and found his eyes fixed resolutely on the road, his jaw tense. He was a good man, and she loved him... but love wasn't going to be enough this time around.

THAT EVENING JEN picked her son up from Lisa's place. Bram had fallen asleep on the couch, and Lisa and Drew had just finished watching a movie while munching on popcorn.

"Thanks for this, Lis," Jen said as her son put on his boots.

"Anytime." Lisa shot her nephew a grin. "It was fun, right?"

"Yeah," Drew said, and he yawned. "Thanks, Aunt Lisa."

"Are you okay?" Lisa asked, lowering her voice. "You look like you've been crying."

Jen shook her head. "I'm fine."

She couldn't talk about this in front of her son anyway. She'd made her decision, and Drew didn't need any added pressure.

"I'm going to come over more often, Lisa," Jen said earnestly. "Like, obnoxiously often. And I'm going to be here for holidays and special days for Bram. I'm going to be a better sister."

"Yeah, sure." Lisa looked at her uncertainly. "Hey, we'll be fine, okay? I know I've been hard on you, but I think we're doing better. Don't you?"

"I think so," Jen agreed. "Good enough that you'll stop writing about me?"

Lisa chuckled. "Don't flatter yourself. You don't feature in that many of my stories. I have my own life, you know."

Jen hoped she stopped being inspiring altogether. All she wanted right now was something safe and warm...somewhere she could piece together her heart all over again.

"I'll see you later," Jen said, and she forced a smile. "Come on, Drew. Let's get home."

For as long as that old house would be home. There was no point in unpacking. Buying this place had been emotional and impulsive, and Drew needed both of his parents in his life. She'd miss the life she'd hoped for, though, and the thought of handing that old place over to Angelina put a lump in her throat. But this couldn't be an emotional decision anymore—this had to be what was best for her and Drew together. So she'd miss that old house, Mountain Springs and all of her plans for a gallery, but she'd miss her son more if she messed this up. She could live with a few delayed ambitions, but Drew came first—always.

NICK DIDN'T SLEEP well that night. He lay awake in bed, his curtain open a little. That hadn't been intentional, but he could see across the road to Jen's place. The old mansion was dark. What would it be like after she left? There would always be a part of him that looked across and hoped to see Jen in the window, phone in hand, and his heart squeezed at the thought of it.

He knew better than to try and stop a woman from doing what she had to do... It wasn't that he'd tried to stop Shari, but he should have looked at the whole package before he'd proposed to her. She'd been wrong for him, just vulnerable in the moment. Her mother had just passed away, and she'd been looking for comfort. Was he doing the same thing again with Jen?

Because Shari hadn't started out being mean, either. That took time. The breakdown of a marriage took two people, and he wasn't ignoring his responsibility in that.

Amelia was heading out to Aspen in the morning. Christmas without her... What was it about him that was never quite enough for the women in his life? He aimed too high—that was his problem. He should find a woman around town who wanted the quiet life that he did—like Bev. But his heart just wouldn't cooperate, even though a woman like Bev would be good for him. Then he stumbled across a woman he knew would be all wrong, and he fell in love.

He did finally sleep, and when he got up the next morning, he started a pot of cream of wheat for Amelia. At the very least, he'd send her off with some hot breakfast in her stomach. He was a dad. This was part of the job.

The cereal was ready when Amelia came downstairs, carrying her packed bag.

"Breakfast," he said.

Amelia put down her bag and came to the kitchen table. She cast him a tired smile.

"How did you sleep last night?" Nick asked.

"Not great. I was chatting with Ben," she said.

Yeah, he'd heard the murmur of her voice late last night while he'd been sitting up with his own heartbreak.

"You miss him?" he asked.

"I really do..." She reached for the brown sugar and began to doctor her bowl of hot cereal. She worked with the same methodical attention to detail that she put into anything she cared about, and he watched her as she poured some milk on top, then took her first bite.

"Can I give you one piece of advice?" Nick asked. "Take it or leave it, but just one little thing."

Amelia looked up at him, then swallowed. "Okay."

"Don't change for him," Nick said quietly. "You're wonderful just as you are. And if he can't see that plain as day, then find someone who does see it."

Amelia sighed. "That's your advice for marriage?"

He could hear the veiled judgment in her tone. He wasn't her expert on happy marriage, that much was clear.

"I was married. You've never been married before. I just might know what I'm talking about," he said and smiled sadly. "You're not going to scare me off, Amelia. You need to hear this. If you want to marry Ben, I'll support you, but take it from someone who has already gotten his heart broken. Trying to be something that someone wants doesn't work in the long run. I tried it with your mom. As time goes by, you just become more of yourself. If the person you marry doesn't like that so much, it only makes life together harder and harder until…you'd rather not be married anymore. So marry someone who sees you, knows you and loves you just as you are."

"Ben loves me," she said.

"I believe you," he said with a nod. "Just… think about it."

He wasn't going to guilt her for following her heart this Christmas. Maybe it would be the beginning of a lifetime love for her, or maybe it would be a learning experience. Either way, he wanted to send his daughter off with his voice in the back of her mind, telling her that she was worth more than this Ben fellow seemed to be offering.

"I have a Christmas gift for you," Amelia said, and she pulled out a gift bag and passed it over. He opened it to reveal a pair of rather expensive-looking suspenders.

It was an Amelia kind of gift—she'd been giving these for years. He had a collection of ties upstairs that he'd worn only a handful of times.

"It's to finish off your whole sexy contractor look," she said and shot him a smile. "Trust me, you'll be irresistible."

Nick chuckled. "Thanks." He pulled an envelope from his pocket and handed it over. "That's for you. I'm not great at picking out things you'll use, so I figured you might want to do the shopping yourself. You've got better taste."

Amelia looked down at the envelope, and she nodded, but the smile slipped. His own fell, too, and he sighed. He'd messed it up again.

"Look, Amelia—"

"No, it's fine," she said quickly. "Thanks."

Cash. Not even a gift card that would show more knowledge of her likes. Yeah, he could see how it had been the wrong move now. But she'd just spent the past week insulting his taste, his style and his decor. He hadn't trusted himself to buy her something. She had very strong ideas about what she did and did not like.

"I actually made you something," he said, the words coming out in a rush before he could think better of them.

Amelia looked up.

"I've been working on it for weeks, ever since you said you'd come home," he went on. "But now that you're here, I figured you probably wouldn't like it, after all. I mean, it's just that we remember things differently. There are things that are really sweet memories for me, and you just see…tackiness."

"What did you make me?" she asked. "Do you still have it?"

"Yeah… Hold on."

Nick went to the garage and retrieved the collection of three singing bears from his workbench. He liked them—their expressive faces and each line he'd carved by hand… He looked down at them and felt another wave of misgiving. This wasn't going to be the right gift, either, and she'd probably just throw them out later. And somehow knowing that made it even worse. But he'd committed himself to it now, so he carried them out to the kitchen.

"I, uh, carved you some versions of those singing bears, before I knew how you felt about them. Thing is," he said, looking down at the bears in his hands, "when you were little, you loved playing with them, and I loved watching you play. You'd lie on your stomach in front of the Christmas tree and arrange your little bear choir..." He smiled sadly. "And then you grew up. And I guess I thought you might have the same happy memories associated with them that I did. So you see, cash might not be such a bad option, huh?"

"Oh, Dad..."

Nick looked up to see tears in his daughter's eyes, and his felt wet, too.

"You grew up," he said. "And you don't have to apologize for that. If I knew you better, I'd have been able to choose a better gift, but—"

"Dad, I love them," she said, and her lips trembled. "Thank you."

"Can you just tell me one thing?" Nick asked.

"Sure."

"Where did I go wrong?" he asked. "I know I lost our connection somewhere, and I go over it in my head over and over again, and I can't figure out when it happened exactly, or what I did."

Amelia was silent for a moment, her gaze locked on the wood carving in her hand. Then she looked up, stronger.

"I just wanted you to be proud of me," she said. "I wanted you to look at me and think, that's my daughter, and brag to your work buddies about what I was doing. I wanted you to think I was...wonderful."

"I do!" he said. "And I did!" He wrapped his arms around her, then gave her an awkward kiss on the top of her head. "Oh, Amelia, that's the easy part. I'm always proud of you." He released her and looked down into his daughter's face. "You're smart, you're determined, you're a force to be reckoned with. And I'm incredibly proud of you!"

"Even if I'm just like my mother?" she asked.

"Hey, your mom is brilliant," he replied. "We might not have been the right match, but your mother is a good woman. She's smart, she's driven and she showed you things I wouldn't be able to. I married her for a reason, you know. And if you end up exactly like her, then I'll be just as proud of you. But you're your own woman now. You'll grow in your own ways. All I want is for you to be happy. That's it."

She nodded, and her chin trembled.

"I just want you to have what you want out of life," he said earnestly. "And maybe you can remember one more thing this Christmas. I know you're in love, and I know love is complicated sometimes. Just...remember what I said and don't change yourself for his family, okay? The thing to change is the guy you're with, not yourself. Okay?"

Amelia picked up the bears and tucked them into her bag one by one. "I'll try."

"And call me when you get a minute? I want to hear how it's going."

Amelia smiled, and for a split second, she was that ten-year-old kid again, and he wished he could step in and take care of her. But she was an adult now, and she'd be making her own choices and her own mistakes. She'd be forging her own future, and it would be amazing.

As they headed outside to the truck, a new

thought was percolating in his head. All his daughter had needed was to know how proud he was of her, and maybe that message had gotten lost in the chaos of the divorce. She'd needed a dad who was proud and cheered her on from the sidelines whether he understood what she was studying or what she was aiming at or not. She needed moral support...

He'd been afraid that things would turn out the same with Jen if he committed to her, but what if that was all it would take to make it work with the woman he loved—letting her know how supportive he was? If she needed a cheering section to let her know just how wonderful she was, whether he fully understood everything she was doing or not, then he could provide that easily enough. He didn't need to be intimidated by the art world she moved in. Maybe he could just be the strong arms and steady heart that she came back to each night—the guy who made sure that she knew she was amazing.

He tossed his daughter's bag into the back seat of the truck, and he looked across the street at the old mansion.

"Dad?" Amelia said as he got into the driver's seat.

"Yeah."

"For what it's worth, I really like Jen. I think she'd be good for you."

"You mean she'd be good for you," he said with a forced laugh.

"No," she said quietly. "I've seen the way she lights up when you come in. And I've seen the way you look at her... I'd like to see you married again, Dad. You deserve some happiness, too."

Nick put the truck into Reverse, then cast his daughter a smile. Was there any hope for a future with Jen? Hope had started to swell inside him. Maybe, just maybe, he had something to offer that was worth a lifetime...

CHAPTER SIXTEEN

IT WAS CHRISTMAS EVE, and outside snow had started to drift down in lazy flakes. The Christmas tree was lit, lights sparkling from the depths of the branches and reflecting off the gifts she'd wrapped for Drew. They looked pitiful compared to the space that was available under that tree, but she didn't mind. At least Drew was home.

She'd be hosting dinner on Christmas Day. Gayle and Matthew were back from their honeymoon, and they'd be there, as well as Lisa and Bram, Uncle Stu and a couple of her cousins. Jen wasn't sure how happy Matthew would be to see Stu there, but she figured he'd have to adjust—blended families could be sticky. It would be potluck style, and everyone was bringing something to share. That massive dining room table was going to be used for its intended purpose for the very first time, and she was glad of that. She needed family right now, and hers were all happy to come and hunker down in this massive, empty mansion. Christmas was about family, wasn't it?

The silver mistletoe ornament glinted on the tree, and she plucked it off the bough and looked down at it in her palm. How many times had she pictured her own life of romance when she'd been young, looking at that mistletoe and imagining silly ways to be kissed underneath it? She smiled sadly. That was a long, long time ago. Was it time to let go of those hopes and be more reasonable?

Jen gazed out the window. She could see Nick's house aglow from across the road. She missed him, deeply. And she stared at the snow falling between them, her heart aching. If she closed her eyes, she could feel what it felt like to have his arms around her, his lips against hers, his beard tickling her face…her heart reaching for his.

"Mom?"

Jen pushed back the memory, feeling the heat on her cheeks. She turned to see Drew coming down the stairs. He must be done with his Xbox for the time being.

"Hi, son," she said.

He came up to the tree and fingered some spruce needles between his fingers, then he squatted down to get a better look at his gifts.

"I hope you like what I got you," she said.

"Can I open them now?" he asked, grinning cheekily.

"You have to wait until Christmas morning," she said with a low laugh. "You know how we do it."

"It was worth a try..." Drew sighed and the laughter evaporated from his eyes. He looked toward the window.

"What are you thinking about?" she asked.

"Just wondering what Dad's doing," he said. "Whatever. I don't care."

Jen ran her fingers through her curls, tugging out a tangle, and then she eased onto the floor next to him.

"You know what, Drew? You're going to have to talk to him about this," she said.

"Maybe you could," Drew said hopefully.

"I think he needs to hear it from you," she replied.

"I don't know..."

"It's not going to be so easy now that your dad and I live apart," she said. "But you're going to have to call him up and tell him what you're feeling. You'll have to make a few demands of your own. You've never been a kid to throw a fit, but there might be a time and place." She smiled softly. "That's my advice."

"You think?" He frowned.

"I'm joking about the fit," she said. "But you'll have to talk to your dad and make yourself heard. I have a friend whose daughter got mad at him a long time ago and she never explained why. To this day, he's really hurt by that. He wants to know. He wants to make it better. And with your father, I know how much he loves you. You need to talk this out."

Drew was silent.

"Son, I know this is hard," she went on. "And I'm willing to move us back to Denver if that's what you need."

"Really?" Drew's eyes lit up and he blinked back some tears. "Do you mean it, Mom? We could go back?"

She sighed. "Yes. I mean it. I know that you need both your father and me in your life, and just because we're divorced doesn't mean I get to run off and have my adventures. I know your dad can be difficult, and that's not your fault."

"It would be easier with us all in the same city," Drew said. "I've been thinking about it a lot. And I could go see Dad on weekends, and have my Xbox there. And then I could be with you during the week, because you help me with homework and stuff, and—" Drew sighed. "Otherwise, Dad is going to do this again. You know he will. And he'll keep doing it. But if we live there—"

"Then he can't get off so easily," Jen finished for him.

"Yeah. Exactly."

Somehow, her twelve-year-old had grown up over the past few weeks, and she looked down at him sadly.

"What's wrong?" Drew asked.

"Nothing," she said, and she forced a smile. "We'll sort it out, okay?"

"Thanks." Drew visibly relaxed and a smile stretched across his face.

"But you call him now and tell him how you feel, got it?" she said.

He nodded.

"Go get your phone," she said.

Just as Drew was heading out of the room

to get his cell phone, her own rang, and Jen felt a rush of hope that it would be Nick. But it was Renata. She picked up the call.

"Hi, Renata," she said. "How are you?"

"Okay, but I need advice," Renata said in a rush. "And Belle and Angelina don't have kids, so I was hoping I could count on you. I need to bounce this off another mom. Is that okay?"

Jen laughed softly. "Yeah. It's fine. What's up?"

"Are you doing Christmas Eve stuff yet?" Renata asked.

"No, we do Christmas morning," Jen said. "What's going on?"

"Seb and I... Okay, so we went out for a couple of dates, and we talked for hours, and he's really something..." Renata sighed. "The thing is, he wants to be my boyfriend— to let people know that we're together."

"And?" Jen prompted.

"And..." Renata sounded slightly breathless. "And I'm scared! What about the kids? They've been through enough, and I'm supposed to be their rock. Their dad is an ass, and I'm the one who holds us all together.

But if I have a boyfriend, and the kids know about him, and..."

"You're scared if it doesn't work out?" Jen asked.

"Even if it does… This *will* affect them," Renata said. "You know what I mean, right? The others won't understand where I'm coming from, not having kids."

"You want my opinion?" Jen asked.

"Yes. Please. Unfiltered. Just tell me what you think," Renata replied.

Jen let out a slow breath. She was emotionally spent, and she didn't have the energy to sugarcoat this if she tried.

"Okay, from what I've heard, Ivan is an ass," Jen said. "I don't know if he was a better guy when you married him, but he's a definite creep now. All your kids have seen so far is their father treating their mother like garbage, and then their father moving on with girlfriends. Maybe it's time they saw their mother treated right—it would be good for them to see you happy! There's always a risk of finding another loser, but you know what? You can dump a loser. Go out with him, and if you want to get more serious with him, I don't think it will hurt the kids at all."

Renata was silent.

"I hope that wasn't too harsh," Jen said after a moment.

"No, that was perfect," Renata said with a shaky laugh. "I really like Seb. He's sweet and strong, and he's really attentive. He's not a womanizer, either. He's been single for a couple of years now. And… I like him."

"Good!" Jen said. "That's a good thing!"

"Okay. Just checking," Renata said. "Thank you… So how are you doing?"

"I'm okay," Jen said, then she sighed. "I don't know. I might be better giving advice than taking it right now. I'm going to be moving back to Denver."

"Why?" Renata asked. "What happened?"

"My son needs his father in his life, and Sam just isn't stepping up. If I'm in Denver, then Drew has his parents in the same city. He'll see more of his dad, and Sam can't sweep his son aside quite so easily. This is about what Drew needs right now."

"Hmm…" Renata sighed. "You do realize that Drew is going to watch his dad move on with whatever twenty-year-old he's dating, and then watch his mom just put up with her situation, right?"

"I'll be the parent he needs me to be," Jen said.

"And you'll be unhappy," Renata said. "What about your gallery? What about that gorgeous mansion, and your family out here?"

"I made a commitment when I decided to have a child—" Jen started.

"For what it's worth," Renata said quietly. "You and I might have something in common. I think it would be good for Drew to see his mom happy, too."

Jen's heart sped up in her chest, and her gaze flickered toward the windows in spite of herself.

"That's something to think about..." Jen said.

"Besides, if you let that gorgeous old house go, it's not going to be available if you change your mind," Renata said.

As much as Jen loved this old mansion, it wasn't the house that was tugging at her heart. If she let Nick go, would she ever fully get over him? Love was rarer than most people realized... Would she find another man who made her feel like this, or would she end up looking back on the guy who got away? But she had a son to worry about, too, and she couldn't put her own heart ahead of his.

"Thanks, Renata," Jen said. "Go get your man."

One of them should, at least.

"I think I will," Renata said with a laugh.

When they said goodbye, Jen hung up the phone and headed back into the living room. Drew was on his phone, talking to his father.

"You can't just dump me like that, Dad!" Drew was saying. "What, am I some kind of embarrassment or something? Or are you planning on just starting over with Tiffany and having more kids?"

Jen raised her eyebrows. Drew was getting right to the point, all right.

"Yeah, well, some things might be for adults, but I don't think Christmas is one of them!" Drew went on. "When you were a kid, did your dad send you away at *Christmas*?"

Jen smothered a smile. Good. Let Drew have it out. It was good for him to say what he was feeling, and it was high time that Sam heard it. She paused at the window again, and this time she saw Nick coming across the street, Goldie at his heels. His coat was open in the front, and the falling snow clung to his hair.

Maybe Nick was just walking his dog, but her heart was tugging her toward him. So she grabbed her coat and stepped into her boots.

"I'll be back in a minute!" she called over her shoulder.

"I don't think sorry is good enough this time..." Drew was saying. "You're sorry, but I still don't see you over Christmas. You'd better make this up to me!"

Jen pulled the door shut behind her. Drew would be just fine in his conversation with his father.

Nick wasn't just walking his dog, it seemed, because he had started up the drive by the time she got outside.

"Jen?" he called.

"Hi," she said, and she headed out into the drifting snow.

Nick didn't say another word, but when he got to her, he pulled her into his arms and lowered his lips to hers. Jen slipped her hands under his coat and held on to his shirt and she let the world disappear around them in the urgency of that kiss. Goldie pushed her head up between them, forcing them to pull back, breathless.

"Can we talk?" he whispered.

"Okay," she said.

"I love you," he said. "And I've been scared of making the same mistake I made with my first marriage—marrying up and having my wife look down on me ever after. But I had a good talk with my daughter this morning, and she said that all she'd needed was for me to be proud of her. And that was so easy! I can do that, no problem. And I realized that I'm never going to be the guy who discusses the deeper meaning of art, but I can absolutely be the guy who supports you in your ambitions. I can be the guy who's proud of you and all you accomplish, Jen..."

"Yeah?" A smile spread over her face.

"I mean, if you could be happy with that," he said. "Truly happy. If you could be seriously proud and impressed with the guy who can redo your house and keep you warm at night."

"It is rather impressive," she breathed. "And I'd be deeply proud."

"I don't know if that changes anything for

you, though—" He caught her gaze, and she could see the hope there, and the agony.

"I was just talking to Renata," Jen said, licking her lips. "Drew does need his father in his life. But Renata reminded me that it's also important for Drew to see his mother happy and following my dreams. On my own two feet."

"I agree with that," Nick said, and he brushed a snowflake off her eyelashes. "Are you willing to let me help you make that happen, though? I know you want to do this on your own…"

"How would it work?" she asked.

"I want you and me to drive Drew out to see his dad, and pick him back up again," he said. "I want to help him have the fullest life he can have. I want to show him how to use a saw and a hammer, and how to work a hands-on job—if you'd let me, that is. I want to support you in raising him, and I want to be the guy who tells him to watch how he talks to his mother every once in a while." He smiled ruefully. "And I want to be there for both of you. And in return… I want you to come home to me."

His words hung in the air, and she caught her breath.

"Come home?" she whispered. "You mean, you want me to stay in Mountain Springs."

"You have dreams here," he said. "And I want to be the guy who you come home to after you build some art empire."

She laughed softly. "I do have dreams here—" Was it really possible to have it all? "I wanted to do this on my own. I didn't want to owe anyone—"

"Hey, I'll be your biggest fan, but I won't be able to take a stitch of credit for what you accomplish. It'll be yours, babe."

She felt her lips tug into a smile at the endearment. "Babe?"

"Can I call you that?"

She nodded, and she felt some heat on her cheeks.

"I know this is crazy," he said. "But I'm in love with you. And I'm willing to have as long of an engagement as you need, but I want to marry you."

Jen's heart gave a leap and she searched his face. "You'd help me with Drew?" she asked. "You mean that? You'd help him connect with his father? Because if I'm going to chase down my dreams here in Mountain Springs, I need help with giving Drew the balance he needs, too."

"You're right. He needs his dad," Nick said. "I understand how important a father is, and yeah, I'm promising you right now that I'll help you with that. You wouldn't be alone in this." His expression softened and he touched her cheek gently. "What do you say?"

She nodded, tears welling in her eyes. "Yeah."

"So..." He hesitated. "You'll stay? You'll marry me?"

"Yes," she said.

He let out a sigh of relief and pulled her back into his arms, his lips coming down over hers as the snow swirled around them and Goldie shoved her nose between them.

"Mom?" Drew called from the door, and Jen pulled back and looked over her shoulder. Drew stood in the doorway, his phone in one hand, a confused look on his face.

"We should get inside," Jen said with a laugh.

"Yeah," Nick agreed, and he closed his hand around hers.

"Dad wants to talk to you," Drew said as they approached, and he held the phone out to her.

Jen looked up at Nick and they shared a smile, then she dropped a kiss on Drew's head. It was time for Drew to see his mother happy, and to see what a supportive, equal, loving relationship looked like.

As Jen took the phone, she overheard Drew ask Nick, "How come you were kissing my mom?" and she knew that the conversations were only beginning. But she felt a calm certainty deep inside her. At long last, love was the answer.

"Hi, Sam," she said. "Merry Christmas."

Nick shot her a grin, his gaze tender, and she couldn't help but return it. Her little ball of silver mistletoe shimmered on the tree, and she let her gaze flow over the room. This was her second chance at following her heart, and she felt certain that there would be many more mistletoe kisses in the years to come.

NICK SAT DOWN on a chair next to the window while Jen spoke to Drew's dad on the phone.

Drew sat eyeing Nick, his expression one of rather mature focus.

"So, do you love my mom?" Drew asked.

"Yeah, I do," he said. "She's pretty amazing."

"I know that," Drew said. "But I don't think my mom is ready for a boyfriend. Besides, we aren't staying here. You'll have to do a lot of driving."

A lot of driving was definitely in Nick's future, but he couldn't tell Drew anything before Jen did.

"My dad made my mom cry a lot," Drew continued. "Are you planning on doing that?"

"What?" Nick shook his head. "No, of course not. I plan on making your mom happy."

"Hmm." Drew didn't look convinced. "I guess we'll see about that."

Drew was drawing the lines here, trying to protect his mother the only way he knew.

"Tell you what," Nick said, leaning forward. "Just suspend your judgment and get to know me a bit, okay? I'm not asking you to leap in and trust me immediately. But if you give me a chance, I think you'll approve."

Drew shrugged. "Like I said, we'll see."

Nick couldn't help but laugh. He was a good kid—and Nick didn't blame him for being cautious. Nick glanced outside, and he saw a cab pull to a stop outside his house and a familiar figure step out. His heart skipped a beat.

"Amelia?" he said aloud, standing up. "That's my daughter. Drew, I'll be right back, okay?"

Drew gave him a bland look and Nick headed for the front door.

"Amelia!" he called, pulling open the front door and his daughter turned and shaded her eyes against the falling snow. Nick grabbed his coat, glanced over his shoulder to see Jen look at him in surprise.

"My daughter's back," he said. "I'll just go get her."

"Of course!" Jen said, then turning back to the phone said, "Sam, I've got to go. We have some family things to take care of over here."

Family things. Nick liked the sound of that. He pulled the door shut behind him and headed down the drive. Amelia's bag was on the ground beside her. She picked it up and crossed the street to meet him.

"What happened?" Nick asked. "Is everything okay?"

"Yeah, it's fine," Amelia said. "I changed my mind, is all. I told Ben that I needed to spend Christmas with my dad, and that I could meet his family at New Year's. If we're going to get more serious, it's better to start out on a balanced footing, don't you think?"

"Yeah, I totally agree..." Nick smiled. "I'm glad." He gave her a hug. "This is good timing, actually. I've got some news."

"Oh, yeah?" she asked.

"Here, give me your bag," Nick said, and he shouldered her pack as they made their way up the drive. "I'm getting married again."

"Are you serious?" Amelia stared at him.

"The engagement might be lengthy, but yeah," he replied. "You were right about Jen. She's really special, and I came to terms with a few things. Long story short, she agreed to marry me."

"I'm really happy for you, Dad!" Amelia beamed up at him. "She's a good choice."

"Now, here's the thing," he said. "Her son, Drew, doesn't know yet, so..."

"Ah." Amelia chuckled. "He might not be crazy about this idea."

"I'll win him over," Nick said. He wasn't too worried about that. Drew wanted his mother to be happy, and Nick was determined to make sure that she was. And he'd make sure that Drew was taken care of. He needed his dad, but a solid stepdad could be a good addition, too.

They got to the door, and Nick looked down at his daughter. Snow spun through the air, and the Christmas tree glowed from the broad windows.

"I'm glad you came back," he said. "Christmas is just better with you here."

Then Nick opened the front door and he felt a rush of gratefulness for the woman he was going to marry, for his daughter here for the holidays and for Drew, who would be his to protect, too. He'd never had a son before, and a stepson felt right. They'd be a family, and for the first time in a very long time, Nick could feel his heart settling into a deeply happy rhythm.

This Christmas, they were making a home.

EPILOGUE

THE WEDDING WAS set on a warm Saturday at the end of June, the weekend before Jen and Nick were set to drive Drew back to Denver to spend the summer with his dad.

Jen and Nick stood in the waiting room of the Mountain Springs courthouse with their bridal party in tow, waiting for their turn to get legally married. Outside, the sun was shining, and indoors the air-conditioning was pumping into the little room packed full of the people Jen and Nick loved most. The rest of their friends and family would be at the reception later on that afternoon, and Jen would dance the afternoon away in her new husband's arms.

Jen had opted for a cream tea-length wedding dress paired with pale blue kitten heels for her something-blue. Lisa and Amelia were both her bridesmaids, and the two of them had hit it off immediately. Amelia was thrilled to not only meet Lisa, but to also be able to call her family. She and Lisa had settled into some long conversations about literature and art, and Jen was happy to see the two of them bonding.

Bram had been bribed with a chocolate chip cookie to keep him quiet and in one place, and he sat on the ground, very seriously licking the chocolate from his palm.

Bert was standing in as Nick's best man, and Drew was going to walk Jen down the aisle, but how much aisle there would be was still unknown. Jen had never seen her son look quite so grown-up as he did in a suit, and when Drew felt her gaze on him, he blushed and dug his shoe into the carpet.

"Mom..." he said.

"You look great, Drew," Jen said, and when she glanced up at Nick, she found her fiancé watching her with a smile tugging at his lips.

"You look pretty amazing, too," Nick said, taking her hand in his. "You ready to do this?"

Jen grinned up at him. "Definitely."

Bram reached out and grabbed a handful

of Jen's dress in his chocolatey hand, and both Lisa and Amelia let out a scream.

"Bram!" Lisa cried, and she scooped him up, looking down at Jen's dress in apology. "Oh, Jen, I'm so sorry…"

Amelia bent down to see if she could wipe away the chocolate just as the judge's door opened and a middle-aged man looked down at his tablet and said, "Nick Bryant and Jennifer Taylor?"

"It's fine," Jen said. "Really! I'm serious. I don't care a bit."

"Are you sure?" Lisa asked.

"I might be able to get it out if we had a few minutes—" Amelia started.

"I'm positive," Jen replied. "It's just chocolate, and I honestly don't have any other plans for this dress beyond today." She looked up at Nick. "Let's get married."

The reception would be later on that afternoon at the lodge, and everyone would be there, including the women of the Second Chance Dining Club. Melanie would come with her husband, of course. Aunt Gayle and Matt would be there, too. Uncle Stu was bringing a date, as well, and Jen was thrilled that he was making use of his plus-one. Belle and Angelina were both coming happily single.

Jen was delighted about Renata's date—Seb was coming, and Renata had finally told everyone that he was her boyfriend. Renata's kids were just fine with that arrangement, since Seb had won them over by being his honest, fun-loving self. And while it was still a secret, Jen happened to know that Seb was carrying around an engagement ring, still working up his courage to ask Renata to marry him. Jen had a feeling it might take a while for Renata to say yes, but Seb seemed determined to win her trust.

When they all went into the judge's chambers, Drew didn't really have anywhere to walk Jen, so she gave him a hug and told him she loved him. The judge asked Jen and Nick to repeat their vows, Jen didn't feel any qualms. She was marrying the right man—there was no doubt. And after Nick pulled her into his arms and gave her a kiss, he reached over and shook Drew's hand.

"Man to man," Nick said quietly. "I'm going to be good to your mom. And I want you to let me know if you think I'm out of line, okay? Between the two of us, we're going to make sure your mom is the happiest woman on the planet. Deal?"

"Yeah, okay," Drew said, and he grinned up at Nick. "Welcome to the family."

When had Drew gotten so grown-up?

Then Nick caught her hand again and looked down into her eyes.

"I love you," he said.

"I love you, too." Jen tipped her head against his strong shoulder. "I'm looking forward to dancing with you this afternoon."

"Cookie?" Bram said, holding up the mushed remnants of his chocolate chip reward, and just at that moment, a court photographer snapped a photo. That picture turned into Jen's favorite photo of the day—a toddler handprint on her dress, her tall, handsome son grinning over at her and Nick's gaze locked on her face with a look of love. Amelia and Lisa made it into the shot, too, their heads together as they laughed over some private joke, and Bram was in the forefront, offering a mashed-up cookie and his little toddler heart. It was perfect!

There would be plenty more messes and mistakes, handprints and apologies—that was part of a family. But there would also be a whole lot of love to cover over the imperfections.

The Taylor-Bryant family was just getting started.

* * * * *

Get 4 FREE REWARDS!

We'll send you 2 FREE Books plus 2 FREE Mystery Gifts.

Love Inspired books feature uplifting stories where faith helps guide you through life's challenges and discover the promise of a new beginning.

FREE
Value Over
$20

YES! Please send me 2 FREE Love Inspired Romance novels and my 2 FREE mystery gifts (gifts are worth about $10 retail). After receiving them, if I don't wish to receive any more books, I can return the shipping statement marked "cancel." If I don't cancel, I will receive 6 brand-new novels every month and be billed just $5.24 each for the regular-print edition or $5.99 each for the larger-print edition in the U.S., or $5.74 each for the regular-print edition or $6.24 each for the larger-print edition in Canada. That's a savings of at least 13% off the cover price. It's quite a bargain! Shipping and handling is just 50¢ per book in the U.S. and $1.25 per book in Canada.* I understand that accepting the 2 free books and gifts places me under no obligation to buy anything. I can always return a shipment and cancel at any time. The free books and gifts are mine to keep no matter what I decide.

Choose one: ☐ **Love Inspired Romance**
Regular-Print
(105/305 IDN GNWC)

☐ **Love Inspired Romance**
Larger-Print
(122/322 IDN GNWC)

Name (please print)

Address   Apt. #

City   State/Province   Zip/Postal Code

Email: Please check this box ☐ if you would like to receive newsletters and promotional emails from Harlequin Enterprises ULC and its affiliates. You can unsubscribe anytime.

Mail to the Reader Service:
IN U.S.A.: P.O. Box 1341, Buffalo, NY 14240-8531
IN CANADA: P.O. Box 603, Fort Erie, Ontario L2A 5X3

Want to try 2 free books from another series! Call 1-800-873-8635 or visit www.ReaderService.com.

Get 4 FREE REWARDS!

We'll send you 2 FREE Books plus 2 FREE Mystery Gifts.

Love Inspired Suspense books showcase how courage and optimism unite in stories of faith and love in the face of danger.

FREE Value Over $20

YES! Please send me 2 FREE Love Inspired Suspense novels and my 2 FREE mystery gifts (gifts are worth about $10 retail). After receiving them, if I don't wish to receive any more books, I can return the shipping statement marked "cancel." If I don't cancel, I will receive 6 brand-new novels every month and be billed just $5.24 each for the regular-print edition or $5.99 each for the larger-print edition in the U.S., or $5.74 each for the regular-print edition or $6.24 each for the larger-print edition in Canada. That's a savings of at least 13% off the cover price. It's quite a bargain! Shipping and handling is just 50¢ per book in the U.S. and $1.25 per book in Canada.* I understand that accepting the 2 free books and gifts places me under no obligation to buy anything. I can always return a shipment and cancel at any time. The free books and gifts are mine to keep no matter what I decide.

Choose one: ☐ **Love Inspired Suspense**
Regular-Print
(153/353 IDN GNWN)

☐ **Love Inspired Suspense**
Larger-Print
(107/307 IDN GNWN)

Name (please print)

Address   Apt. #

City   State/Province   Zip/Postal Code

Email: Please check this box ☐ if you would like to receive newsletters and promotional emails from Harlequin Enterprises ULC and its affiliates. You can unsubscribe anytime.

Mail to the **Reader Service:**
IN U.S.A.: P.O. Box 1341, Buffalo, NY 14240-8531
IN CANADA: P.O. Box 603, Fort Erie, Ontario L2A 5X3

Want to try 2 free books from another series! Call 1-800-873-8635 or visit www.ReaderService.com.

LIS20R2

THE WESTERN HEARTS COLLECTION!

19 FREE BOOKS in all!

COWBOYS. RANCHERS. RODEO REBELS.
Here are their charming love stories in one prized Collection:
51 emotional and heart-filled romances that capture the majesty and rugged beauty of the American West!

YES! Please send me **The Western Hearts Collection** in Larger Print. This collection begins with 3 FREE books and 2 FREE gifts in the first shipment. Along with my 3 free books, I'll also get the next 4 books from The Western Hearts Collection, in LARGER PRINT, which I may either return and owe nothing, or keep for the low price of $5.45 U.S./$6.23 CDN each plus $2.99 U.S./$7.49 CDN for shipping and handling per shipment*. If I decide to continue, about once a month for 8 months I will get 6 or 7 more books but will only need to pay for 4. That means 2 or 3 books in every shipment will be FREE! If I decide to keep the entire collection, I'll have paid for only 32 books because 19 books are FREE! I understand that accepting the 3 free books and gifts places me under no obligation to buy anything. I can always return a shipment and cancel at any time. My free books and gifts are mine to keep no matter what I decide.

☐ 270 HCN 5354   ☐ 470 HCN 5354

Name (please print)

Address   Apt. #

City   State/Province   Zip/Postal Code

Mail to the **Reader Service:**
IN U.S.A.: P.O. Box 1341, Buffalo, N.Y. 14240-8531
IN CANADA: P.O. Box 603, Fort Erie, Ontario L2A 5X3

50BWH20

Get 4 FREE REWARDS!

We'll send you 2 FREE Books <u>plus</u> 2 FREE Mystery Gifts.

FREE
Value Over
$20

Both the **Romance** and **Suspense** collections feature compelling novels written by many of today's bestselling authors.

YES! Please send me 2 FREE novels from the Essential Romance or Essential Suspense Collection and my 2 FREE gifts (gifts are worth about $10 retail). After receiving them, if I don't wish to receive any more books, I can return the shipping statement marked "cancel." If I don't cancel, I will receive 4 brand-new novels every month and be billed just $7.24 each in the U.S. or $7.49 each in Canada. That's a savings of up to 28% off the cover price. It's quite a bargain! Shipping and handling is just 50¢ per book in the U.S. and $1.25 per book in Canada.* I understand that accepting the 2 free books and gifts places me under no obligation to buy anything. I can always return a shipment and cancel at any time. The free books and gifts are mine to keep no matter what I decide.

Choose one: ☐ **Essential Romance**
(194/394 MDN GQ6M)
☐ **Essential Suspense**
(191/391 MDN GQ6M)

Name (please print)

Address   Apt. #

City   State/Province   Zip/Postal Code

Email: Please check this box ☐ if you would like to receive newsletters and promotional emails from Harlequin Enterprises ULC and its affiliates. You can unsubscribe anytime.

Mail to the **Reader Service:**
IN U.S.A.: P.O. Box 1341, Buffalo, NY 14240-8531
IN CANADA: P.O. Box 603, Fort Erie, Ontario L2A 5X3

Want to try 2 free books from another series? Call 1-800-873-8635 or visit www.ReaderService.com.

COMING NEXT MONTH FROM

HARLEQUIN
HEARTWARMING

Available November 10, 2020

#351 MONTANA MATCH
The Blackwell Sisters • by Carol Ross
Fiona Harrison's dating app attempts haven't gone according to plan. What better way to make things worse than allowing Simon Clarke to play matchmaker? She's falling for the handsome bartender, but he doesn't see marriage in his own future.

#352 THE COWBOY'S HOLIDAY BRIDE
Wishing Well Springs • by Cathy McDavid
Cash Montgomery is stuck covering his sister's absence from their wedding barn business with event coordinator Phoebe Kellerman. Then come his three former fiancées, all to be wed and each ready to impart their advice about the bride who's right under his nose.

#353 AN ALASKAN FAMILY CHRISTMAS
A Northern Lights Novel • by Beth Carpenter
Confirmed skeptic Natalie Weiss is in Alaska to help a friend, not spend the holidays with a stranger's family in their rustic cabin. Tanner Rockford finds himself drawn to the cynical professor, knowing full well her career will take her away.

#354 MISTLETOE COWBOY
Kansas Cowboys • by Leigh Riker
Ex-con Cody Jones discovers that the love of his life is engaged to someone else. Is there any way the cowboy can turn his life around and convince Willow Bodine to choose him over her successful lawyer fiancé?

YOU CAN FIND MORE INFORMATION ON UPCOMING HARLEQUIN TITLES,
FREE EXCERPTS AND MORE AT HARLEQUIN.COM.

HWCNM1020